BETROTHAL OR BREAKAWAY

D.C. EAGLES HOCKEY
BOOK 3

LEAH BRUNNER

EDITED BY
MIDNIGHT OWL

ILLUSTRATED BY
MELODY JEFFRIES

Copyright © 2024 by Leah Brunner

All rights reserved.

No portion of this book may be reproduced in any form without written permission from the publisher or author, except as permitted by U.S. copyright law.

❦ Created with Vellum

TRIGGER WARNINGS

This work of fiction contains mild language.

This book has themes of child neglect (past), bullying (past), and the death of a pet (non-descriptive).

*To all who have felt like too much while simultaneously not enough.
To all who have always felt out of place, like they don't belong.
To all who have felt uncomfortable in their own skin, wondering why they can't just be "normal."
To all my favorite people, the ones who break the mold, the ones who make me see life through a different lens.
Normal is a tragedy. And this book is for you.*

PROLOGUE
AMBER: 2ND GRADE

I WALK into my classroom feeling confident and ready to make new friends in second grade. Mom ironed my pretty green dress and told me it looks okay with my red hair. I wanted to wear a pink one, but Mom said she had a teacher once who made her read a boring book, and the book said redheads don't look good in pink. I have no idea why she listened to a book called—what was it called again? *Banned in Green Marbles*, I think.

I still think my pink dress would've been better.

"All right Amber, have a good day," Mom says, standing above me. She doesn't crouch down to get on eye level like other parents seem to do with their children. She also doesn't hug me goodbye.

Her blonde hair and blue eyes are so pretty, and I remember a comment she made about how I got my looks from my dad. I've never met my dad, but my mom doesn't like him. And she definitely doesn't like that I look like him instead of her.

"And remember, you're just as good as everyone in that

classroom. Don't let anyone look down on you because of where you live or the clothes you wear."

I have no clue what she's talking about. My clothes are fine, and our apartment might be small, but it's clean. I even have my own room. We painted it pink. I can have pink walls, but not pink dresses.

"Okay, Mom," I say, hoping she might bend down and kiss my cheek. But she simply glances at her wrist watch—one of her boyfriends gave it to her—and leaves.

I head inside my classroom, and smile at a few of the girls already seated at their desks. The desks are in groups of four, and each one has a name taped on top. I look around for mine.

When I find it, I drag my hand over the top. It's laminated and has colorful apple stickers surrounding my name. A snuffling sound grabs my attention. It sounds like someone's crying. I spin in a circle trying to find where the sound is coming from. After a few seconds, I realize it's coming from under the group of desks where I'll be sitting. Getting down on all fours, I see a boy curled into a ball, rocking back and forth as he cries.

"Hey, are you okay?" I ask, even though he's obviously not okay.

He doesn't answer.

I glance from side to side, noting that our teacher, Ms. Montgomery, is in the front of the classroom speaking to a few of the students, and not noticing the boy.

After checking to make sure no one is watching, I slip under the tables and sit beside him. The space is cramped, so I have to hug my legs to my chest.

The boy who is crying has short but messy hair. It looks like he's been tugging on it. The dark strands rest against his light, clammy skin. He's sweating, and his hair looks a little damp. I wonder if he's always pale and sweaty, or if it's because of whatever's going on right now.

My mom would be furious if she knew I was under a table on my first day of school. She doesn't like it when I draw attention to myself.

The boy's crying quiets, and he momentarily stops rocking. His arms slide down, and he peeks up at me through his tears. He looks into my eyes for a few seconds before moving his gaze up slightly… like maybe he's looking at my hair?

"Hi," I say, offering a hesitant smile. "I'm Amber."

He blinks with eyelashes so long and so dark, I know Mom would be jealous of them. Even though he's not looking at my eyes, I can tell his eyes are dark brown. Kind of shiny and pretty too. I like them. They're kind eyes.

He doesn't speak, but he tilts his head down in a nod. "Hi," he finally whispers.

"What's wrong?" I ask, hoping the question won't send him back into his meltdown.

His head jerks away, and he looks down at his feet.

"Are you nervous about the first day of school?" I ask.

His head tilts back in my direction, and he nods.

I release a deep breath, glad that's all it is. "It's okay to be nervous."

I notice his hands are trembling, and instinctively, I cover them with mine. I'm hoping the touch comforts him.

The boy jerks like I scared him and pulls his hand away. "A-a-a-re you?" He stutters the question out. "Nervous?"

I smile easily. "No, but my mom says I'm a social butterfly."

His nose scrunches up. "That doesn't make sense. Butterflies are solitary insects."

"It's just a saying, I think."

His shoulders drop. "I don't like sayings. They never make sense."

I shrug. "What *do* you like?"

His dark eyebrows draw together. They're kind of big for his face, but I suppose he'll grow into them, eventually. His eyes close tight, like he's thinking really hard, then they fly open. "Hockey," he whispers, his voice laced with excitement. But he doesn't offer any more information.

"That's cool." I smile again and this time my smile is returned. I hedge, noticing the feet moving around us. Everyone must be finding their desks.

"So, you wanna come out of hiding and sit at our desk? I think class is about to start."

His face crumples, and I wonder if he's going to cry again.

"I'll be here with you," I tell him. "You're my first friend in second grade."

His eyes widen. "Y-y-you want to be my friend?"

"Of course," I say quickly. "I'm gonna need you to teach me about hockey."

The boy's mouth turns up in a crooked grin. "Okay," he whispers, sliding out from under the tables with me. His skin is still pale, but his eyes are dry.

I take a seat at the desk marked with my name and he smiles nervously, then takes the seat beside me. The name on the desk says *Ford*.

"Are you Ford?" I ask, and he nods. "That's a really nice name."

He gives me another crooked grin.

CHAPTER
ONE
FORD

STANDING at the Delta Airlines baggage claim, I study the stupid sign I made earlier today. This morning making a glittery sign for Amber's first visit here as a mom seemed not only fun, but like I was extending an olive branch. A proverbial, "look how fun this welcome sign is! I don't care that my best friend since childhood now has a baby with a man I can't stand. Oh, and welcome to D.C.!"

But as I shift awkwardly on my feet, the sign seems way over the top. It looks like I'm trying too hard, or not being genuine.

Because the fact is, Theo is a scumbag, and he not only broke my best friend's heart, but left her with a baby and pretty much no support.

I close my eyes and try not to let my anger at Theo ruin Amber's visit before it even begins. Taking a deep breath, I attempt to swallow my irritation, but my throat feels thick. I bring my hand up to tug at the collar of my long-sleeved D.C. Eagles hockey tee.

The soft fabric of my tee begins to itch where it touches my skin. My dark-wash jeans pull on my legs like they're too tight.

The glasses resting on my face feel too heavy. Everything is closing in on me, strangling me. I close my eyes and thrust a hand into my jeans pocket to find my dad's university hockey championship coin he gave me as a kid. It's dumb, childish even, but the smooth texture of the cold metal and the tiny grooves along the edge have always calmed me. It probably just takes my mind off the feelings overwhelming my brain sometimes, but nevertheless, I always have it with me.

I focus on the coin's varying textures as my winding thoughts calm down. My heart is still beating fast, but my clothes don't feel tight and scratchy anymore.

Before I can open my eyes, Amber's sweet voice filters through my ears, and all the overwhelming feelings float away.

"Hey, Ford. You look good."

She's the only one who still calls me Ford, while the rest of the world knows me as Remington, or Remy… team captain of the D.C. Eagles. A smile spreads across my face as my eyes fly open. The sight of Amber, with her red hair, now pale pink at the ends, and bright green eyes makes my heart stop—and then race. But not in a bad way.

A soft coo pulls my attention down to a tiny head covered in a pink knitted hat. My gaze shoots back up to Amber. She's watching me closely, and I hate that she looks nervous at my reaction to her baby. But even more so, I hate that I'm nervous about my own reaction. What if she looks like Theo? Worse yet, what if she acts like him? I know she has her mother's red hair, that much was obvious in photos. But it's hard to make out a baby's features.

"Nice sign. You even added glitter."

I meet her gaze and offer a shrug with no other explanation, then take a step forward. Leaning over, I look at the tiny human strapped onto my best friend's body. Her little face is chubby and rosy-pink, with the widest green eyes I've ever seen. She's a carbon copy of her mother. The baby blinks up at me, with long lashes that are blonde at the base and reddish on the tips. Her lashes flutter as she looks at me… and then her mouth pulls up into a toothless grin, making one dimple pop on her left cheek. The dimple is from her father, but even that thought doesn't squelch the affection expanding inside me for this little girl. Meeting her feels different than I imagined, and now I feel stupid for being nervous about it.

My mouth pulls into a smile. I couldn't stop it even if I wanted to.

Amber laughs, a light tittering sound. "She likes you."

A breathy laugh escapes me. "Can I hold her?" I ask before I know what I'm doing. *What the hell, Ford. You haven't held a baby since your sisters were born.*

Amber blows out a dramatic sigh. "Not sure the ladies in here can handle Ford Remington, NHL captain, and America's heartthrob, holding a baby. You're going to be the cause of many swoons. Possibly even fainting."

I roll my eyes. "Fine, I'll get your bag. I'm assuming it's pink?"

"You know me too well." Her eyes twinkle with mischief, telling me I'll recognize her bag as soon as I see it.

"And I'm sure Nella would love for you to hold her once we get back to your place." She shifts on her feet, making me wonder if her back hurts from carrying Nella around all day. "But if I take her out of this baby carrier, she'll scream bloody murder when I try to tuck her back into it."

I study my friend's pretty face for a moment, noting the purple smudges under her eyes and the messy braids keeping her hair out of her face. To anyone else, nothing would seem out of place, but I know this woman almost better than I know myself. And I've never seen her looking so exhausted. The desire to hold her is so overwhelming, I have to ball my fists to keep myself in place. Because I'm a split second away from moving into her space and pulling her into my arms. To protect her and comfort her, to give her the safety and rest she needs.

But she knows me well too, and she knows I'm not a touchy-feely guy. So, she'd likely think that was pretty odd. I clear my throat and nod my head instead, moving toward the conveyor belt where the luggage from Amber's flight starts piling on one by one with loud thuds.

Luckily, the fifth bag to land on the luggage carousel is pink, covered with hand-painted flowers, and has a pink ribbon attached to the handle. I move forward and grab it off the belt, it's followed by a smaller bag that's baby pink and has a matching ribbon tied to it. I grab that one too, assuming it's Nella's.

I try to pull the handle up on Amber's suitcase to roll it, but the handle is broken and won't budge.

"Sorry, it broke last year. The wheel is busted too, so I just carry it by the side handle," Amber says, her voice coming from beside me.

She moves to grab the smaller bag, but Nella starts fussing. It's a pathetic, heart-breaking sound. Amber begins to bounce up and down, and making a *shhh* sound.

I easily grab both bags and think to myself how much easier it is to travel with my pain-in-the-ass teammates than it must be to travel with a baby. Often, I feel like a babysitter with the guys, but at least they don't cry...usually.

"Just these two bags?" I ask her, and she nods while still bouncing and *shhh*-ing. I offer her a small smile then jut my chin toward the sliding doors that lead to the parking area. She follows closely behind as we walk to my Land Rover. I already installed an infant car seat so Amber wouldn't have to bring one. It was the only thing she'd let me buy, along with something called a pack-and-play. Nella needed a place to sleep during their visit, but the bed thingy that feels like cardboard doesn't seem that comfortable to me.

After lifting the bags into the trunk, I close the hatch, then come around and open the back door on the driver's side, where I have meticulously installed the safest car seat money can buy. And I stopped by a fire station earlier today to make sure it was installed correctly.

Amber giggles as she removes Nella from the baby carrier and tucks her into the car seat. "I should've known you'd purchase the most expensive car seat on the market."

I peek my head in and see Nella sleeping as her mother jostles her around to buckle the car seat. "I didn't pay attention to the price; I just got the one with the highest safety ratings."

Amber jumps at the sound of my voice. She must not have realized I was so close behind her. Her back collides with my front, and I place my hands on her hips to steady her.

She laughs and brushes my hands away. "Sorry, you kind of snuck up on me."

I smile. "I've always been able to do that, haven't I?"

She smiles back, a million memories moving through those emerald eyes. "Yes, you have."

During the hour-long drive to my house, thanks to D.C. traffic, Amber yawns half a dozen times. Nella sleeps the whole time, or maybe she's awake and just really quiet. I don't know much about babies.

I pull into my garage, and Amber releases a dreamy sigh that makes my head spin, imagining a dozen different ways I could get her to repeat that sound.

"Finally," she says. "I've been dreaming about your mattress since last time I visited."

I blink rapidly, trying to slow my racing thoughts. Because

my twisted brain has had several dreams that include me, Amber, and my mattress over the years. But there's no way that's what she's referring to.

She glances over at me and bursts into laughter. "Calm down, I meant your guest room's mattress. I wish you could see your face!" She laughs again. "You look so horrified."

I force a laugh and scratch the back of my head, going for a casual look. "Ha. I'm just tired from early practice this morning. My brain isn't functioning at full capacity."

Still giggling, she unbuckles her seatbelt and walks around the vehicle to get Nella.

Closing my eyes, I take a deep breath before removing my own seatbelt and getting the bags from the trunk.

We step inside my large home, every surface sparkling because I clean when I'm nervous, or stressed, or sad... or happy. But today it was nerves making me clean. The other guys on the team pay house-keepers, but not me. Don't need one since I'm what they call a *neat freak*.

Amber glances around, as if looking for any changes since she was here a year ago. Her eyes land on the infinity countertop made from concrete, then the rest of the modern kitchen. Every appliance is made to match the cabinets, giving a streamlined appearance. Her head swivels to take in the dining room. The table and chairs are white and sleek, not an item out of place.

"I swear, nothing has moved since last time I was here," she finally says, walking farther inside the house and smiling when she sees the living room. My sectional is white, the rug is white, and the large flatscreen is mounted to the wall, with every cord hidden for optimum tidiness.

"I don't like change." I shrug and carry the bags upstairs to the guest room, which is right across from my master. I offered her the bigger space since she's sharing with Nella, but she refused, saying she didn't want to be high maintenance.

Since my guest room is almost as big, and has its own attached bathroom, I didn't argue.

I can hear the light sounds of Amber's footsteps behind me. "I'll never understand how you can keep things so clean all the time. You should see my apartment, Ford. It's a mess of bottles, diapers, baby toys." She groans and I study her, noting once again how tired and worn down she looks.

"Well, that makes sense, since you have a baby. It would be kind of weird if my place was a mess, seeing as I live alone." I keep my voice quiet since Nella is still asleep in her infant car seat, which Amber is carrying along. She's standing lop-sided, like the car seat is getting heavier with each passing second. I quickly carry the bags into the guest room, then take the car seat from her and set it gently on the bed.

I still for a moment, studying the teeny version of Amber sleeping in front of me. Her tiny lips form a cupid's bow, slimy with drool. Her pink outfit looks damp in the front, like she spit milk onto it during the flight. Then, something amazing happens. Nella sneezes. It's the cutest sound I've ever heard. I pinch my lips together, trying to play it cool.

"I know. Cutest sound ever, right?" I can hear the smile in Amber's voice.

I turn to look at her and finally relax, allowing a smile to lift my lips. "Damn, it really is."

My eyes go wide. "I mean, dang it. Sorry."

She covers her mouth, stifling a laugh. "She's three months old, Ford. She's not going to learn swear words any time soon."

I breathe a sigh of relief. In the dimly lit room, I notice the dark circles under her eyes again. "You doing okay, Ambs?"

Her smile fades, her expression turning troubled. I hate that look; I want to wipe it away.

"Let me put her to bed, then we'll talk, okay?"

"Yeah, sure. The baby bed thingy is set up already." I point to the corner of the room where I put her pack-and-play. "I'll go make some tea."

"Perfect." Her smile momentarily returns before she yawns loudly.

Something inside me settles at having her here. Even though she's exhausted, and we have a lot of catching up to do. Having her and Nella here just feels right.

CHAPTER
TWO
AMBER

AS I TURN on Nella's white-noise machine, I peek at her in the pack and play and make sure she's still sound asleep. This pack-and-play is infinitely nicer than the one she sleeps in at our apartment back in Ohio. This is the Cadillac of baby beds. Because of course it is.

I grab my phone and sneak out the door, pausing to appreciate the grand curved staircase that leads downstairs, where Ford is waiting on me. It's been longer than usual since I've seen him, since he was busy with his teammate's wedding over the summer and I was working extra hours to save up for my maternity leave. I swear he's aged since I saw him in May after his last season ended. But not in a bad way. He looks mature and debonair, with just a few more creases around his eyes, and deeper smile lines. He also got glasses over the summer for reading and driving, and they look so good on him.

Why do men age so well? Or are they just allowed to age, and women aren't?

When I step into the kitchen, I smell the familiar scent of the sweet tobacco mixed with cleaning supplies. I smile, loving how I can always count on his steadiness. He's always been particular about scents, but those sweet tobacco candles from Target have been his favorite since college.

As I round the corner into the living room, I find Ford holding two small white teacups in his giant, paw-sized hands. He extends one to me, and I take it.

"Couch?" he asks, dark eyes twinkling in the overhead kitchen lights.

I nod and follow him into the living room where we sit beside each other. Close enough to chat but not touching.

"You look tired," he starts.

"Gee, thanks. You sure know how to make a new mom feel good," I tease.

"That's not what I meant," he says urgently, not picking up on my teasing tone. "You always look great." He blushes slightly, and I wonder briefly if I've ever seen him blush before. "It's just that you're yawning, and—"

I hold up my hand up to stop him, unable to help the laugh that escapes me. "Ford, I was teasing. I *am* tired. Exhausted, actually."

His already frowning mouth, turns into an even deeper frown. Ford isn't one of those broody types, but he's serious. He thinks before he speaks—or acts. I think he was born with the brain of a forty-year-old man. He's always been protective of me, even when we were kids. I guess even me becoming a mother won't stop that protective streak.

"I hate him. I hate him for leaving you. And I'm not a big fan of your mother at the moment either."

"I know. I know." I place a hand on his bicep, and his shoulders relax. "There's no use being angry, though. I'm not. I have a beautiful baby girl, don't I?"

A moment of silence stretches between us. Ford takes a sip of his tea, studying his bare white wall with interest.

A contented sigh escapes me. I'd forgotten how nice it is to be with my best friend. He doesn't need to fill every silence with chatter. He's my calm, steady presence. My big protector.

"How's the season going?" I ask, wanting to talk like we normally would, even though the tightness in my chest reminds me of something I want to talk to him about. Or maybe that's the literal hole in my heart causing the tight feeling? Either way. A reminder.

He swivels his head to look at me, close enough now for me to see the masculine lines around his eyes, the lines that are adding to the whole mature but handsome effect I noticed earlier.

One corner of his mouth turns up. We both know I know how the season is going. I haven't missed watching one of his games since we were kids.

Ford finally huffs out a laugh and sets his tea back on the tray. "Did you see my breakaway a few nights ago?"

I grin. "I did. Very impressive. Me and Nella were cheering you on."

He smiles back, drawing attention to that little dip in his chin that I used to poke just to annoy him—one of the few touches he'd allow. I'm tempted to do it now, but his body language seems stiff, like he's nervous.

"Knowing you're watching always helps me focus. I can ignore the crowd and the clatter and just think... Amber is sitting on her couch watching right now."

I laugh. "Maybe someday I'll make it to a game in person."

"I'd love that. I might be able to get you good seats." He raises his eyebrows.

"Think they could spare a few for the team captain?"

"Probably." He shrugs.

I let my head fall back onto the couch with a laugh.

His face is stoic and serious, even when he's jesting. I used to have to tell the people around us when he was joking or not, but I can tell easily. It's all in the eyes. They get all shiny when he's joking.

Ford leans forward, resting his elbows on his knees. Even hunched over he's huge, taking up twice as much space on the couch as I am. "All right, Ambs. Enough chitchat. What's going on?"

I blow out a long sigh. "You know me too well."

He doesn't say anything, just looks at me expectantly.

"First, don't be alarmed. I'm fine. Totally fine."

"Then, why would I be alarmed?"

Ignoring his question, I continue, "Second, I may need a favor in the near future, but when... if I ask, you can't give me an answer until you've taken time to think about it. Like, a week, at least."

"I already know the answer is yes," he says, his eyes not leaving mine.

My fragile heart skips a beat. I knew he'd say something like that. He's just that kind of person. Always there, no matter the ask.

Clearing my throat, I force myself to keep going, "So, the thing is... I might need a tiny, little, no-big-deal surgery."

Ford's dark eyes go wide, his thick eyebrows rising in alarm. "What kind of surgery?"

I look down, avoiding those intense brown eyes even though they are glued to my face. "For my heart." Closing my eyes, I collect myself. I hadn't meant to jump into this conversation so abruptly. "There's a small hole in my heart. It's been there since I was born, most likely. But it went unnoticed all this time, until I was giving birth and my heart rate was all over the place." Taking a deep breath, I will my shoulders to relax. The last thing I want is to pour all of my anxiety onto my best friend. "Which is why I ended up having a c-section. They kept me an extra day at the hospital to monitor things, and everything seemed normal, so they discharged me." I roll my lips together and glance at Ford, who looks like I just told him I'm dying. "But my heart rate remained erratic. Sometimes it felt really fast, and I couldn't tell if it was anxiety, or my heart. I went to see a cardiologist, and they had me wear a heart monitor for a few weeks, and when I get back to Ohio, I have an appointment for an EKG and a stress test." What I don't add, is how expensive it all is. And I try not to think about it, either. "My cardiologist is positive I have a hole in my heart, they're just covering all the bases to be sure they need to operate on it. At my appointment Monday, we'll discuss the options. But surgery is likely."

Ford pushes his glasses up on top of his head and pinches the bridge of his nose with his thumb and forefinger, his forehead shining with sweat.

"Ford, it's okay. I swear, it's a very minor heart surgery."

Ford jumps up from his seat, and I rise from mine too. I place my hands on his arms and rub my thumbs gently back and forth. He's not someone who enjoys being touched, but tonight it seems to soothe him. He closes his eyes and takes a deep breath.

"Minor heart surgery? I'm pretty sure any heart surgery is major, Ambs."

"It's a tiny hole, itty-bitty. A cute miniature hole, really "

He arches an eyebrow, unamused.

I grimace, realizing that making light of it isn't easing his worry. So, I decide to go with facts—he will appreciate facts. "If they decide to operate, they'll use a method called cardiac catheterization. A catheter will be placed in my wrist, or my neck. The entire procedure is done through the catheter. It's non-invasive. Most likely, I'll only stay one night in the hospital, then I'd be back home and good as new."

Ford doesn't look any less stressed by my explanation. He brings up his hands, places them on my shoulders, and forces me back into a sitting position. "Sit down. Should you even be standing? Hell, are you even supposed to be walking? Or flying?"

"Ford, please. Calm down. It's a procedure they do all the time, literally every day."

Ford's square jaw flexes as he closes his eyes. His nostrils are flared, and it's obvious he's getting angry. I prickle for a second, wondering why on earth he'd be mad at me. But then his eyes open, and the turmoil playing in the deep brown of his irises nearly breaks my heart. Wait, no that's a terrible metaphor to use at a time like this.

"So, Theo not only got you pregnant and then broke off your engagement… but now your health is suffering?" He looks down then holds abruptly still, as if something just dawned on him. "Wait, do you even have insurance to pay for your procedure? Have you told him about this?"

I sigh. "No, I don't have insurance. That's actually what I needed to talk to you about. And I haven't told Theo either. I don't want him coming back because he feels guilty. He didn't want me, and he didn't want Nella. As far as I'm concerned, he doesn't deserve to even know what's going on in my life."

He nods, seeing my point. "So, if you and Nella don't have insurance, what about the cost of her birth?"

"No, Nella does. She qualifies for insurance through the state of Ohio until she turns 18. I've gone without health insurance the past few years. Since I was too old for Mom's insurance plan. And at the salon I rent my booth, which makes me self-employed. I stupidly never got an insurance plan, because Theo was going to add me to his plan as soon as we got married, and he has great insurance—which I would've had access to, had we gotten married. But that's not how things went down."

"What can I do? Let me help," Ford says, his voice low and pained.

I tuck a stray piece of hair behind my ear. It must've snuck out of my braid during the flight. I really should've peeked in the mirror before coming down here. I probably look like a troll. "If we do need to schedule a procedure, I could use some help. Financially." I close my eyes, hating the thought of asking my best friend for money. "The procedure would be expensive. And I don't expect a handout, Ford," I say quickly. "If you lend me some money, I'll pay you back with interest. I never want you to think I'm friends with you for your money, and I hate even asking."

"Yes," he says adamantly. "I don't care how much it is, and you're not paying me back."

"Please think about it for a few days. It's a lot of money. No decisions about it now. I have money, savings even, just not enough...yet. And if you agreed, after thinking it over"—I shoot him a knowing glance and he rolls his eyes—"I'd want to write up a contract stating I'll pay you back, for my own peace of mind. I never want money to come between us."

He stares at the floor, hands on his hips. I know this is a big ask, because Ford is generous, and he really doesn't care about money. But I saw how money made my mom crazy and fueled all of her relationships. I don't want that for myself or Ford.

Finally, his eyes meet mine again. "Just let me do this for you. I already know you're not friends with me for my money. You were there for me when I was an awkward eight-year-old, then when I was a scrawny pre-teen, and of course through my broody teenaged years. You've been there through it all, so let me be there for you."

I sigh heavily. "Just humor me and take a few days to think about it, okay?"

He rolls his eyes again. "My answer will still be yes in a few days. And didn't you say that was just one of the things you wanted to talk to me about?"

I clear my throat. "Oh, right. Yes, there's one more thing."

He waits for me to continue.

"Like I said, the procedure isn't a big deal." I smile, putting on my bravest face, even though I'm terrified of being put under anesthesia and all the things that could go wrong. Which is why I have to ask what I'm about to. "But if something were to go wrong..."

His eyes widen.

"I said *if*. I need someone to agree to be Nella's guardian. With my mom no longer speaking to me and Theo out of the picture, I don't have anyone to raise her if something terrible happens. In or out of the operating room. What if I was in an accident or something?"

His face falls, and he does something that takes me completely by surprise. He hugs me.

CHAPTER
THREE
FORD

I CAN'T SLEEP. I'm feeling too murderous. I'm not this hotheaded guy. I'm mature and calm. The one who holds everyone else back when they're trying to start fights. I hate feeling out of control.

I've already tried all my usual tactics when I have trouble sleeping, which is often. Melatonin, white noise, heated blanket. Nothing is working. Nothing short of kicking Theo Peregrine's ass would help me relax enough to fall asleep.

Also, I can't stop thinking about Amber. Is she alive and healthy in the other room? Is her heart okay? How soon would they schedule the surgery? Are there any other options? I should've asked more questions earlier.

And why would she want me to take a week to think about it? Surely, she knows I would do literally anything for her. I'd give her a kidney if she needed one. And apparently, I'd raise her child if something happened to her. I know I would. But am I the best person? Maybe not. A little girl being raised by a single hockey player seems like a recipe for disaster. I push the thought out of my mind because nothing is going to happen to Amber. Like she said, they do this surgery every day.

Finally, I give in and pad softly through my room and across the hall to peek in on her. Maybe if I see her breathing, I'll finally be able to get to sleep. Sometimes, I wish we could go back in time, when we were little and camped out in a tent in the backyard, huddled together reading books with a flashlight. What I wouldn't give to curl up beside her and sleep with her all night like when we were kids.

Keeping my steps quiet on the hardwood floors, I bring my hand up and rest it on the doorknob. If she locked the door, I'll be up all night worrying about her for sure. The doorknob turns easily, and I slowly push open the door. Creeping to the side of her bed, I see her in her usual sleeping position, which hasn't changed in the last twenty years. She's on her stomach, hair tossed over her face, mouth open. Amber isn't a pretty sleeper to most, but seeing her hair flying around from her deep, sleepy breaths, makes my shoulders finally come down from my ears. I hadn't even realized how tense I was, until I saw her breathing. Quietly, I step over to the pack-and-play, where Nella is sleeping in almost the exact same position as her mama. I smile down at her.

I turn to leave the room, telling myself everything is fine and now I can go to sleep. But my feet won't move. There's some instinct deep inside me gluing me to this spot on the carpet. I decide not to fight it and sit down on the plush rug between the pack-and-play and the guest bed. Resting my back and head against the side of the mattress, I close my eyes.

I drift off to sleep, finally, as I think, *I'm no cardiologist, but heart issues are pretty serious? Aren't they?*

"Wahhhhh! Wahhhhhhh!"

Starling awake, I jump to my feet, coming face to face with

a bleary-eyed Amber. Now that she's out of bed, I can see she no longer sleeps in oversized tees. She has on a pink spaghetti strap nightgown that ends just above her knees. It's not showing a ton of skin, but enough for me to appreciate it.

"Ford, what are you doing in here?" Her brow furrows in confusion, then she turns and picks up Nella. Nella quiets instantly in her mother's arms. "Did Nella wake you up?" Amber asks, deftly grabbing a diaper and wipes from the bag on the nightstand, then laying Nella on the bed to change her.

"No, sorry." I reach up and scratch the back of my head, feeling awkward. "I couldn't sleep and came in to check on you. I was worried your heart would like...stop or something. Then I must've fallen asleep in here on the floor."

She looks up at me, her hands still moving to change the diaper. Her eyes are soft as she studies me. "Oh, Ford, you poor thing. I'm okay."

"Poor thing? *I'm* not the one with a heart hole."

She releases a sleepy chuckle. The raspy sound does something to my chest, making me wonder if maybe I do have a hole in my heart.

"You worry too much. Always have." She refastens Nella's outfit and picks her up again, standing from the bed and walking toward me. "Here, do you mind holding her while I get situated to nurse her?"

My throat feels tight, but I force myself to swallow. "Um, yeah, sure." I hold my hands out to take her and Amber laughs softly. "Bring your arms in toward your chest, almost like you're giving yourself a hug."

I do as she says, leaving just enough room for her to rest Nella between my arms and my chest. Her hands brush my pecs as she pulls them away from her daughter. I try not to notice.

Amber's face brightens in a huge grin as she looks at me.

"Oh, my gosh. This is so cute. Let me grab my phone and snap a pic." She rushes to the nightstand and unplugs her phone, taking a few photos of me holding Nella.

The baby who's getting very, very wiggly. And not appreciating my firm chest at all. Amber grabs a weird looking pillow in the shape of a half circle and gets into her bed, resting her back against the headboard. She circles the pillow around her waist, then unsnaps one of the straps of her nightgown.

The fabric loosens, not falling down completely. I blink rapidly, willing away the desire to look at that patch of exposed skin. But that's not for me, it's for Nella. I bend my knees, making a bouncing motion, trying to soothe the fussy infant. It doesn't do any good. The baby's just rubbing her mouth around my pec, trying to find a nipple.

"Sorry, Nella, You're not going to get any milk out of that."

Amber bursts into laughter, extending her arms. "Okay, I'm ready. Bring the hungry baby over here."

I gently hand her over then look away, trying to find something to look at besides Amber's breast.

If she notices my inner turmoil, she doesn't mention it.

"Hey, grab the remote and find something for us to watch while she eats."

Thrilled to have a distraction, I practically lunge for the remote. I turn on the small flat screen sitting on top of a dresser and turn the volume way down. Flipping through the channels, I smile when I see that an old rerun of The Joy of Painting has just started. I select it then sit on the end of the bed.

"Get your butt up here, Remington. Don't let a little boob freak you out."

I shoot her an annoyed glance but scoot up to sit next to her.

"Oh! It's the Dark Waterfall episode. My favorite."

I smile at her, making sure to keep my gaze on her face and not any lower.

Thanks to Amber, I've seen every single episode of The Joy of Painting at least twice. Despite being a terrible painter, I always thought Bob Ross's voice was soothing. Honestly, It's just a good show.

We watch the episode while Nella eats, and time passes quickly. Amber brings a sleeping Nella up to rest on her shoulder and pats her back gently. Nella's mouth is open as she sleeps, and I chuckle at how uncivilized she looks. There's even some breast milk dribbling out of her gaping mouth.

"She's gross, right?" Amber whispers, wrinkling her nose to get her point across.

"She's not very ladylike. You've got your work cut out."

Amber's sleepy giggle makes my stomach flip.

She gets up and puts Nella back in the pack-and-play then climbs back into bed. I turn the TV off and get off of the bed. Taking a few steps toward the door to head back to my own room, I put on a brave face because I really, really don't want to leave. I'm going to stare at my ceiling in my bedroom for the rest of the night.

"Ford, just stay."

I turn to look at my best friend over my shoulder. She's lying on her side, facing me, and releases a wide yawn.

"The bed is big enough for us both, and it's not like we haven't shared a bed a million times." She smiles softly. "Besides, you're just going to worry about my heart hole for the rest of the night if you leave."

I sigh and walk back to the guest bed and climb in beside Amber. We're facing each other, but her eyes are already closed. She looks beautiful in the dim light coming from the nightlight that she must've brought with her. I hadn't thought of getting a nightlight. Her red hair looks darker now than it did in the bright airport lighting. I've always loved her hair color. The red always made it easy to spot her in a crowd. The bright red is still visible at the roots, but the dyed pink ends are a cute addition, and *so* Amber. A cascade of light brown freckles splays across her pretty face and pert little nose. I fall asleep counting them.

CHAPTER FOUR
AMBER

NELLA WAKES us up early in the morning, and I'm relieved when I roll over and see Ford looks well-rested. I hate that my health issues are causing him stress. Which I realize sounds ridiculous, since they are causing *me* stress. But Ford has enough on his plate, what with being the leader of one of the top teams in the NHL.

While Ford excuses himself to cook breakfast, I nurse Nella. I spend extra time soaking up our moments while nursing, knowing I won't be able to nurse for several days before and after my procedure because of the medications.

When I come down the steps holding my daughter, I can hear the sizzle of bacon and the clanging of pans. It smells delicious.

As we come into the kitchen, Ford is too distracted to notice us. He turns the bacon and pancakes with a spatula, splattering some pancake batter on himself in the process. I know he hates being messy, so I'm expecting him to grab a towel and wipe up the mess, but instead, he puts the spatula down, reaches behind his head, and tugs the white tee off over his head. He turns and tosses it on the counter and continues cooking.

Perhaps it's because I was with Theo for so long, and that's why I've forced myself not to notice just how attractive my best friend is. But now Theo isn't in the picture, and apparently, there's nothing stopping me from ogling Ford's pristine form guilt-free.

Goodness. Not only has he aged well, but I think he's gained several pounds of muscle since last I saw him. His perpetually tanned skin is taut and smooth everywhere, with just a smattering of dark hair across his chest, then picking up again right above his belly button and trailing down…I shake my head, ending that thought immediately.

His honed muscles ripple and pulse as he flips the pancakes and moves around the kitchen. His abs flex when he reaches for something in the cabinet near the stove.

My mouth goes dry as I study him, wondering how someone can possibly be this fit. I guess it's literally his job, but still, I feel suddenly self-conscious. Ford isn't vain, but I wonder if he's noticed how I've changed in the past year. A few more wrinkles, a few more pounds…and *not* of muscle. The stretch marks that make my once-flat stomach now look like a tiger mauled it. Thankfully he can't see my belly.

Nella coos, drawing Ford's attention. His head whips over to look at us and the most stunning smile stretches across his face. And there's that chin dimple again.

I squeeze my eyes shut for a second, willing these thoughts away. Making things awkward between myself and the most important person in my life—besides Nella—is not on my list of things to do. Ever.

I don't even know what's gotten into me today. I've always been able to recognize Ford's attractiveness, without *being* attracted to him.

Damn these post-partum hormones.

"Good morning, girls," he says before turning back to the bacon and pancakes.

I swallow, trying to dampen my dry throat. "Good morning. It smells great."

Nella coos again and I look down to see her staring up at me. Her fine, red hair is wild around her face, and her green eyes are shining. She's always happiest in the morning.

Ford finishes up and makes two plates. The way he arranges the pancake stacks is so precise, like he used a level. The man could make food for magazines. Or be one of those guys on TikTok who makes sexy cooking videos.

I follow him to the long dining table and sit down. He places a plate in front of me and I can't help the laugh that bubbles out of me. "You know, I'm just going to stuff these pancakes in my face. You didn't have to arrange them so neatly."

He shoots me a shy grin. "I don't even think about it. It just happens."

"I wish I could have just an ounce of your tidiness," I admit before cutting off a section of pancakes and popping it into my mouth.

Nella fusses and Ford studies her. "Do you want me to hold her while you eat?"

I study his face, looking for signs of apprehension, but I only find genuine helpfulness. "Sure." Gently, I hand him Nella.

She stares at him as he fumbles to get the right hold on her. I notice that his stomach doesn't even bunch when he sits down. The rows of abdominal muscles just do this fascinating stacking thing.

He props Nella up on his shoulder, and she snuggles in

there, dipping her tongue out and drooling on his skin. He laughs. "Whoops, I forgot to go get a clean shirt."

Nella licks his skin, not even knowing what she's doing, probably hoping to find milk.

He laughs again and I join him. Babies are so unhinged.

I start eating quickly so I can take Nella back and let Ford eat.

Ford clears his throat, his deep voice low when he asks, "So, not to be annoying, but what exactly *can* we do this weekend?"

I snort a laugh, but his stony expression doesn't budge. "As long as I'm not running a marathon or giving birth, I'll be fine. Try not to worry, please? It's been forever since I got to hang out with you, and I don't want the whole weekend to be ruined."

With a resigned sigh, he nods.

After eating breakfast and getting dressed, Ford takes us to a local shopping area in Alexandria. He only has the morning with us before he has to head to a team photo shoot for the afternoon, but Nella and I are going to tag along and watch.

The area we're in is newer, but the builders obviously worked hard to make everything match the historical part of town. The buildings are white and fresh, with gold sconces and brick accents. The sidewalks are red brick, distressed so they don't look new. The shopping center is quaint, but it also feels fancy. It's adorable. Every shop has its own entrance opening onto the brick path, everything from restaurants to clothing boutiques to salons. One shop, in particular, that catches my eye. It's a salon called Luxurious Lather, and it stands out amongst the other establishments, with black details instead of gold and a blush pink rug out front. I stop in front of the large windows and glance inside, noting the marble counter tops, huge floor-length mirrors in front of each station, and blush pink salon chairs. There's even a black velvet couch in the center of the stations where clients can wait. It's the prettiest salon I've ever seen. The kind of place I always dreamt of working but ended up in a dumpy little salon in Ohio instead.

Nella fusses from the baby carrier, and I sigh. She prefers to be moving and is probably mad I stopped for so long.

"I get my hair cut there," Ford says. "The stylist I go to doesn't know who I am. It's refreshing."

I chuckle. "Ahhh, or do you just go here because they have the hottest stylists?"

"Well, I always go to a guy named Peter. So, no, that's not the reason."

I burst out laughing. "Peter isn't a hockey fan?"

"If he is, he's never said anything."

Looking over my shoulder, I glance longingly at the chic salon once more. "I'd love to work at a place like that. It's so pretty."

"Why don't you?" he asks, looking straight ahead as we walk.

"I already have a solid clientele built up where I work. Our prices are lower than the fancier salons, so if I switched, not many of them would follow me."

He nods. "You should move here. I could send you clients."

"Ford." I huff out a laugh. "I can't just move to D.C."

He stops walking and looks at me. "Why not? What's keeping you in Ohio?" His deep brown eyes bore into mine, and when he makes this much eye contact, I know he's serious. "If you're closer, I can help you with Nella."

It warms my heart that he's thought about this, and if I'm

honest, there's nothing besides my clients keeping me in Ohio anymore. But starting over when this year has already brought so much change feels daunting.

"You travel all the time. I'd rarely see you. And I don't want to be a burden, I don't want you to feel like you have to help me." I take a few strides forward, the movement giving me something to focus on besides Ford's intense gaze.

He catches up with one long stride. "If I needed help, would you feel burdened by me?"

I tilt up my head, leveling him with a look that says *I know where you're going with this.*

He raises his eyebrows and shoots me a cocky smirk, knowing he made his point.

"And what about your recovery?" he says, lowering his voice. "Who's going to help you while you're healing?"

I pause, scrambling to give him a solid answer. Ford won't be content with just any made-up answer, but that's all I have to give him. Because the only option I have is to hire help, which is more money that I don't have. Not to mention the days of work I'll miss for the procedure and recovery. "I'm not 100% sure I need the procedure, and *if* I do, the downtime is nothing. I'll hire help if I need it."

One of his dark—but perfectly groomed—eyebrows shoots up. "Won't that be expensive?"

I release a sigh that turns into a groan. "I'm an adult, Ford! Let me figure it out." I know my annoyance is misplaced and he's just trying to help. But it sucks being the needy one here. Ford can try to reverse our roles in theory, like he's the one who needs help, only to make me see his point. But the fact is, he doesn't need help. He never does. He's stupidly successful and I hate asking him for things. I suppose it's my pride getting in the way, but what do I have left if not my pride?

CHAPTER FIVE
FORD

AMBER IS SULKING. Why is this woman so stubborn? I'm not trying to treat her like a child, I just want to help. I have millions of dollars sitting in my bank account and she needs money. Problem solved! Except this ridiculously independent woman wants to do everything herself.

We walk in silence, something I'm usually more than comfortable with, but I hate that she's upset. I wanted to ease her worries, not add more to them. I glance at her right as we pass by a colorful shop window. By the look of the window display, it seems to be a furniture and decor store. Amber's face finally brightens.

"Oh, my gosh. Let's get some things for your house." She grabs my wrist and tugs me along behind her.

Now, of course, I could easily resist her. I'm a 250-pound, 6'4" professional hockey player…and she's a foot shorter than me and a good hundred-ish pounds lighter to boot. But now that she's smiling again, I'm not about to ruin it.

As soon as the door shuts behind us, I'm hit with a dozen different scents. I school my features, trying not to scrunch up my nose. I look to my left and see a candle display filled with candles of varying scents, shapes, and colors. That's probably where the overwhelming smell is coming from. I remind myself it still smells better than our locker room.

To my right, there's a large red sofa with so many pillows on it, there's no way anyone could actually sit on it. Amber is eyeing the same couch, but her expression is delighted.

What is it with women and throw pillows? What's the point? You need two throw pillows exactly. One for each end of the couch.

Amber squeaks a sound of excitement. "Ford, we have to get you some pillows."

I'm not sure what expression my face twists into at that moment, but it makes her laugh.

"A little color will brighten up your living room. Just trust me."

I heave a resigned sigh. "Fine. Two pillows."

She places her fists on her hips. A difficult pose to pull off with a baby strapped to her front. "Five."

"Three."

"Four," she pleads, making her green eyes all big and round and pretty.

I clench my jaw. "Okay, four."

She claps her hands together above Nella's head, then turns around and gets busy picking out four pillows. She holds one up that has a flamingo on it, complete with actual feathers. She touches the feathers with an evil grin on her face.

"No."

She tosses it back into the pile and grabs a pale yellow one with a pineapple on it.

"Does everything in this shop have a symbol for swingers on it?" I ask with a groan.

She slaps her free hand over her mouth, trying not to laugh. "Get your mind out of the gutter," she whispers, looking around just as an older woman with a name tag walks over toward us.

The grey-haired woman, whose name is apparently Barbara, smiles at Amber. "Well, good morning! Can I help you love birds find anything?"

I open my mouth to correct her, but it's too late. She's spotted the baby.

"Oh, lord! Look at this little doll!" Her voice goes all soft and motherly as she looks at Nella with twinkling eyes. "You guys are just the cutest little family," Barbara gushes, smiling at me and Amber.

Amber takes it in stride. "Thank you so much." She looks up at me and sighs. "Isn't my husband a tall glass of water? I could just drink him right up." She turns and winks at Barbara.

I can't see my own face, but the heat I'm suddenly feeling would indicate I'm blushing. Hard.

Barbara giggles and loops an arm through Amber's. "Well, I wasn't going to say it. But yes! You lucky thing, you."

Amber flutters her lashes at me, loving this entire spectacle.

"Listen," Barbara says. "I own this shop, and I'll give you guys 20% off everything today, just because y'all are so stinking cute." She smiles and starts to walk away, waving over her shoulder. "Just let me know if I can help you find anything!"

Once Barbara is out of ear shot, Amber breaks into laughter.

I roll my eyes and cross my arms. "All day, every day I feel like I'm babysitting unruly hockey players…and you're no better."

She ignores me, back to rummaging through the throw pillows. "Okay let's pick out your pillows and get out of here. I'm sure the candles are driving you crazy."

I smile. It's nice having a person in this world who knows me almost as well as I know myself. Someone who can sense the things I don't always want to say out loud, someone who really sees me, even when I want to be invisible. Amber has a way of siphoning my thoughts out of my own head...except for my thoughts about her. But that's probably a good thing.

She picks two of the simplest pillows in the pile, one a pale blue, and the other white with a subtle floral pattern. Amber hands them to me, and I hold one under each arm, feeling ridiculous. She selects two more, both similar to the other two, with blue details.

"These four are simple but will still add a little color to your house."

I nod, surprised that I don't mind the colors or patterns she chose. Amber starts toward the register in the center of the shop where Barbara is waiting for us. I lean in, making my voice low so only Amber can hear me. "You do realize I don't need the 20% off, right? I could buy this entire shop with cash." I'm not trying to brag; I'm giving her facts. She doesn't have to pretend to be my doting wife to get me discounts. And money isn't an issue for me, so helping her isn't a big deal. I *want* to help her.

"I know, Mr. Money Bags. I was just having a little fun."

CHAPTER SIX
AMBER

STEPPING inside the D.C. Eagles ice plex brings a smile to my face. Actually, a full-on cheesy grin. Being in the icy cold building, finding a seat on the bleachers, brings back so many good memories from when Ford played varsity hockey at our high school.

After shopping, we stopped back at Ford's place just long enough for me to restock the diaper bag, grab some warm layers for myself and Nella, then head out again. Thank goodness Nella sleeps well in her carrier. My back is aching from carrying her around all morning, but that's okay. I wouldn't miss the chance to watch my best friend's photo shoot for the convenience of putting her down for a nap in her pack-and-play.

Ford points me toward the stands behind the glass where a smattering of family members have congregated, then walks toward the ice where they have lights and camera equipment set up. Today's photo shoot is for a calendar the team puts out every year. The guys pose with dogs and cats from a local animal shelter, and all proceeds from calendar sales go to the shelter. Ford loves dogs and looks forward to this every year.

I'm about to sit in the front, on an empty row of cold bleacher, when a pretty blonde starts waving at me. She comes toward me like she knows me, and I stare at her in confusion.

"You must be Amber!" she says once she's right in front of me. She's just a little taller than me and has shoulder-length blonde hair. Two other women trail closely behind her. One is tall and slim with short, curly hair. And the other looks like a Disney princess, with light brown hair and round, sparkly eyes.

"I'm Andie, Mitch's fiancée," The blonde woman says with a friendly smile, gesturing to herself, then juts a thumb behind her toward the Disney princess. "This is Mel. She's married to West." The petite woman smiles and wiggles her fingers in an awkward wave.

The taller one steps forward. She seems more serious than the other two, but she's wearing a kind smile. "I'm Noel. I'm with Colby Knight." She blushes and Mel nudges her playfully. Noel shoots her a playful glare then turns back to me. "It's so nice to meet you."

"It's nice meeting you, too."

Mel gets up close and personal so she can get a better look at Nella. "Oh, my gosh. Your baby is a-freaking-dorable."

I chuckle, finding it refreshing how friendly these girls are. Ford isn't one to share a lot of details about his friends. I know some of his teammates' names, mostly from watching games on TV. But I didn't realize I would meet some of their girlfriends and wives today.

"Thank you," I say, looking down to discover that Nella isn't even asleep. She's just staring at Mel.

Mel is a strange name for such a dainty-looking person. I wonder if it's a nickname. Before I can ask, she looks up at me with those blue eyes. "Can I hold her? If you don't feel comfortable, that's totally okay."

I withhold a sigh of relief. The chances I have to give my arms and back a break, are few. I'm alone in Ohio, except for the daycare I started using when I went back to work a few weeks ago. Actually, this might be the first time someone has offered to hold Nella for me just because they wanted to. My eyes begin to burn at the realization, and I have to control my facial muscles to keep my chin from shaking. "Yes, of course," I manage to choke out.

I unbuckle the baby carrier and carefully hand Nella to Mel. I just met the woman, but now I want to be best friends with her.

Mel cradles my baby in her arms, looking at her with all the adoration this little girl deserves. My chest tightens at the reminder Nella doesn't have any uncles or aunts…or even a father. Not any she'll ever know, anyway. It's surprisingly emotional for me to see her being loved on by someone other than me.

Andie leans in and stares at her, using one hand to smooth Nella's wispy red hair. "She's gorgeous," she whispers.

"She really is. I'd die for vibrant red hair," Noel says, studying Nella.

I chuckle, hoping it doesn't sound watery. Because my emotions are definitely getting the better of me.

"Come sit with us. We saved seats right in the middle so we can watch the puppy cuteness," Noel says, waving a hand for us to follow her.

When we make it up to the center of the bleachers and get comfy in our seats—as comfy as one can get on a metal bleacher—the guys walk out onto the ice. They're in jeans, tennis shoes, and their jerseys. The team walks straight toward the crates and starts interacting with the animals. The dogs wag their tails, excited to make new friends. And the cats hiss and cower, not wanting to be disturbed. This should be interesting.

Noel stares at Colby and sighs.

"You're a goner," Mel teases, then snuggles Nella a little closer. Nella is slowly drifting off to sleep in her arms.

Andie, who's farthest from me, leans over so she can see me past Noel and Mel. "Noel was a little resistant to Colby's charms at first, so it's fun to see her all googly-eyed."

"Really?" I ask, looking at Noel and then at Colby Knight, who's walking—no, swaggering—across the ice. "But he's so dreamy."

Noel smirks and rolls her eyes again.

"How long are you in town?" Mel asks from her seat beside me.

"I have to fly back to Ohio Sunday night." Does my voice sound as depressed as my heart feels? Oh yeah, my heart. My stomach dips at the reminder that I have my appointment Monday after arriving back home. My heart begins to race with the possibility of being in an operating room. I breathe in a calming breath and push it from my mind, for now.

"Aw, such a short visit," Andie says, looking at Nella in adoration. "Can I hold her too?"

With a smile, I nod.

Mel narrows her eyes at her friend briefly, but sighs. "Okay, fine. I'll share the baby cuteness."

Andie makes grabby hands as Mel adjust Nella so she can hand her off.

Andie snuggles her close and sniffs her hair. "Why do babies always smell so good?"

I scoff. "Trust me, they don't always smell good."

The girls laugh. Now that Nella is closer, Noel studies her. "Wow, they're just so sweet and innocent at this age. It's nice to know they don't come out as cocky eighteen-year-olds trying to get out of homework."

My eyebrows raise slightly, wondering what the hell she's talking about.

"Noel is a history professor at Arlington U. She has some difficult students," Mel explains.

Noel blows out a deep breath, as if sloughing off her annoyance. She leans over Andie and Nella to look at me. "What do you do, Amber?"

"I'm a hair stylist," I say with a smile. I'm proud of what I do, and I'm really good at it. Sure, I'm not thrilled with my current salon, but I love that I get to be creative every day.

"No way!" Noel ruffles her curls. "I wish you lived here. My stylist just retired."

Mel combs a hand through her curtain bangs. "My last stylist messed up my bangs."

Andie looks up from the sleeping baby. "I have a stylist who's great with hair…but she has no filter. She always asks creepy questions about Mitch."

They all groan.

"Oh, I hate that!" This comes from Mel.

Noel glances across the ice and bursts into laughter. "Don't look now, but I think Mitch 'The Machine' is a little terrified."

We all look up and see Mitch, West, Colby, and Ford staring at us. Mitch's eyes are wide, and his skin is pale. He's clearly a little freaked to see his fiancée doting over a baby.

Andie grins at him and blows him a kiss before returning her focus to Nella.

Colby says something to Mitch, and they all break into laughter, except Mitch. The joke must've been at his expense.

I chuckle. "Mitch realizes babies aren't contagious, right?" I ask in a teasing tone.

"He'll be okay." Andie grins. "It's good for him to be a little scared once in a while, ya know?"

"When is your wedding?" I ask, having a hard time picturing the large, grumpy athlete marrying this bright ray of sunshine.

"Right after Christmas! I can't wait." Her gaze flits up to her fiancé again, who's now holding a kitten while a photographer moves him in front of the cameras.

Mel snickers. "Mitch with a kitten is something I never thought I'd see. He's usually plowing into his opponents. Sometimes after a hit the other player will fly several feet before landing."

Noel and I grimace. But Andie looks on and sighs happily. "I love how powerful he is."

"Better wear a helmet on your honeymoon," Mel teases, making Andie laugh.

"Don't worry, I'll be prepared." Andie winks.

"Ew." Noel rolls her eyes. "Okay, my turn with the baby."

Noel's face morphs into a gooey expression as she reaches for Nella. Nella is sleeping through all the fuss. Up until now, Nella had been held by myself…our doctors and nurses, my daycare lady, and Ford.

I kind of wish she was awake to appreciate it all, I think to myself but regret it a few seconds later when she abruptly wakes up. Noel is trying so hard to hold Nella in a way that will make her comfortable, but it's just not working. I wrinkle my nose and stand to take her from Noel.

"Sorry, she's probably getting hungry."

Noel reluctantly hands her back to me.

CHAPTER
SEVEN
FORD

"MOMS ARE *HOT*," Bruce says, his eyes as wide as they can possibly go as he stares at the girls sitting on the bleachers. The girls who are taking turns cooing over and adoring the baby.

I swallow, suppressing the sudden urge to slam my fist into his sharp jaw. She's my friend. There's no reason to be jealous. She's my *friend*.

Colby studies me with concern, an astuteness in his eyes that wasn't there before he met Noel. Before Noel, he thought only of himself most of the time.

I clear my throat, which Bruce either doesn't hear or completely ignores. "I mean, wow. I would've never guessed she just had a baby."

West slugs him in the shoulder, and since he's not wearing his goalie padding, he rubs at the area where West's fist landed. "What was that for?"

West, Colby and even Mitch glance at me. Am I that transparent? Surely, the feelings I've harbored for Amber since I was eight aren't that obvious. What if Amber has sensed them all this time and felt sorry for me? The thought makes my gut twist.

Colby elbows Mitch in the side. "I think your girl wants a baby, dude."

Terror washes over Mitch Anderson's face before he eases it back into his familiar scowl. "One year of wedded bliss, then I'll give her all the babies she wants."

West beams. "Aw, Daddy Mitch."

We all laugh at that, the stiffness in my back easing and my gut unclenching. Thank goodness I have these gigantic goofballs to keep my mind occupied.

Our new defenseman, who looks barely twenty, walks over carrying a fluffy white cat. With his freckles, curly brown hair, and blue eyes, he looks even younger than most of the other rookies.

"Hey guys," he says with a nervous smile.

I rifle through my brain for names. I'm not great with people I don't know, and I'm especially horrible with names. I do this word association thing, have since I was a kid, to remember names. Only, now I can't remember my word association for the kid.

I glance at West and Colby. They're good with people. "Hey, Thomas!" Colby says, giving the kid a big smile.

Thomas. I keep my face neutral but wince internally. Thomas the Tank Engine. Now I remember.

West ruffles the fur on the cat's head playfully, apparently forgetting it's a cat and not a dog. The cat's ears go down and West doesn't even notice. "You played amazing last week, kid."

Thomas's mouth pulls up into a crooked grin, like he's trying to play it cool and not smile but he can't help himself.

"Thanks, man."

"Yeah, Thomas, great work," I say, following social cues

from my teammates. I think one of the reasons I've always loved playing hockey is because it gave me endless opportunities to watch people interacting and, in turn, learning how to interact with people myself.

Here I am, the leader of the D.C. Eagles…the captain, but I feel like a fraud. If it wasn't for my teammates, I'd be lost.

Needing a distraction, I find the crate of a friendly dog. It looks a little younger than the others. The dog's tongue hangs out as it breathes and its bushy tail wags. Glancing at one of the animal shelter workers, I point to the crate. The man nods, and I unlatch the crate and pull out the small puppy. Looking at the name plate, I see her name is Rose. As I hold her, I note that she looks like a different version of a dog I once called my best friend. My childhood dog, Moose, was a Bernese mountain dog. And this one has similar coloring, but with more white and less black. Rose licks my face and I run my hand through her soft fur. Her bottom wiggles happily, and it's simultaneously comforting and sad. Moose used to greet me the same way.

I allow myself to think back to when I was a kid, when I'd hold it together at school all day…coming home to Moose felt like a reward. I could always relax and be myself with him. He didn't care if I made too much eye contact, or not enough. He also had an uncanny way of knowing when I was close to a meltdown. Any time I felt itchy all over, he was by my side distracting me and calming me before I knew what was happening.

It's cool they train dogs for kids with autism now, and I'm glad I had those years with Moose even though he wasn't an official service dog.

Glancing down at the puppy in my arms, my throat feels thick, and her face becomes a little blurry. My teammates probably wouldn't care if I cried in front of them, but I'd like to avoid it anyway. I blink back the emotion and rest my chin on top Rose's soft head. She jerks her head away and licks me right on the lips. I laugh, unable to help myself.

If I didn't travel so much, I probably would've already gotten myself another dog.

"I can't believe your visit is over already," I tell Amber as I drop her off at the airport Sunday evening.

Amber hedges, thinking before she speaks. Her eyes are filled with a sadness that's unusual for her. "I'm glad you have people here, Ford," she finally says, her voice sounding like she's holding back tears. "I loved meeting your hockey family. Your teammate's wives and girlfriends." She pauses, smirking. "And hanging out with you, of course." Her green eyes twinkle in a way that makes it obvious she's teasing. Amber is easy to read, which I appreciate. Most people's expressions are difficult to understand.

Despite her teasing, there's still something sad in her expression, or maybe the way she's standing, or maybe I'm reading into it. Deciphering the way people are feeling has never been my strength.

The sounds of cars stopping and going whirls around us, the scent of gasoline keeping me from getting one last inhale of the way Amber smells... and Nella. Babies smell strangely nice. Now I know what my mother is talking about when she talks about her memories of me and my sisters when we were infants.

"I'll see you for Thanksgiving, yeah?" She breaks the silence. Nella stirs in her baby carrier, always strapped to her mother, and Amber bounces a few times to soothe her.

"Yeah, Ambs. I'll see you girls next week. My parents are excited to see you… and Nella."

Amber chuckles. "I'm sure they're more excited about the cute baby, but that's okay."

I smirk, sticking my hands into my pockets. "Maybe my mom, but you know she loves babies."

Amber's phone pings. "That's probably my check-in notification. I better go."

I keep my hands firmly inside my pockets so I don't reach for her and holding her for a while before she leaves. I remind myself I'll see her next week and that makes me feel a little better. "Have a safe flight."

She waves and smiles, heading inside the airport.

I stand there, staring after her like a sad puppy. I always feel this way after her visits, but something about the look in her eyes made me feel like she wished she didn't have to leave. Maybe just because she doesn't have Theo to go home to any longer.

Or maybe it was more than that.

CHAPTER EIGHT
FORD

THE FOLLOWING WEEK, I'm at my parent's in Ohio for Thanksgiving. I don't always get to come home for holidays, but we happened to have four days between games, so I took advantage of the lapse in our schedule.

I'm in the kitchen with my mom, where she has me stirring the gravy. I glance around the room while I stir. Their house is the complete opposite of mine. But I love it, nonetheless. Being home makes everything...easier. I can relax in my parent's dated nineties-style home in the Dayton suburbs and be myself. If I don't make enough eye contact or say the right thing, Amber and my family won't judge me or think I'm weird. My family, and Amber, are the only people in my life who know about my Asperger's—er, high-functioning autism. I've carefully guarded the information so the media won't bombard me.

Mom knows I'm comfortable with silence. Unfortunately, my peaceful moment doesn't last long. She abruptly turns to me, pinning me with her blue eyes, and asks, "So sweetie, are you dating anyone?"

I blink a few times since I wasn't prepared for this question. "That was abrupt."

Her slim shoulders sag, and she wipes her hands on her checkered apron and leans against the counter. "You're handsome, successful, wonderful…" She fusses with her salt-and-pepper bob as she speaks—it's what she does when she's worried.

I interrupt her. "Mom, stop. You don't need to worry about me."

She pushes off the counter and grabs the large goggles beside her, fixing them on top of her head. She always wears them to slice the turkey since getting turkey juice in her eye a few years ago. "I don't want you to be alone. I know it's hard for you to open up to people. But you're such a wonderful person. Your sisters are settling down and falling in love, while you're all alone in D.C." She sighs. "Farrah is already married, and even thinking about children, even Felicity is getting serious with the young man she's been dating. I just hate the thought of you being lonely while your younger sisters are moving forward with their lives."

I meet her gaze, knowing it puts her mind at ease for some reason. Why do people want eye contact? It's so weird. "I'm very successful, Mom. Some parents dream of their sons making it to the NHL."

"I don't care what you do for a living, Ford. I just want you to be happy. We're proud of you, always have been…but it's hard sometimes to know how wonderful you are and to see you all alone." She pats me on the chest lovingly. "I want you to have someone to share all that success with."

I heave a heavy sigh. I hate that all these years after my diagnosis, my parents still worry about me. As if I haven't proven I can be a thriving and successful adult. It feels like no matter what, they will always, always worry about my well-being.

But being alone has never bothered me. And I have friends, I have a life. I'm not cowering under tables when I get overwhelmed anymore. I've learned to live with the challenges of being neurodivergent. I know Mom didn't mean to offend me, that she means well...but her words still make my whole body feel tense. My skin prickles in that irritating way that it has since I was a kid whenever I get upset.

"When will Amber be here?" Mom asks, changing the subject. It's like she can read my thoughts. And honestly, maybe she can. The woman has always seemed to have eyes and ears everywhere.

I count to three and exhale a calming breath before I glance up at the giant rooster-shaped clock above the stove. It's almost three in the afternoon. "She should be here any minute." A smile tugs at my mouth, and all those itchy, prickly feelings start to fade.

My sisters must hear the mention of Amber and bound into the small but cozy kitchen that's lined with oak cabinets in an ugly, orange wood-stain.

"Did somebody say Amber is here?" My youngest sister, Felicity, asks. Her dark hair is pulled up in a bouncy ponytail and she has a white ribbon tied around it like she's thirteen instead of twenty-eight.

My middle sister, Farrah, has the same dark hair as Felicity and me, but hers' is styled neatly and flows down her back. I think she must've used one of those hair straightener thingies. Her wedding ring flashes as she demurely tucks her hair behind one ear, but I notice Connor isn't here with her. He always seems to put work over everything else, even his own wife. I've never liked the guy. I remember Mom's comment about her thinking about having kids, and my eyebrows draw together.

"I can't wait to hold Nella," Farrah says, her face lighting up.

"Women and babies," I mutter, earning a smack on my shoulder from Felicity.

The neutral expression I have plastered on my face is making me a big liar, because I can't wait to see Nella again. It's weird how having Nella and Amber in my home for a weekend felt more normal than it ever did without them.

The doorbell rings and my dad yells from the living room, where he's been watching the Thanksgiving Day parade, that he's getting the door.

I eye my sisters, and then we all bolt out of the kitchen, through the living room, and to the front door in a race to see who can get there the fastest.

Not much has changed since we were kids.

"Whoah, whoah, whoah!" Dad puts up his hands up, laughing. "You're gonna knock this old man right over."

I roll my eyes. My dad is in great shape, always has been. And despite his dark hair being about fifty percent gray now, he looks younger than his sixty years.

Dad shoves us all behind him and swings open the door. Amber comes into view, holding a sleeping Nella, and my breath is suddenly stuck somewhere in my lungs I just saw her last week, but knowing she's right here, brings me a joy I can't put into words.

"Amber, so good to see you, kiddo!" Dad says loudly, causing Nella to stir.

"Thank you for having me," she says as Dad ushers her inside.

My sisters rush in to hug her, and I find myself once again

wishing I hadn't held back embracing her all these years. As a kid, I hated being touched. I'm still not a touchy guy. I *could* be with Amber, though.

"Oh, Amber, she's a doll," Felicity whispers, not wanting to wake the baby.

"She really is," Farrah agrees.

"Thank you. I agree," Amber says with a wink.

"Hey, you," I finally say. I'm the only one in the room focusing on Amber and not Nella. No offense to Nella, but I could just look at her mom all damn day. It's always been like that, my eyes navigating straight toward her like I'm a ship lost at sea and she's dry land.

Mom scurries into the living room where we're all still standing. Her apron is a mess, and her goggles are still on top of her head. "Amber!" Mom says, rushing in to give her a hug.

My family might be loud, brash, and a little dorky. But they treat people well, and I'm especially thankful they love Amber like family with all she's been through this year.

"Wow, I've missed this house," Amber says softly, then sighs. "It hasn't changed a bit. And neither have the Remingtons." She grins, eyeing my mom's goggles and then my dad's ugly Christmas sweater.

Dad chuckles. "It's been too long, sweetheart. How's your mom?"

Amber stills. I open my mouth to change the subject, my go-to for when a topic makes things uncomfortable. But Amber recovers, giving my dad a smile that doesn't meet her eyes.

"I'm not sure. We actually don't talk." Amber glances down at her baby girl, and Dad's eyebrows raise in understanding.

"I didn't realize that. I'm sorry." He clears his throat. "Well, we're thrilled you're both here."

Mom nods in agreement, then ushers us into the kitchen where the Thanksgiving meal is ready and waiting, aside from the turkey that she's about to trim with her electric knife. Everything is arranged on the countertop in a buffet-style. We're not one of those fancy families who lay out a picture worthy spread in a formal dining room. We're plastic tablecloths and buffets all the way in the Remington household.

Excited chatter fills the room as Mom cuts up the turkey and tosses the chunks into a big, foil pan. Dad watches with his arms crossed, always a little sour he doesn't get to carve the turkey but knowing better than to interfere in his wife's kitchen.

When Mom gives the all-clear, we usher through the kitchen, filling our plates with turkey, mom's famous stuffing, green bean casserole, and all the Thanksgiving fixings. We take our seats in the formal dining room. Formal is a strong word since there's a plastic tablecloth lining the dated table. It has a turkey-and-pumpkin print all over it. Also, we're eating on paper plates. The nice, thick ones…but still paper.

Nella wakes up the moment Amber sits down to eat, but she's quickly stolen by my oldest sister, who snuggles her happily while Amber eats.

"So, tell me what's new with the Remingtons," Amber says after swallowing a bite of stuffing.

"Well." Felicity jumps in first, as usual. "You'll get to meet my man today, Harvey. He should be here any minute." She sighs dreamily, looking up at the ceiling. "He's amazing."

Amber waggles her eyebrows. "Oooh, Felicity's in looooove," she teases.

Felicity blushes, but the grin on her face tells me she doesn't care who knows how smitten she is.

Amber turns to Farrah with a smile. "And where's that hubby of yours?"

Farrah's face falls for a split second before she plasters on a smile. "Connor had to work today. His company is closing on a really big deal."

Amber nods, but I don't miss the worried glance she shoots me. I notice my parents give each other a weird look, silently communicating, the same way me and Amber just did. Before anyone else can speak, the doorbell rings.

Felicity jumps up from her chair so fast, it almost tumbles backward. "That must be Harvey!"

She rushes out of the room to greet him, and Farrah's comment is all but forgotten…by everyone but me.

Felicity returns, holding the hand of a young man with blond hair. He looks like the human version of an Australian Shepherd, with a happy-go-lucky grin, bright blue eyes, and his tongue half hanging out as he makes cow eyes at my little sister. My lips tug upward in a smile. How could they not? These two look so happy to be in each other's orbit, you can almost feel it in your soul.

"Everyone," Felicity says with a cheesy grin, "this is Harvey." She looks up at him again and his smile is just as big as hers.

"Great to see you again, Harv," Dad says with a smile, having already met Harvey several times, I'm sure. Mom gets up and hugs them both.

Harvey comes around to shake my hand, and I stand, towering over him. I'm not trying to be intimidating, it's just that he's barely taller than my little sister. But if a short king makes her happy, who am I to judge?

"Nice to meet you," I say, shaking his hand firmly.

I'm pleasantly surprised that his handshake is firm and confident. Not insecure about being smaller than me. You'd be surprised how skittish men get if you tower over them.

Harvey and Felicity walk over to their seats at the table, glancing awkwardly at each other and giggling instead of taking their seats.

They whisper to each other, and finally, Harvey clears his throat. "Before we sit, we actually have an announcement."

Felicity bounces a little, showing her excitement. "We're getting married!" She blurts, then the room goes into chaos mode. Everyone's standing, ushering toward the couple for hugs and congratulations, asking to look at the large diamond we all hadn't noticed until now. So, she must've been hiding it in her pocket. My parents and Farrah, seem genuinely excited, so Harvey must be a pretty good guy. Unlike Connor. None of us were excited when Farrah and Connor announced their engagement. Sure, we put on a happy face for Farrah. But I think we all had a bad feeling about him.

Once everyone sits back down, the questions roll in: *How did he propose? When's the wedding? How long will you wait to have children?*

Yes, my mother really asked that. At least it's not just *my* life she meddles in.

When the room finally calms down again and everyone starts eating again, I feel my spine relax. I don't always realize I'm uncomfortable, not in the moment. But when everyone talks at once, it puts me on edge.

Amber studies me from her seat beside me. She lays a hand firmly on my shoulder, probably sensing my stress somehow. Nella is looking at me too, with those wide green eyes that match her mother's. I smile at her, my hand coming up and pressing lightly on her nose. Her face morphs into a drooly grin, and damn if it doesn't just melt my heart right inside my chest. How does she do that?

When I turn away from the adorable baby to focus on my

plate of food, I meet my mother's sympathetic gaze. Her eyes move from me to Felicity and Harvey and then back again. My father follows suite. They're looking at me like I just told them I'm dying.

Since when does being single earn so much sympathy?

CHAPTER NINE
AMBER

ONCE DINNER IS OVER, Ford asks if I'd like to sit in the backyard. Mrs. Remington is happy to hold Nella for me since it's chilly outside. I need to leave soon, it's supposed to snow later, and I don't trust my car to drive in the snow. But I can't resist a quick walk in the Remington's backyard, a place that brings so many good memories. And I'd rather focus on those memories, than the fact that my appointment on Monday confirmed that I *do* need the procedure.

I look over at the man next to me. He sits on the bench near the rose bushes that bloom during the summer. A small wooden cross has been hammered into the ground next to the roses, and Ford stares at it.

Moose's grave.

I'm sure he's sad thinking about his old friend, but there's something else too.

He looked so happy when his baby sister announced her engagement, but soon afterward, something shifted. He's barely uttered a word since. He won't even make eye contact. Sure, eye contact has never been his favorite, but he usually does pretty well, especially with me. Something unspoken happened at that table, something that took the wind out of his sails, but I don't know what.

I allow the silence, sitting next to him on the bench and making myself comfortable before I try to get him to talk about whatever's bothering him.

He sits there stoically, hands interlocked on his lap. He might as well be a garden statue.

When he finally speaks, it's startling. Speaking is actually too soft of a word, because his voice sounds solidly determined when he says, "I think we should get married."

I blink a few times before bursting into laughter. "Oh, my gosh. Ford! You were so serious. You really had me there for a second." I can barely speak through my laughter.

"Amber, I'm not joking."

Still chuckling, I look at him. His soulful brown eyes meet mine, looking ever the little boy I met all those years ago. He looks completely serious, his expression unchanging as I watch his features for some clue that he's teasing me.

"Ford," I bring my hand to my chest. "What?"

He finally breaks eye contact, ruffling his hair with one hand. "You asked me for my help, for your procedure. Well, I have excellent insurance. Marry me, and you wouldn't even have to pay me back. My insurance will cover most of it."

"You can't be serious."

"Ambs, think about it. It makes sense. I could help you with Nella, I could replace your stupid car that's barely running, I could give you insurance and security."

I swallow the lump in my throat. "It makes sense?" I scoff. "What about the fact that we'd be *married*? And we're not in love with each other."

He flinches. It's barely perceptible, but he flinched.

"I mean, we love each other, of course. But not like that," I add quickly.

Ford exhales, making his broad chest move up and down. "People get married for all kinds of different reasons."

"Like what?" I ask, crossing my arms in anticipation of what he'll come up with.

"You remember Andie? She reads a lot, and the people in her books get married for citizenship, mafia protection, and even a woman's chastity being compromised. You name it."

A humorless laugh comes out of my mouth. "Ford. That's *fiction*. And it's a little too late for the chastity argument."

He huffs a laugh. "Okay, but we could help each other. This would solve both of our problems."

"How could this possibly solve *your* problems? You don't even have any problems!" I throw my hands up in frustration. Did my best friend have a brain aneurysm during dinner? Where is this conversation even coming from?

"You think I don't have any problems?" His voice sounds tortured, almost like he's holding back tears. "My parents are constantly worried about me. Always expecting me to revert to my childhood self and start throwing tantrums and hiding from people I don't know."

He stands up abruptly, turning and pacing around in a circle. I get up as well, moving in front of him so he'll stop pacing. I have to look up to meet his gaze.

"My mom thinks I'm going to die alone."

I huff a laugh. "That's ridiculous."

"Why?" His expression breaks my heart. His brow is furrowed, hair ruffled, shoulders slumped forward. The man literally thinks no one wants him.

Taking a step closer to him, I place my hands on his upper arms. Arms that are really, really firm beneath my fingertips. My breath hitches, and I think to myself how silly it is that *this* extremely attractive man thinks a woman wouldn't want him. I'm a touchy person, especially with serious conversations like this. I feel the need to touch him to say what I'm about to say, and I hope he's not offended at the connection.

"Ford, listen to me. You are not only wildly attractive..." I pause, watching as his eyebrows shoot up to his hairline. "You're wealthy, talented, and a genuinely amazing human."

He looks thoughtful, those dark eyebrows quirking, then straightening, then arching. He has so many emotions splaying across his face, it looks like an eyebrow workout. "Do you really think I'm...wildly attractive?"

I snort a laugh. "Have you looked in a mirror? You're tall, dark, and handsome... plus you have a hockey butt."

His eyebrows shoot up again. "A hockey *what*?"

I shake my head. "We're getting away from the subject at hand. My point is, some lucky woman will snatch you up before you know it. And you can't be insurance-married to me when you meet *the one* and fall in love."

Ford shakes his head, his dark hair still messy from his hands. "I can't open up to people, Ambs. I've never been able to. The only people who really know me are my family and you."

"What about your teammates? You guys seem close," I say, curious why he didn't include them.

"They don't know I have autism."

I keep my mouth shut tight, trying to avoid gaping at him, before I ask, "Why wouldn't you tell them? There's nothing wrong with being neurodivergent. Obviously, it hasn't stopped you from being an NHL team captain."

He smiles softly before his mouth turns down in a frown. "I know. But when I got my first NHL contract, I was so worried that it would be too overwhelming...too loud, too many people. I thought if people knew, they'd be watching, waiting for me to fail." He pauses, taking a deep breath. "And then, I made friends." He shrugs those massive shoulders. "When I was younger, people would give me that *poor you* gaze when they found out. And I couldn't stand the idea of my friends looking at me that way.

"I don't know your friends that well, but I can tell they look up to you. You're their captain, their leader. A position you earned, a position they respect. There's no way they would pity you." He opens his mouth to speak, but I put a hand up, motioning for him to stop. "You have every right to your privacy. I'm just saying, if you ever wanted to tell them, I think you could, and they wouldn't react the way you think."

"Maybe you're right," he agrees, leaning against the tree we used to swing on, crossing one long leg over the other. "We keep getting sidetracked. I'm just saying, we could be married for a few years. Show my mom I'm not a completely lost cause." He smirks. "And you'd have your procedure paid for. And no rent. You could save a lot, be in a better financial position when we go our separate ways again. If that's what we wanted to do."

I lean against the large oak tree beside him, allowing my body to rest against his warmth. I should've grabbed my coat. Ford doesn't tense or shrug away. Maybe he's getting better with touch?

Leaning my head against his shoulder, I close my eyes and allow myself to imagine being married to my best friend. Could our friendship survive such an arrangement? He does have a point—the stress of paying him back tens of thousands of dollars would take me years. On top of everything else I need to be saving for. What if Nella breaks her arm some day? Or needs braces? I'll have no savings because of this stupid surgery repayment.

And I *would* repay it. Despite what Ford says.

"Promise me you'll think about it?" Ford whispers, his mouth close to my ear. "You know I'll help you no matter what

—the money you need for medical care, whatever else you need. I'm just offering another option. One that might benefit us both."

With a sigh of resignation I promise, "Okay. I'll think about it."

CHAPTER TEN
AMBER

THE DAY AFTER THANKSGIVING, I have to run to the store for diapers. I'm running so low on time and diapers, I pop into Dorothy Lane Market. Dorothy Lane isn't for me, it's for rich people. A supermarket so pristine and well-coiffed, I feel like I can't touch anything, or I'll leave a stain on it with my peasant-hands. It's one of those stores where you buy two things and it somehow costs a hundred dollars. But it's almost eight, and I need to get Nella to bed. This happens to be the nearest store that carries diapers, and I don't feel like wading through the Black Friday shoppers.

As I strut through the store at night with a tired baby, bags under my eyes from exhaustion, and barely enough money in my checking account to purchase the diapers I need, my mind goes back to Ford's crazy idea, and I wonder if it's not so crazy after all. What would it be like to live with Ford? For him to run to the store late at night, for us to be a team. It almost sounds…nice.

Nella is in the baby carrier strapped to my front as I navigate the glossy aisles all the way to the back where the baby section is. I'm passing by a large shelf of health food when a woman rounds the corner, and we nearly slam into each other.

My hand protectively cups the back of Nella's head. "I'm so sorry," I say, looking at my daughter instead of the person who I almost slammed into.

"Not at all, completely my fault," the woman argues.

I look up at the woman's face and an uneasy feeling moves through my body. This woman is familiar, but it takes me a few seconds to pinpoint where I recognize the perfect, blonde shoulder-length bob and hazel eyes. Theo's mother. I've only met her once, since he rarely brought me around his friends or his mother. He always told me it was because his parents were divorced and he didn't have much of a relationship with either of them—something I could tell was false the moment I stepped inside his mother's home and heard their conversation. Theo's mother knew more details about his schedule than he ever told me. And she even seemed familiar with his friends.

"Oh." Recognition lights up her eyes, the same hazel color as her son's. She sweeps two perfectly manicured hands down the front of her button-down top and pencil skirt. "Amber, right?"

"Yeah. Yes." I stumble over my words. "Nice to see you, Mrs. Peregrine."

She smiles faintly, but I can tell by her posture she feels just as uncomfortable as I do.

Nella fusses from the carrier, a silent plea for me to start walking again.

Nella's unhappy sounds prompts Mrs. Peregrine to notice the infant for the first time. She cocks her head to the side to study my little girl, her eyes growing wider the longer she looks.

"She's darling," Mrs. Peregrine finally says. Her words

coming out careful and slow, like her brain is calculating. "Is she yours?"

My eyebrows raise. Why would I have a baby in Dorothy Lane Market at eight at night, on a weekend if she wasn't mine?

"Um, yes."

The woman nods, her eyes shifting as if doing algebra in her head. "May I ask how old she is?"

I swallow, my throat suddenly thick. It's not until this moment, right here next to the almond flour and stevia in Dorothy Lane Market, that I realize Theo never told his mother I was pregnant. He probably didn't tell his father either. Maybe he simply told them he ended our engagement, and they sighed in relief and went back to their perfect lives.

I meet Mrs. Peregrine's pretty brown-green eyes. "Three months old."

Her eyes go all shiny in the supermarket lighting. I bite my bottom lip, unsure what to say and even more unsure how to feel. On one hand, I feel bad for her. She's meeting a grandchild she didn't know she had, a baby fathered by her only child. But on the other hand, she never tried to get to know me and wasn't overly warm or even friendly the one time I was around her. Theo took me to his mother's home right after he proposed, and I was so excited to finally meet her. But I was met with a historic mansion that was as beautiful as it was tragic. I still remember the forested lot and how eerie it all felt. A home that seemed cold and unwelcoming…a house that was merely wood and plaster, with no color or laughter.

It was that day when everything seemed to change between us. He became busier with work, which didn't seem that strange since he was doing his residency. And he stopped texting me throughout the day. Again, I thought he was just a busy medical resident. Stupidly in love, I was. Ignoring all the signs.

I don't think he could bear to soil the Peregrine name—so rich with old money, so cultured—by adding a hair stylist into its midst. He never brought me back to his mother's home again, and he was also never introduced me to his father. Like I'd failed some unspoken test.

Theo used to joke he was the black sheep of the family because he went into medicine instead of law. As if even being a doctor was even beneath his parents. I'd thought he was joking. But I don't think he was.

The day I met Theo, he'd come into my salon wearing scrubs and looking exhausted. He was in his last year of medical school, and he charmed me instantly. After that, Theo came in for a haircut every week until finally, he asked me to dinner. I thought I was the luckiest girl in the world.

Mrs. Peregrine shuffles on her heeled feet, drawing me out of the bitter-sweet memories. Her back is as straight as a flagpole as she stares at me and my daughter, her expression unreadable. If I didn't know better, I might wonder if she was holding back tears. But she doesn't strike me as a person who has emotions, let alone one shows them to her son's ex-fiancée.

The woman clears her throat. "Well, I apologize for almost bumping into you. Have a nice evening."

I nod and watch her walk away from us. Halfway to the checkout, she stops. I think she might turn back and say something else. But her steps begin again, and she never looks back.

CHAPTER ELEVEN

AMBER: 2ND GRADE

I'M at the park near my house when I see Ford sitting on a park bench. I'm not surprised he's sitting alone in a quiet, shady spot instead of swinging or running around the playground. He's been better at school the past few months, though. I think he just had to get used to it or something. When he spots me walking in his direction, his face lights up.

"Hey, Ford!" I smile and wave.

He stands and meets me in the wood chips scattered on the ground of the park. Two dark-haired little girls wave at Ford, and he studies the area surrounding them before he waves back.

"I'm keeping an eye on my sisters." He points to a simple, but nice house right behind the park. "We live just there, and my mom's making dinner."

"Cool," I say, wondering what it would be like to have my mom home every day for dinner. She's usually working. Or on a date. "I live just down the street." I point to the apartment building nearby. "My mom's not home from work yet," I whisper. "I'm not supposed to leave the house, but I get bored."

Those thick eyebrows, that are too big for his face, rise just a little. "You stay home alone?"

I nod. "It's just me and my mom. I entertain myself until she gets back."

"We were just about to head back home. Want to come with us? My mom's a great cook. She'll feed you." He smirks, and for just a moment, he looks kind of cute.

I glance down at my Barbie wristwatch. It's not quite five… and Mom won't be home until seven. "Sure, that sounds fun. You sure it's okay with your mom?"

He huffs a laugh through his nose, like I asked a ridiculous question. "Come on," he says, waving toward his house. He calls his sisters, and they follow. One is probably two or three, and the other one is maybe five. He must be really responsible for his mom to let him watch them at the park.

His little sisters each hold onto one of his hands as we walk down the sidewalk and to their front door. Ford lets go of their hands to turn the doorknob, but the door is barely open an inch before a giant dog bursts through the crack and pounces on Ford. Ford falls on his rear end, but he's smiling bigger than I've ever seen him smile before as he pets the furry black dog. The girls run inside, closing the door behind them.

The dog notices me for the first time and rushes over to lick my face. I giggle and pet the dog's thick fur.

"This is Moose." Ford grins. "He's a Bernese mountain dog, and my best friend."

I pet the dog's head and admire the white fur on his chest and the light brown patches where eyebrows would be. They seem to make the dog extra expressive. "Hi, Moose. You're so handsome."

The dog pants happily.

"Come on, Moose, let's get inside," Ford tells the dog in a serious tone, opening the front door again.

Moose trots back inside, and once Ford and I follow him, Ford closes the door. The house is comfortable but not fancy. I like it. I feel like we could sit on the carpet in the living room and play video games while eating snacks and no one would yell at us for spilling crumbs. Even the red throw pillows resting on the brown couch look rumpled, like they've been used for pillow fights and naps.

"Follow me," Ford says to me over his shoulder.

He takes me into the next room, which is a modest-sized kitchen. His mom is at the sink peeling potatoes, and I notice there's a window right above the sink where she can see the park. Ah, so she was keeping an eye on the kids even though Ford was out there. The knowledge that she's a protective mom makes me instantly like her.

"Well, hello there!" His mom says with a pretty smile. "Who's our guest?"

Her hair is a lighter brown than Ford's, and her eyes are blue instead of brown. She looks like she's nice.

Ford tells his mom my name and that we're in the same class.

"Does your mom know you're here, sweetie?" she asks.

"Her mom's at work. Can she eat dinner with us?" Ford asks, before I can speak.

"She won't be home until seven," I add.

Ford's mom wipes her hands on her checkered apron, glancing up at a big rooster clock above the stove. "Of course you can eat dinner with us. But can you make sure to let your mom know where you are next time? I wouldn't want her to worry."

I nod my head. "Yeah, I will." I want to keep coming over. And my mom probably won't care either way. She's too busy trying to snag a husband to take care of us. Her words, not mine.

"Ford, do you mind setting the table?" his mom asks with a smile.

"Sure," he answers.

Ford grabs silverware and plates from various drawers and cabinets, handing me the forks so I can help him set the table for dinner. Moose follows us the entire time, always appearing as if he has a big smile on his canine face. He seems to have a special bond with Ford, and Ford always has a hand on him. Like Moose is a life source for him.

Ford is lighter here in his home, like there's an invisible weight pressing on him at school that isn't here when he's in his own space. He's happier here in his element, here with his dog.

By the time the table is set, a man walks into the kitchen. He looks like a giant version of Ford, and it makes me wonder if Ford will be this tall someday.

The man sneaks behind Ford and ruffles his hair. Ford doesn't tense or shy away from the touch, like I've seen him do when kids at school get too close. Instead, he turns and tries to mess up the man's hair. It's an impossible feat since the man is so much taller.

"Who's our guest?" The man asks in a deep voice, shooting me a grin.

"This is my friend from school, Amber," Ford tells him, then looks at me. "This is my dad."

"Welcome to the Remington house, young lady," his father says before striding farther into the kitchen and planting an unabashed kiss on his wife's lips.

I look away quickly and notice Ford is wrinkling his nose.

"They're so gross," he whispers.

A moment later, Ford's parents call the girls, and we all sit at the table for dinner. The Remington's dining room is warm and full of conversation and laughter, flirtatious touches between Mr. and Mrs. Remington, and little spats between the girls. This simple house is full of life, and it makes me feel like something is missing at my house. Not because I don't know my dad, or because I don't have siblings, but because my mom and I don't laugh and talk like this. We don't have fun or sit down to eat together. The Remington children are cherished, but my mom probably thinks I'm a nuisance.

"You okay?" Ford whispers from his seat beside me. He has an uncanny way of knowing when I'm feeling down. He always finds me when I'm having a bad day, and I suppose I do the same for him.

"Yeah," I lie.

We finish our food and Ford makes a *psst* sound and jerks his chin toward a sliding door at the back of the house. I glance at the rooster clock—it's just after six, so I can stay a little longer.

As I follow him to the backyard, he leads me to a swing that's just a slab of wood held up by two ropes tied to a high branch in a tall oak tree. The tree is surrounded by a pretty garden with many different types of flowers. I can see where Ford's mom spends her time when she's not caring for her children or cooking meals. I smile at a particularly pretty pink flower. Ford goes straight to the swing and sits down, but I'm too distracted by the flowers to join him.

"What's this?" I ask, gently cupping the bright flower in my hand.

He studies it for a second. "My mom calls those Pink Piano roses."

I grin. "Pink is my favorite color," I say, feeling my smile fall slightly. "My mom says it's not a good color for me, with my red hair."

Ford pouts, his face scrunching in an adorable but angry scowl. "I think you have the prettiest hair I've ever seen," he says, his voice sounding cool and calculated. "And you'd look nice in any color."

I stare at him, a little stunned by how defensive he's being. And even more surprised that it makes me want to smile. "Thank you."

CHAPTER
TWELVE
FORD

TWO DAYS. It takes two days for Amber to call me—frantically. Her name appears on my phone just as we're exiting the Eagles' private plane at the Thunder Bay airport. Dressed and ready for game one in a stint of three away games.

"Ford, I have to use my tiny bit of savings on my car. It won't start. According to the passive-aggressive mechanic, who thinks I'm a moron, the transmission is on its last leg."

It sounds like she's holding back tears, or perhaps even a full-on emotional breakdown. I wish I was there with her—not that I'd be brave enough to pull her into my arms, but just to be nearby. To help somehow.

"Let me Venmo you some money, Ambs. Please. It's not a big deal," I offer.

Bruce is walking with me, both of us towing our carryon suitcases behind us, and dressed in our game day finery. Me in a navy suit with a houndstooth print, and Bruce in a dark purple suit that only he could pull off. Bruce arches an eyebrow, obviously wondering what Amber and I are talking about. I look away and slow my pace for more privacy.

Amber clears her throat. "If we got married, would it actually help you somehow?" she asks, sounding breathless, as if she's forcing herself to say the words out loud.

I sigh. "Of course it would. My mom would stop fretting over me, and I'd get to see my best friend every day." Lowering my voice to a whisper so Bruce can't hear, I say, "Amber, getting married was just an idea so you wouldn't worry about paying me back. I'd add you to my insurance now, but I checked my policy, and we'd have to be married. I'm not trying to blackmail you into anything."

She huffs a laugh. "You're not capable of blackmail. You're too pure of heart."

I smile at that, and there's a pause, and I don't know what to say to fill the silence.

"I'll do it. I'll marry you…for two years, or however long it takes to benefits both of us, or until you fall in love with someone."

I stop in my tracks. Bruce looks behind him and sends me a worried glance. I nod my head, a silent signal that I'm fine and the guys don't need to wait for me.

"Amber," I say slowly. "I don't want you making a decision about this because of car trouble. I'll send you however much money you need. You don't have to marry me for me to help you."

"I know," she says, her voice defensive. "I've been thinking about it, getting married, nonstop for days. We'd basically just be roommates, roommates that are married in name and help each other out. People do weirder things than this all the time, right?" She breathes a humorless laugh. Nella begins fussing in the background and Amber groans. "I have to go, but let's do this, okay? Call me later when you have time to talk."

"Okay," is all I can say before she ends the call, leaving me standing in the middle of the airport tarmac with all the blood drained from my face.

Married. To Amber. It's what I've always wanted, what I've always dreamt of. Obviously, the circumstances are all off. But maybe the proximity, maybe living together, might somehow help her see how good we could be together?

Realizing that's a pipe dream, I shake my head and rush to catch up with the guys.

Bruce notices me first, his usually bright features somber with curiosity. "Hey, Cap'n. You okay?"

"Yeah, I'm good. Amber's just having some car trouble and I was trying to help."

West's head snaps up from the mint he's unwrapping. He pops it into his mouth and sticks the wrapper in his pocket. "Girls are so stubborn. She won't let you pay for it, huh?"

I smirk and shake my head. "Nope."

Mitch makes a grunting sound, his grumpy face as stormy as always. "Why won't they just let us use our money to help them? We have plenty, and we're happy to use it for something good."

Colby snorts a laugh. "Yeah, Noel still feels guilty about how much I spent on books for her library. But with the thanks I got, I'd do it again in a heartbeat." He winks.

Mitch shoves him. "Gross. Keep that to yourself."

"Never stepping foot in that library again," West teases.

We shuffle into the large bus that will shuttle our team to the hotel. Once inside, I sit in an empty row, and the silence feels stifling. I usually love silence, but now there's this looming secret in the air. And for once, I want to talk to the guys about my personal life, to tell them about what Amber and I are thinking of doing. But I don't know if she'd want me to say anything, and I don't know who we'll tell about our arrangement and who we won't. If it even happens. I'm 99.9%

sure she's going to change her mind in the next twenty-four hours. But her procedure is in two weeks, so I suppose we need to make a decision soon either way.

I like to be prepared, so I checked my insurance policy after talking to her about this whole crazy idea on Thanksgiving. My policy doesn't have a waiting period, so if we get married, she'll be fully covered on day one. Her and Nella.

Something about that makes my chest puff out a little, the thought of taking care of them. Of those girls being mine.

CHAPTER
THIRTEEN
AMBER

"I'M NOT GOING to change my mind," I tell Ford for the millionth time. "I get to hang out with my best friend for a few years. Why would I change my mind about that? And I finally have an excuse to move to D.C." I'm actually not lying about the moving part—that's what I'm most excited about. But the marriage part? It makes my tummy hurt a little...not because it's Ford, I trust Ford more than anyone. Last year I was planning a real wedding, though. To a man I was really in love with. A man who shattered my heart.

"Because," he says, then pauses, his deep voice sounding even deeper with how tired he is from traveling and from their game tonight. "It's marriage."

The word *marriage* brings heat to my cheeks. I've avoided wedding stuff for so long. It's just a reminder of my failed engagement—and a fiancé who had a million red flags, all of which I ignored.

"We do need to hammer out the details," I say, pushing off of my disastrous kitchen counter. Not a countertop that's custom made like Ford's, but one with peeling laminate that's supposed to look like granite but failed miserably.

I attempt to open my junk drawer, yanking hard to get it open. Something inside is caught and keeps it from opening. Finally, it pulls free. I dig around in the mess, hoping to find a pen and paper. I find several tubes of acrylic paint, a few paintbrushes, some lip-liner, and a clean-ish napkin. Good enough. I grab the lip-liner and flatten the crumpled napkin on the countertop. Which is difficult, since the tiny amount of counter space I have is littered with dirty bottles and dishes.

I might not be a neat freak like Ford, but my apartment isn't usually this bad. Today was insane, dealing with the car, a teething baby, scheduling a procedure—one that I'll need to reschedule now—and of course, planning a wedding.

"Okay, I have a pen and paper," I say, opening the cap of my lip liner.

Ford makes a pleasant, throaty sound. It sounds like he's half humored and half annoyed. "You just have a napkin or something, don't you?"

I gasp. "How do you *do* that?"

"I know you, Ambs." I can tell he's shrugging one of those big shoulders as he says it. "I have a Word document pulled up, so put the napkin away."

"At least one of us is a responsible adult," I tease.

"It's easy to be a responsible adult when I only have to worry about myself," he says. "You have a whole extra human to worry about."

The simple but honest words bring tears to my eyes. Something about it makes me feel seen. For such a large man, Ford has a way of making me feel just as tall as he is. Of making me feel *known*.

It's easy now to see that Theo never knew me, not really. From the ring he bought me, a simple solitaire with a white gold band, to the presents he gave me...designer handbags from brands I'd never even heard of before. And where Ford has always welcomed me into his family, Theo avoided bringing me around his.

I close my eyes and push thoughts of Theo from my mind. I stopped loving him the moment he didn't want me and our baby girl. But all this marriage talk has that part of my life sneaking into my thoughts again, bringing back all those bitter memories.

Ford clears his throat, and I can hear the keys of his computer clacking. He's probably typing a professional-sounding title for the document, something like Ford Remington and Amber Park's Marriage Contract.

"So, first I think we need to discuss if anyone know the… um…circumstances of our marriage."

Dropping the lip liner, I move from my tiny kitchen into the living room that's only three steps away. A living room that's also…tiny. I slump down on the worn, blue sofa I found at a local thrift store. "Honestly, I think it's best if it stays just between you and me. You're in the public eye so much, it would be too easy for word to get out. And can't you go to prison for insurance fraud?"

Ford sighs. "How could anyone prove that? We've known each other since second grade, we have a thousand photos together, text messages, emails. It would be easy to prove our relationship."

"True. But it would also be easy to see that we've never been romantic with each other."

"Alright. So, we don't tell anyone," he says, typing something again. "That means we'll have to convince people… friends, family, teammates…that we're really, you know…in love." He's stuttering and pausing so much, I have to stifle a laugh.

"Does pretending to love and adore me sound so difficult?" I tease.

Silence...nothing but silence comes from the other end of the phone.

"Ford?"

He clears his throat. "Uh, sorry. I was typing."

I think he's lying, and I wish we were having this conversation in person so I could see his face, his expressions and reactions. I don't want anything to be awkward between us. And that's definitely my biggest worry about this whole arrangement.

"So far, I have that you and I are the only ones who know, and that we need to convince everyone around us that we're really in love. Which won't be difficult, because I'm an amazing actor," he deadpans, making me laugh and disintegrating the weird tension I was feeling before.

Ford is a terrible liar, always has been. So the acting part of this will probably be difficult for him.

"You and Nella can have your own rooms, of course," he says. "And I think, financially, we should act like a real married couple. You're on my insurance, I pay the bills, groceries, vehicles, etcetera."

"It's not the 1980's, Ford. You don't need to pay for everything. And I'm not about to be a stay-at-home mom. Not that there's anything wrong with that," I add. "But I enjoy the creativity my job brings. I missed it so much during maternity leave that I started painting again." I glance at the painting I did of a Pink Piano rose, and smile. "Hey, I thought maybe you could give me the number of your stylist, and I could apply at that chic salon we saw?"

"I can do that. But you have to follow your doctor's orders and rest until they clear you to work again."

I smile to myself, appreciating his concern. "Okay, deal. And speaking of doctors, I'll need to get a referral from mine to a cardiologist closer to you. If I stayed in Ohio for the surgery, it would seem really weird...if we were married and all."

"I agree. And since you'll be my wife..." his voice falters on the word wife. "The NHL will allow me to take a few days off for a family emergency. So, I can be with you the day of the procedure and two days after. Unfortunately, that's all the time I'll have before jumping back into the regular season schedule."

"That's okay. I didn't think you'd be able to have much time off, if any. Do you know anyone I could hire to take care of Nella during recovery?"

"I'm positive my mom would come help if we asked her. But if you're not comfortable with that, I won't mention it to her."

I take a moment to ponder the idea. She would stay with us, thinking we're married. The thought makes my stomach flip with nerves. The lying is going to be the worst part of this whole thing. Especially fooling Ford's family, who has always treated me with kindness and respect. But it has to happen sooner or later, and I would trust her implicitly with Nella.

"Yeah, I think that would work. If she wants to, of course. No pressure."

He laughs softly. "I'm pretty sure she'll jump at the chance, Ambs. We'll probably have to stop my sisters from joining her."

She would. I know she would. Which is why I adore her and she's the best. More of a mother to me than my own mom ever was, and it kills me to lie to her. Although, we will really be married...so maybe it's not entirely a lie?

I swallow the thickness in my throat and clutch the phone a little tighter. "So, we're really doing this?"

A pause. "I'm in if you're in."

"Okay. I'm in."

CHAPTER
FOURTEEN
FORD

THE MOMENT I arrived home from our Canada trip, I hopped on a plane to Ohio. I hate feeling rushed, but we have to make this legal as soon as possible so her procedure will be covered. And Amber got a referral with a respected surgeon in Virginia, and her surgery is now scheduled for next week. *Next* week. If I'm being honest with myself, marrying this woman doesn't make me that nervous, but her having work done on the most important part of her? That terrifies me.

The way my palms are sweating is almost enough to gross me out. I slide my hand into the pocket of my dress pants. My fingers find the old, gold coin that's nearly smooth now from my hands feeling the lines and grooves. I run my thumb over it as I walk through the crowded Cincinnati airport and out to the parking lot to find Amber's unreliable car. A car we won't be taking to D.C. with us, a point I still need to make Amber aware of.

When Amber spots me, I swear I see her shoulders relax as she breathes a sigh of relief. And that fact that my presence can do that to her, give her peace, makes my own heart feel like it's beating a little funny.

"Ford," she says, her voice sounding watery. "Aren't you a sight for sore eyes."

Before I can stop myself, I wrap my arms around her in a tight embrace. She hugs me back just as fiercely, like she needed the hug just as much as I did.

She sniffs as I hold her, and I feel the tears soak through my shirt. "It's all right. I'm here now."

I swallow, thinking of a little joke I could make. Is this a time when a joke is appropriate? But then again, sometimes Bruce and Colby make jokes at the wrong time, and everyone seems to love it. I decide to go for it. "Or are you crying because I *am* here and I'm about to become your husband?"

Her tears turn to laughter and her shoulders start shaking. I blow out a breath, thankful I made her laugh and not the opposite.

She pushes away from me and looks up to meet my gaze. I'm momentarily struck dumb by her glossy green eyes and how I could lose myself in them. Looking into the depths of those emeralds is how I imagine it would be to frolic around a lush, green meadow would be.

"Yeah, poor me, marrying a handsome athlete." She snorts ungracefully, but it's adorable. "You do realize most women would cut off their right arm to trade places with me, yeah?"

I grimace. "That was…graphic. I'm not that great."

She looks down, noticing that my arms are still loosely draped around her shoulders. "Is this okay? Hugging… touching?"

I laugh. "Yes, Ambs. I don't mind hugs, not from people I know well. There are still touches I hate, like someone tapping on my shoulder." I shiver at the thought, and she chuckles.

Amber moves away from me and reaches out to open her driver's side door. "Well, it's cold. And our time slot at the courthouse is in forty-five minutes."

"Right," I say, gently moving her away from the driver's side door. "I'll drive, if that's okay."

"Are you kidding? I can't remember the last time someone chauffeured me." She peeks in the back seat, checking on Nella in her car seat, before meandering around to the passenger side. "This married thing is the best." She winks and I roll my eyes.

If she thinks me driving is spoiling her, then her eyes are about to be opened to a whole new universe. Because I'm about to spoil the hell out of this woman, the way I've always wanted to.

We arrive at the Cincinnati courthouse fifteen minutes early, which is good, because I had no idea how much longer everything takes with a baby. When Amber and Nella came to visit me in D.C., we didn't have a schedule to follow, we just hung out. But today, we have an important appointment, and Nella is bound and determined to make us miss our own wedding.

She has been changed, nursed, and burped, and I can tell by the frown lines Amber is getting frustrated. She's wearing a really pretty dress that I didn't notice until she took off her coat. It's a rosy-pink velvet, and it looks soft and warm for winter, but the material clings nicely to her body. The shoulder now has a large drool splatter on it from Nella, but not even that takes away from her beauty. Her red hair is up today, in some kind of whimsical braid that circles around her head.

"I'm so sorry, Ford," Amber whispers, bouncing and trying to get Nella to calm down.

"Don't apologize. She's a baby, and we're on her schedule." I pause. "Can I try?" I ask, reaching out for the unhappy baby girl, her cheeks red and splotchy from crying.

Amber shrugs and hands her over. I place my hands right under Nella's armpits and she dangles there, staring at me for about two seconds, before she starts crying again.

A happy couple comes out of the room where we're headed next. They're smiling and holding hands, then they kiss passionately, ignoring the hallway full of people.

Nella cries louder, and they pull away from each other and shoot me and Nella an annoyed glance.

I snuggle her into my chest, and whisper against her head, "Wow, Nells. How rude. Have they never seen a crying baby before?"

She grunts, as if agreeing with me. Her big green eyes look up and meet mine, holding my gaze for a long moment. It's funny how she can look just like her mother, but there's something wholly different about her. She's entirely her own little person with her own personality.

"Can you believe the nerve of those two?" I whisper again since she seems to like it. "As if they're more important than you."

She makes a gurgling sound, with her mouth full of drool.

"You, Nella, are the most important person in this building. I don't think they realized that."

She coos in response.

"Take comfort in the fact that I, Ford Remington, know how important you are and that your demands must be met—and met immediately."

Nella grins, reaching for my face and grabbing at my chin.

Amber laughs softly, and I realize she's been watching us and listening intently this whole time. "I see how it is. You two already ganging up on me? Teaming up?"

"Never," I say, looking into her eyes. "The three of us, we're a team. No man—er, woman—left behind."

"Amber Park?" A middle-aged woman, her hair pulled into

a low bun and dressed in a black pantsuit, calls from the doorway. I'm assuming the double door behind her leads to the justice of the peace.

"That's us," Amber says, lifting an eyebrow as if giving me one final chance to escape.

I hold out my free arm to her, and she slowly drapes hers through mine as we walk into the room where everything is about to change.

We follow the lady with the bun into the large courtroom, and the judge is already standing at the front of the room. The woman looks at the door and then back at us. "Will you have any witnesses? Or would you like me to stay and witness?"

"Does the baby count?" Amber teases, her voice sounding strained, like she's nervous.

Of course she's nervous, because she's not in love with me. This whole situation is probably way more nerve-wracking for her. I'm marrying the woman I love, and I don't have to have surgery. Therefore, I'm not nervous. My chest feels tight, and I want to comfort her, but I don't know how, so I just continue silently holding Nella, who's still playing with my chin and thankfully, not crying.

The woman laughs softly. "I'm afraid not. No matter how adorable she is, she's under eighteen. But that's okay, I'll stay as witness. I'm Susan, by the way, Judge Carter's assistant."

We smile and she ushers us to the front of the room to stand near the judge. "Well, aren't you all the cutest family," the older gentleman says, his grey hair swept neatly to the side and his black legal robe perfectly pressed. "I'm Judge Carter," he smiles. "I'm assuming you're Amber Park," he looks at Amber, and then glances over at me. "And you're Ford Remington?"

"Yes, sir," I answer.

His eyebrow quirks. "You look familiar…" He taps his chin with his index finger. "Do you play hockey?"

Amber laughs. "I can't take you anywhere, Ford. Isn't the wedding day supposed to be all about the bride?"

I feel my cheeks and ears heat. The total lack of anonymity is something I've never gotten used to—and probably the hardest part of being in the NHL. The good outweighs the bad, but there are still times I hate that I can't hide and be invisible.

"Yes, I play for the Eagles," I respond. "But today is all about my beautiful bride." I wink at Amber, something Colby does to Noel a lot, and she seems to like it.

Amber beams at me, so she must be okay with it.

The judge laughs heartily. "Good man. You already know how marriage works, my boy. Happy wife, happy life."

Amber bats her lashes at me, and I hold back a laugh.

We go through the basic vows of a wedding ceremony, and I realize we don't have rings. The Judge smirks, probably thinking we couldn't wait to marry each other and forgot rings because we're too in love to think straight. He's probably right, on my end, but not on Amber's.

Judge Carter wraps up the vows and announces, "It's my honor, by law of the state of Ohio, to pronounce you husband and wife. You may kiss your bride."

My brain goes a little hazy, and for whatever reason, I look down and notice Nella is still in my arms. I think I was so distracted by the ceremony I didn't realize I was still holding her. She gives me a gummy grin, then I glance back at her gorgeous mother. Who's now my wife. And I'm supposed to kiss her.

Amber moves toward me, bringing her small hand to my cheek, then leaning in and kissing the other cheek. The scent of her skin and her shampoo nearly knocks me off my feet. When she pulls back, I have to blink a few times to remember where I am. And for the disappointment to sink in that I had an opportunity to kiss this woman, and I missed it.

I mean, the cheek kiss was nice, don't get me wrong. But having my lips pressed against her pillowy soft ones, so pink and glossy? With her feminine scent dancing around me? Ugh. Damn it, I want that kiss. I want to go back in time and start the ceremony again. To grab her and kiss her and see if it was as good as I know it would've been.

"Congratulations!" Susan says, coming toward us with paperwork to make this all official.

Amber signs the documents, then takes Nella from my arms so I can sign them too. I instantly miss the small weight and the warmth of her little baby self. It was oddly comforting, like a tiny weighted blanket.

Nella instantly starts fussing, and Amber sighs. "I guess she only wants you today."

I sign my name on the documents, then turn and look at the red-haired mother and daughter duo. Something inside my head—and heart—throbs at the sight of them. My heartbeat now thrums with the word, *mine*, as I look at them.

CHAPTER
FIFTEEN
AMBER

HE BOUGHT ME A TRUCK. A truck. A brand new one. A shiny, red Ford F-150 that he says is very safe. Apparently, Ford purchased the truck via cash transfer two days ago, after our phone conversation about getting married. The title is in both of our names and everything.

The man doesn't waste time, that's for sure. We spent our wedding night packing up my meager belongings and crashed for the night in my lack-luster apartment. Definitely not the wedding or honeymoon Ford Remington deserves, but he never once complained.

And then he left to get breakfast and came back with my brand new, shiny red truck. The beast is loaded up with half the contents of my apartment, which is, of course, why he bought me a truck of all things. Only Ford would have the forethought to purchase a truck so I could bring as many of my belongings with me to D.C. as possible.

But how am I going to park this thing?

We're now halfway into the six-ish hour drive to Ford's place just outside D.C., in a luxurious Virginia neighborhood.

Nella is fast asleep in her car seat behind me when I finally say, "I cannot believe you bought me a truck."

His face doesn't leave the road as he drives us home. Home…will it feel like home? Did my apartment in Ohio really feel like home? No, I suppose it didn't. I think the only place that ever felt like home to me was when I was a child and I spent afternoons in the Remington house.

"It's a wedding gift," he says simply, his face giving no hint of humor.

"You can't just buy me a vehicle, Ford."

"Yes, I can."

I cross my arms and look out my window, trying to ignore the large man sitting next to me, the man who takes up so much room I almost forget how big this truck is.

He sighs, and I can tell he's looking at me. The skin on the back of my neck prickles, knowing his gaze is just there. "Ambs, your car was having too many issues for a road trip. The salesman gave me a decent trade-in value for it despite its transmission troubles, and your doctor said no more flying until you're cleared after surgery. I want to take care of you. And Nella. And you need a safe and reliable vehicle. It's just that simple."

Slowly, I swivel to look at him. He's looking at the road again now but glances at me for a second. His mouth in a thin, straight line. He's worried. And I hate it when he worries.

"I'm not trying to be difficult. It's just, I can never buy you gifts like this. It makes this feel uneven, you know? Like, I get all the benefits of this whole arrangement and you get nothing."

I study his chiseled profile and relax when his mouth pulls up in a smirk.

"That's ridiculous," he says, removing one hand from the steering wheel and brushing it through his dark hair. He's wearing his glasses, the dark rimmed ones that make him look even more handsome, somehow.

"Is it? What are you really getting out of this?"

He huffs a quiet laugh through his nose. "Everyone thinks I'm a loner, that I'm broken or something. You're saving my reputation." He looks at me again, his mouth still in a smirk. "You're making me look like a cool husband and girl dad."

I burst out laughing. "That's the reputation you want? Sounds very…wholesome."

He smiles. This is his rare but genuine smile, the one he gives when he's totally relaxed and at ease with the person he's talking to. A smile I always feel honored to be on the receiving end of. "That's exactly the kind of reputation I want."

I smile back because that's so Ford. He's never been a womanizer, or a rebel. He's exactly the type to want a quiet life with a doting wife, sweet children, and probably a dog. And in two years, when our gig is up, I have no doubt he'll find exactly that.

"Hey, why don't you have a dog?" I ask out of the blue. His head tilts in my direction quickly before focusing on the highway again.

"Well, for a while it felt like no dog could ever compare to Moose. Seeing dogs makes me feel…sad?" His forehead scrunches as he thinks about what emotion he felt. Something he's always done when big feelings were involved. "Yeah, sad," he decides.

"And now?"

He sighs. "I'd like a dog. But I travel so much, it doesn't seem fair to him… or her."

I grin, and when he sees my expression, his eyebrows draw together. "No, Amber. You're going to be taking care of a baby and healing from your surgery. This is not the time for a dog."

I stick out my bottom lip as far as I can. "Come on."

"No."

"But this is finally something I can do for you! After I'm cleared for normal activity, which should be two weeks since it's a minor procedure, we can get a dog. I'll be home to care for it, and when I find a job, I'll come home for lunch to walk him or her. It's perfect. Please let me do this. It makes this whole thing feel less one-sided."

He groans and grips the steering wheel tighter. "We'll talk about it after your surgery."

I clap my hands together. "I'll convince you. I can be very persuasive." I waggle my eyebrows for effect, and it's not until I notice the deep blush spreading across Ford's face and ears that I realize how suggestive that sounded.

Clearing his throat, he changes the subject. "I have a question, and it seems kind of personal, so you don't have to answer."

I nod my head. I'm not concerned about the question being personal because I'm an open book, especially with Ford.

"Should we be worried about Theo? Like, does he have any parental rights or anything?"

Ford's strong throat works as he swallows, and I wonder if it pains him to talk about Theo. He's always hated him. I'm pretty sure Ford has harder feelings toward the man than I do. And I'm the one who Theo ended an engagement with…when I was pregnant with his child.

I turn my body so I'm facing him. "You don't need to worry about that. Theo could establish paternity, but I haven't heard from him in a year. He wasn't interested, at all, in being a father when he had just finished his residency." I believe his exact words were, *I can finally enjoy life again, I can't take care of a baby*. But I'm not telling Ford that—he already hates Theo enough as it is.

Ford blows out a long breath. "Okay, that's good." His eyes widen. "I mean, not that he wasn't there for you…but that he shouldn't be a problem."

"I knew what you meant." I lay a hand on his arm, and he doesn't flinch or act annoyed. Instead, his ears turn red again.

"Since we're talking about the big stuff, we should probably come up with a story. I imagine your teammates, and your family, are going to wonder why we got married after never even dating… and so quickly."

He relaxes, his hands easing on the steering wheel again. "You're right. Any ideas?"

CHAPTER
SIXTEEN
FORD

IT'S the day after Amber, Nella, and I drove back to D.C., and I just finished early morning practice. I'm exhausted, and the guys, of course, wanted to know why I took off to Ohio without a word. I told them, word for word, what Amber and I discussed in the car. Basically, her impending heart procedure made her really think about her life, and she knew in that moment she loved me. I felt the same way, and we got married.

Bruce, West, Colby, Mitch, and myself are the last ones in the locker room, and after telling them about our quickie marriage, they're staring at me with their mouths open, but none of them are saying a word.

I swallow and adjust my shoulders. "So, you see. The whole heart surgery thing made us both realize we want to be together. And why wait? You know? We're already thirty-four, and life is too short."

They continue staring, not one of them even blinking for a solid five seconds.

Colby finally breaks the horrifying silence. "Well, Remy, I'm happy for you! I know you've held a candle for that girl forever." He moves toward me and slaps me hard on the back. "I'm throwing you a party. Or do they call it a reception? Either way, we're celebrating."

I smile, but it doesn't feel real. It feels like a disguise.

West's eyebrows are still high on his forehead, but he follows Colby's lead and gives me a side hug. "Yeah man, I'm happy for you. It just seems so unlike you to get married all of a sudden. But it makes sense, with her heart issues and all, I guess. Let us know if you need help while she's recovering, yeah?"

"Thanks, I appreciate the offer. And Amber will too."

Mitch grabs his duffle bag and takes a step toward the exit. But first, he slams a hand awkwardly against my arm. "Congrats, man. This is weird as hell, but whatever."

Unable to hold back, I laugh at his blunt statement. "Thanks, Mitch."

One by one, my teammates shuffle out of the room to get home to their ladies. But not without glancing back at me over their shoulders, concern lining their features.

Bruce stays seated on the bench, where he removed all of his goalie gear for Jeff, the equipment manager, to clean. He's showered and changed but hasn't said a word. Which is very unlike him.

Bruce's icy blue gaze makes me feel like I'm frozen in place. Waiting to see what he's gonna say. His shaggy, blond hair hangs limp, damp against his scruffy face. "Listen, Rem. I'm happy for you, I am. I think we could all tell you were in love with that girl. But this is really fast."

I open my mouth to defend our situation, but he holds a hand up to stop me. "I'll stand behind you, no matter what. But if you need someone to talk to…or open up to, or whatever. I'm here, okay?" He quirks a brow and I nod my head.

"Yeah, thanks, man."

"And I really hope her procedure goes well." He pauses. "Are you scared?"

My shoulders slump. I don't think I knew how much I needed someone to ask me that question. His asking makes me feel normal for being scared, like it's to be expected to feel this way. "Yes. It scares the hell out of me to think about her heart stopping."

Bruce stands and gives me a big hug. He's not the person I want to hug right now, but I don't mind it just this once and hug him back quickly before stepping away from him.

We both grab our duffle bags and head for the exit, walking out to our vehicles together.

Bruce unlocks his old Chevy pickup. And by unlock, I mean he has to put the key in the keyhole because his pickup is *that* old. "I mean it, Cap'n. You call, and I'll be there. I don't know what all is going on here." He uses one hand to draw a circle in the air in my vicinity. "But there's something sketchy."

I roll my eyes and press the remote start on my key fob and get in before Bruce can hound me anymore.

Maybe my teammates know me a little better than I thought they did. Maybe I should tell them why I am the way I am. Why I can be a little…different.

With a sigh, I grab the spare set of glasses I keep in my vehicle and slide them on, settling in for the drive home. The commute feels longer than usual, possibly because I'm excited to get home to Nella and Amber, to see how they're settling in. Now I know why the guys always have summer weddings and don't get married in the middle of the season. I can't take time off to be with them and spend time making Amber feel at home. I can take off some time next week for her procedure, now that Amber is my wife. But then I'm back to practicing and traveling as per usual. It's part of my contract. The D.C.

Eagles own me. Not something I've ever considered a bad thing. But now it feels a little stifling.

When I finally pull into my driveway, my body relaxes. I slide out of my Land Rover, and the tension in my shoulders disappears, and when I open the garage door and enter through the laundry room of my house, it feels like a home for the first time.

Music is playing, something by Miley Cyrus I think, Amber is singing, and Nella coos like she wants to sing too.

I step lightly into the kitchen, not wanting to interrupt whatever is going on in there. Amber is in one of those nursing nightgowns she was wearing last time she visited, but she's thrown an oversized Eagles sweatshirt on the top of it. Her red, and pink, hair is down—and wild. She's barefoot even though it's winter, but I have heated floors, so it doesn't really matter.

She's using a whisk as a microphone and singing to Nella the lyrics for *Wrecking Ball,* as the song plays from her phone where it rests on the infinity countertop. It looks like she's in the middle of making breakfast, Nella sits happily in her bouncy seat we packed into the truck with most of their other belongings.

"Well, good morning," I say, announcing myself from where I'm leaning against the kitchen archway.

Amber gasps, jumping a little. The whisk drops from her hand, and she clutches her chest. "Ford! You scared me to death!"

I rush toward her, reaching out and putting my hands on her shoulders. "Are you okay? Is it your heart?"

She bats my hands away—now she's laughing. "Would you stop fussing over me? I'm not going to have a heart attack." Amber bends at the waist and picks up the whisk.

"You're a giant man, and I just didn't know you were home is all."

I inhale deeply, feeling suddenly out of breath myself. "Oh, right. Sorry."

"You want biscuits?"

"Really? With gravy?"

"What kind of wife would I be if I made biscuits without gravy?" she asks, shaking the whisk at me with one hand and resting her other hand on her hip.

I laugh. "Are you going to take my shoes off and massage my feet too?"

Her pert, freckled nose scrunches up adorably. "Ugh. No. I've seen your feet. I'm pretty sure they get worse every time you lace up those skates."

"Hockey players really do have the nastiest feet," I agree. Especially Colby.

Amber smirks, then turns and continues her wifely endeavors. I turn to Nella and say hello. She smiles at me whenever I talk to her, and there's just something about it that makes me want to keep talking so she'll keep smiling.

As soon as I'm facing Amber instead of her, she fusses, arching her back like she wants out of the bouncy seat.

I look to Amber, raising an eyebrow in silent question.

"Yeah, you can take her out. She's been sitting there for a while. Breakfast is almost ready."

It takes me a few minutes to figure out how to unfasten the five-point harness, but I finally have her secured in my arms, and she's happy again.

We look at each other, and it's comfortable. The eye contact isn't awkward with a baby. Maybe because they have no concept of personal space.

"She's weirdly obsessed with you," Amber muses, drawing my attention.

I look over to see her studying us with a bemused smile on her pretty face. A face free of makeup but just as beautiful as ever. Amber is always pretty, and I get that women like makeup and being creative—especially someone like Amber who sees it as an art form—but there's something about fresh-faced Amber that I've always adored. Maybe because I can see her freckles better this way.

Not sure how to respond, I opt for a joke. "According to Sports Illustrated, I have one of the handsomest faces in hockey."

I don't smile when I say it, or even use a teasing tone, but Amber still knows I'm joking. She bursts out laughing, throwing her head back. "Did you hear that, Nella? You should feel privileged to look at that face."

Nella coos in my arms, and I look down at her just as a stream of drool runs from her mouth and then down to my arm.

Amber grabs the two plates of biscuits and gravy she prepared for us and takes them to the large dining table in the opposite room. I follow behind her with Nella and take a seat.

The moment I'm seated, Amber reaches for Nella. She laughs when I'm reluctant to hand her over. "It's about time for her to eat. Do you want to feed her? I pumped a bottle earlier; she needs to get used to bottles since I can't nurse her with the pain medication I'll take after surgery."

"I'd like to, yes."

Amber smiles and walks back into the kitchen, quickly returning with a bottle of breast milk. It's bluish in color and, honestly, doesn't look very appetizing for something that came out of a breast. The milk warms the plastic of the bottle, and it makes my stomach churn unexpectedly. I clear my throat and man up. Boobs are for more than looking nice. They feed humans. Nella whines, and I place the bottle close to her mouth. She latches on and sucks enthusiastically.

"Wow," Amber muses. "She'll hardly take a bottle from me. I think she wonders why I'm using one."

I smirk. "And she knows my nipples are useless, so she doesn't mind me giving her a bottle."

Amber laughs, the sound filling the dining room and making me feel lighter.

Once Amber finishes her breakfast, she takes Nella to burp her. I watch so I know what to do next time.

Remembering the breakfast Amber made me, I shovel a large bite into my mouth and groan at how good it is. If Amber keeps up this kind of cooking, I'm going to get what Colby and Bruce call a dad-bod.

CHAPTER
SEVENTEEN
AMBER

AFTER BREAKFAST, Ford Facetimes his parents while I put Nella down for her nap. When I come back down the stairs and peek in on him sitting on the living room couch, the nerves start kicking in.

We planned this during the drive here from Ohio, but it doesn't ease the sloshing in my belly. My stomach feels like it's the Black Sea blowing one of those giant ships around—complete with the deep baritone sea shanty playing in the depths of my gut, of course.

Biscuits and gravy probably weren't my smartest idea.

I can see Ford's parents on the screen, both smiling at their son the way they always do. But they have no idea the bomb we're about to drop on them. Ford wanted a few minutes to talk to them before I pop into view, so I'm standing to the side waiting to make my appearance.

I catch Ford's eye, and he gives me a small but reassuring smile. Even with his black sweatpants and hoodie, seated in a man-spread position on his giant sofa, there's still something in his posture that makes me think he's more anxious than he's letting on. Maybe it's the way he's barely blinking...or how tightly he's holding onto his phone.

He swore his parents would be thrilled about us, but that seems too good to be true. And if life has taught me anything...it's that if it seems too good to be true, it *is* too good to be true.

Mr. and Mrs. Remington are smiling through the screen at Ford. His dad's deep voice comes through, "You all rested up after your Canada trip, son?"

Ford shuffles so he's holding his phone with one hand and runs the other one through his short hair. His hair is a little longer than usual. I'm guessing between traveling and our impromptu wedding, he didn't make it to his standing bi-weekly haircut appointment. Actually, now that I'm here, I should offer to cut his hair for him.

"Uh, not really. It's been pretty busy," Ford answers, his voice just a little deeper than his father's. Even as a kid, he had a deeper voice than the other boys in our class, but then once his voice changed, I swear he had to bat the girls away. Not that he ever seemed to notice their attention.

"You look tired, sweetheart," his mom says, looking at him with concern. There's love all over her face, you can see it even through a phone screen.

"I'll be okay," he says with a smile. "There's actually a pretty great reason I've been so busy."

He glances in my direction, quirking one of those dense eyebrows. This is my cue.

I walk toward the couch and take a seat next to him. I have to sit close, really close, so we both fit on the screen. His quad is so firm, I can feel it pressed against my soft thigh, even through his thick sweatpants. He also smells really nice. He must've showered at the Eagles ice plex after practice. And I smile when I note that he uses the same bodywash now that he did in high school. I've never been so thankful that he skipped over the Axe phase entirely. He's always been more into masculine, earthy scents. Something about the lingering soap smell reminds me of a sea breeze.

Ford drapes an arm across the back of the couch, not around my shoulders, but close enough that I can feel the heat of him through his sweatshirt.

His parents stare at us in shock and confusion before their faces break into grins. "We knew it!"

Mrs. Remington nudges her husband. "Didn't I tell you they were looking at each other some kind of way at Thanksgiving?"

"You did!" he exclaims, his voice full of laughter. "You totally called it, honey!"

Ford's mom claps her hands together. "Oh, this makes me so happy. I've always been so worried about you, Ford. That you'd never find someone who understood you and loved you the way we do." Her face goes soft, and she wipes a tear from her eyes. "But Amber has always just *gotten* you, you know?"

"So," His dad grins. "How long have you two been dating?"

Ford stiffens, and I glance over at his hard profile. He swallows, and his throat bobs with the effort. His arm drops from the back of the couch and rests on my lap, palm up so I can hold his hand. I thread my fingers with his, noticing the contrast of his calloused hands with my soft ones. My stomach goes from the crashing Black Sea to a spinning, swirling whirlpool. I'm not sure exactly what I'm feeling. But it's not entirely...unpleasant.

"Actually, we're not dating...we're married."

The happy faces on the screen disappear, replaced with surprise, or perhaps, worry.

"*Married*?" His mom squeaks out.

Mr. Remington balks, his mouth opening, then closing again, then opening again. "When in the hell did you two even have time to get married?"

Ford tightens his grip on me, and I'm unsure if it's for my benefit or his. "I know it seems sudden," he begins, keeping his voice steady, solid, responsible. Totally Ford. "But Amber found out she has a small heart defect, and it requires a minor procedure, but still. We knew how we felt about each other and didn't want to wait."

"Oh, sweetie." His moms voice goes soft as she focuses solely on me now. "Are you okay?"

"Yes," I say with a light laugh, trying not to worry them. "I guess I was probably born with a small hole in my heart, but it didn't cause any issues until I was in labor with Nella. So, now we're getting it fixed. Easy-peasy."

Ford's dad slides his glasses down his nose. "And you guys thought marriage would somehow...help the situation?"

The man beside me flinches slightly, his thumb lightly rubbing up and down on the back of my hand in a subtle up and down motion. I'm not sure he even realizes he's doing it. His jaw ticks, and that's how I know he's getting irritated.

"Dad, with all due respect, we're thirty-four years old. I think we're old enough to know if and when we want to get married."

His dad nods. "Sure, but you could've dated first."

I bring our joined hands to my lips and press a kiss on the top of Ford's hand. Smiling at the screen, where his parents are looking back with concern, I say, "I know it seems fast, but we've been best friends since we were in second grade. Dating is for getting to know each other, and that step just seemed unnecessary." I chuckle, hoping to make this conversation a little more lighthearted.

Mrs. Remington's hand comes up to pat her husband on

the shoulder. "She's right, Gordon," she says softly before turning her attention back to me and her son. I note how her eyes drop to where our arms are entwined before popping back up to our faces. "Although I hate that we didn't get to plan you a wedding."

"It's okay," I tell her. "Neither of us wanted the fuss."

"When is your procedure?" she asks.

"In four days," Ford answers.

"Four days!" She starts to stand then sits back down. "Well, I need to pack."

"Mom, calm down," Ford says with a sigh, his dad following with an identical sigh of his own.

"I need to get down there to help with the baby! And I'm not taking no for an answer." Her face is about as fierce as I've ever seen it.

"We'd love the help, Mom. Thank you." Ford smiles at his mom and so do I.

"Yes, your help would be amazing, Mrs. Remington."

Truthfully, her kindness is a little overwhelming. While my mom wants nothing to do with me, Ford's mom jumps at the chance to help us without us even having to ask. I should've known she would, but it still surprises me anyway.

She waves a hand. "No more of this Mr. and Mrs. Remington nonsense. You're family. Call us Gordon and Sally, please."

I laugh. "Okay, deal."

"I'd come too," Mr. Remington—er, Gordon—says, "but I can't take off work on such short notice. I bet one or both of your sisters would love to join your mom for the trip though, if you're brave enough to host multiple Remington women," he teases, earning a playful shove from his wife.

"I think one Remington woman is enough for now," Ford says, and his mom shakes her head in dismay.

"Well, Nella is my grandbaby now, so I'm afraid you'll have to get used to me being there! A six-hour drive can't keep me away!" She smiles.

I choke back tears. A grandma for Nella. And a grandpa… and aunts. One piece of paper from the courthouse, and now my daughter has so many people in her corner. But what happens in two years when Ford and I amicably separate? Will Nella have to say goodbye to people she will come to adore? In my head, she wasn't going to remember any of this, she's just a baby. But what about two years from now? Will she have a cute name for Ford's mom, like Gigi? Will she call Ford Daddy?

My eyes begin to burn, my vision blurring. I close my eyes, shoving down the tears, and all of these heartwarming and also terrifying thoughts. I push them far from my mind, to keep myself from breaking down in tears during a Facetime call.

CHAPTER
EIGHTEEN
FORD

THE MORNING after announcing our marriage to my parents, I wake up early, unable to sleep any longer. With how fitful my sleep is, I tend to sleep in late on the mornings I don't have practice. But how does one sleep in when they suddenly remember they have a wife and a baby?

Grabbing the phone from my nightstand, I see a text from my dear mother telling me she's arriving tomorrow.

I sit up straight in bed, fully awake now, and run a hand down my face with a loud groan.

Tomorrow.

And she's bringing Farrah with her. Felicity wanted to come too, but thankfully she has a wedding to plan. I love my sisters, but both of them together is…a lot.

Two house guests, a new wife, and an infant.

Cue the panic attack.

I do not enjoy unexpected things, and yet, all the unexpected things are happening. The marriage was my choice, but everything is happening at a rate I can't slow down. The snowballs just keep being thrown at me, and I can't duck to avoid them. Instead, they're pelting me in the face repeatedly.

Knowing I need to warn Amber of the onslaught of Remingtons coming at us in the next twenty-four hours, I stumble out of bed and into the hallway. I'm about to put my ear against her bedroom door to see if she's awake, but a wail beats me to it. The wailing is coming from downstairs. I rush in that direction, a little concerned about the screaming and why it's happening this early in the morning. I raise the phone in my right hand, double checking that it is, in fact, only seven in the morning.

I stumble unceremoniously down the last two steps, only to find Amber on the couch, in another little nursing nightgown. This one is pale blue, trimmed in white lace. It makes her skin look angelic, and her dark brown freckles stand out from the pale fabric. One of her breasts is freed from the garment as she tries, unsuccessfully, to contain a wailing and flailing, Nella.

I'm out of breath as I come near the couch and realize I'm still making eye contact with Amber's areola. My chin raises and my eyes move up to the ceiling of my home. There's an interesting light fixture up there. The designer called it a modern Sputnik chandelier. A wonderful, fascinating ceiling. Honestly, people don't appreciate their ceilings enough these days, you know?

This platonic husband thing is already harder than I imagined it would be. And not for any of the reasons I expected it to be challenging.

"Ford, it's just a boob. You don't have to pretend the ceiling is so interesting. Could you hold her for a second?" Amber asks, her voice tense.

I look at her, her nightgown fastened again. "Yeah, of course." I reach out and take the infant from her grasp, settling her on my bare chest and bouncing up and down. She liked that last time I did it. But she is not liking it right now.

"I'm sorry," Amber says, her voice wobbly like she's about

to cry. "She was up most of the night. I don't know what's wrong."

"You were up all night?" It comes out louder than I wanted it to. "Why didn't you come get me? I could've helped."

"Ford." She scoffs. "That's not really what you signed up for here."

I pause, making sure my voice is soft and even, not harsh. "That's exactly what I signed up for. We're a team here, Ambs. You don't have to do this alone anymore."

A tear cascades down her cheek, and she sniffs. I pull her into my chest too. Comforting both my girls at the same time. Amber leans against me, her hand coming to rest on my back. She seems comforted by my presence. Nella does not. The normally adorable and coo-ing infant, is really freaking pissed.

I sit down, remembering something Mom used to do with Felicity. Felicity was a horrible baby; it wasn't her fault. She had colic and was just miserable, the poor thing. I lay Nella on my lap and start moving her legs like she's riding a bicycle.

She continues writhing and fussing, but after a full minute, she starts to calm down a little. The poor thing seems really uncomfortable, her arms moving rapidly.

There's a vibration on my thighs where her back is resting, and then warmth. Something wet, and very warm, is moving up her back and onto my legs. Ignoring it, I keep moving her legs. Once the vibrations from her rear-end stop, and she sighs, I stop my ministrations. I raise her up, to see my fears have come true. She's had a blowout.

Amber giggles, and the sound almost makes me happy enough not to notice the disgusting smell coming from Nella's diaper. A diaper that obviously didn't do its job well.

"Oh, Ford. I'm so sorry." Amber's hand comes up to cover her mouth.

"What do I do now?" I ask. "She probably needs a bath."

Amber looks down at my legs. "Yeah, and you probably need one too."

Glancing down, I see my grey sports shorts are twin to Nella's soiled pink sleeper. I'm glad I'm not wearing a shirt, because that prickle of discomfort that's always followed by itching is creeping up. If I was wearing a shirt right now, it would be feeling too tight. Too rough. I close my eyes and count to two, allowing myself to take a deep breath. When I open my eyes again, Amber is watching me. Concern written all over her face.

"I want to help you, but I just need to change first. Okay?"

Amber nods. "How about I give her a bath while you take a shower?"

I shake my head side to side. "I just need to change, then I'll give her a bath while you go back to sleep for a while."

Bad smells aren't my favorite thing, that's no secret. But Nella doesn't smell any worse than a hockey locker room. There's no stench equal to hockey equipment that's been worn by a bunch of big, sweaty athletes.

Amber hedges, shifting her weight from one foot to the other. "It's really fine, Ford. Go shower."

"I can handle a little poop," I tell her, knowing she's been up all night and needs some rest. "I'm going to change, and I'll meet you in the guest bathroom."

With a sigh, she follows me up the steps.

I duck inside my bedroom, change into a clean pair of shorts and throw on a t-shirt while I'm at it, then head across the hall. Amber is in the guest bathroom, sitting on a plush rug. She has Nella laid out on a towel and is stripping off her sleeper.

I kneel beside her. "I'll take care of it. You go get some sleep."

Looking at her face for the first time since practically falling down my steps earlier, I see the dark circles there. She's exhausted.

"You're sure?"

"Positive. I'm cleaned up and good to go."

Nella babbles happily, whatever was bothering her tummy no longer causing any issues.

She stands and starts to walk toward the bedroom, then turns back. "You've never bathed an infant before."

"Until three months ago, had you ever bathed an infant?" I ask, raising an eyebrow to drive my point home.

Amber crosses her arms, and my eyes drop, very briefly, to her ample breasts. Amber has always had nice curves, but some parts of her are definitely...more generous now. "Please wake me if you need help, okay?"

Glancing at Nella, I say, "We've got this, don't we?" Nella coos, and I give Amber a salute.

Amber heads straight to her bed and rolls onto it, taking the blankets with her.

I stand and close the bathroom door so Amber can sleep, then start the bath water before crouching in front of Nella again and cleaning her up with baby wipes.

The guest bathroom is almost as big as mine, so there's plenty of room to move around. It has a sleek white freestanding bathtub which now hosts a smaller, pink baby bathtub. While the pink tub fills up, I move to the cabinet where the towels are stored and remove a few for Nella and lay them out for when her bath is finished.

Gently, I pick up the wiggly baby girl and ease her into the tub. When her body hits the water, her face scrunches up like she's mad, but she soon calms down and gives me a gummy smile. She splashes her hands merrily in the water, causing it to spray all over my face, but I just chuckle. How could I be annoyed when she's so happy? Especially after seeing her so miserable not even fifteen minutes ago. I never want to see her scream like that again, but I know she probably will.

Amber has arranged a caddy beside the tub with baby soap, lotion, small wash cloths, diapers, diaper cream, and fresh sleepers. I smile at her tiny bit of organization. Tidiness has never been Amber's strength, so you can tell that her number one priority in life is... taking care of her daughter. I grab a washcloth with a little pink duck pattern and squirt some lavender-scented soap onto it, then get to work washing the slippery baby. She coos and smiles like she wants to have a conversation, so I oblige.

"I never had a chance to tell your mom that we're going to have company tomorrow."

Nella stares at me.

"I know. Not even three days into marriage, and family is already visiting."

She pokes her tongue out.

"Hey, now. Cut me some slack just this once, okay?" I dampen her red curls with the washcloth. "At least you'll get spoiled by your aunt and grandma. Honestly, you can't complain."

She smiles and flails her hands again, making water splash on my face once more.

"All right, Nells. Let's get you dried off before your fingers and toes go pruney."

She splashes in protest, but I manage to get the clean baby dried, diapered and dressed.

As Nella and I sneak out of the bathroom, I peek toward the bed and see Amber facedown amidst a pile of pillows and smile to myself.

Thankfully, Nella stays quiet as I close the guestroom door. When I pass my room on my way back downstairs, I stare at my bed, denying the itch to make it the way I do every morning of my life. Instead, I force myself to ignore it and carry Nella downstairs, where I lay her on her playmat that has little toys hanging above it. She loves the simple contraption.

As I'm making myself a cup of coffee in the kitchen, where I can still see Nella in the living room happily grabbing for her toys, I take a deep breath for the first time since waking up early this morning.

I'm quite literally about to plant my ass on the sofa—the first time I've sat down this morning—when my doorbell rings.

I close my eyes and count to three, that annoying prickle of overwhelm creeping its way in. I've held it together the past few days, through all of the changes in life, routine, tidiness of my house...but that one little doorbell sound is what's about to set me off.

Checking that Nella is still on her mat—not sure where I was expecting her to go—I run to the door.

Colby Knight stands there, grinning his signature smile. I groan and spin on my heel, back to the living room. I can tell he's following me from the sound of the door clicking shut and the patter of footsteps.

"Okay, what's your problem? That's no way to greet your next-door neighbor and favorite teammate, now, is it?" He asks, taking a seat on the floor by Nella as I sit on the couch and grab my mug of coffee.

I roll my eyes and take a sip, welcoming the caffeine to my system. "None of you are my favorite," I grumble, sipping my black coffee again.

"Everything okay? Where's Amber?"

"You wouldn't believe the morning we've had, especially since we've only been awake for like two hours." I set my mug down. "I woke up to a text from my mom that she and my sister are coming tomorrow, went to find Amber to tell her, then got completely derailed by this adorable thing." I pause, pointing to Nella. "Who was having a massive meltdown and pooped all over the place...all over *me*." I huff a laugh. Now that the moment has passed, I can admit it's a little bit funny.

Colby bursts into laughter then bumps his fist against Nella's. The contact draws her focus to the man on the floor beside her and she smiles up at him. Colby's eyes go soft, and he runs a hand across her now dry curls. "Dude, how can you be annoyed with someone this cute?"

"I'm not annoyed at her," I defend myself. "She couldn't help it. I think I'm just..." I pause again, thinking of a description for what I'm feeling. "I think all the change is sinking in, you know? I'm more than happy to have Amber and Nella here, but this morning was my first dose of reality. Nella comes first over everything, obviously, but babies are a lot of work. I know it's stupid, but I didn't think about how hard it would be. How hard this has all been for Amber. Like I'm exhausted from two hours when she's been doing this on her own for nearly three months. She's freaking super mom." Leaning forward, I rest my elbows on my knees. "Every day I wake up and have the same routine, I have only myself to think about, until I get to work and have the team to think about. My time has been my own, everything was just easy. And I need to learn to spread that time to three people now."

Colby nods, blowing out a breath. "That's definitely a lot of change at once. But if anyone can do it, it's Ford Remington. Captain of the unruly D.C. Eagles."

I snort a laugh. "Nella and Amber are much cuter than you guys."

Colby's hand comes to his chest in mock offense. Nella coos, and he looks at her, his bottom lip poking out. "Okay, you have a point. She's really f—"

"Language," I warn.

"Right. Really freaking cute," he corrects. "Can I hold her?"

Holding my hands up in front of me, I say, "Hold at your own risk. She may have another blow out."

Colby narrows his eyes at me then carefully places one big hand under Nella's head and another behind her back. He lifts her into his arms and beams at her. "Girls don't have blow outs," he tells her. "I don't believe that guy for a second." He shoots me a glare.

A loud yawn comes from the stairs, and I glance over to see Amber walking into the living room, looking a little more rested. And a little too sexy, in her nursing nightgown, for my comfort. Colby looks over, hearing her enter the room. He must want to stay alive, because his gaze quickly darts back to Nella.

Colby is a great guy, and he's good to his fiancée, Noel. But Amber is wearing too little clothing around another man for my liking. Honestly, *I* shouldn't even be seeing her like this. But I won't stand for any other man to see her in her nightie either.

I stand, whipping off my hoodie, walking toward her, then swooshing it over her small frame. It nearly comes to her knees, which is still more leg than I'd like anyone to see. But it's an improvement.

Amber blinks at me but pushes her arms through the sleeves. Her green eyes widen when she spots Colby holding Nella, and she offers me a coy smile and a nod of her head in silent thanks for the hoodie.

"Well, good morning," she says brightly, moving farther into the room and sitting on the couch. "I didn't know we had company."

Colby shoots her that winning, dimpled grin that makes all the girls swoon. She remains smiling, but she doesn't faint or blush. I release a silent breath, relieved she doesn't seem to have an insta-crush on Colby Knight like every other female on the planet.

"I'm Colby. I'm Remy's teammate, but I also live next door."

"You belong to Noel, right?"

Colby grins. "Yes, ma'am."

"I didn't realize you lived right next door," Amber says, glancing at me. "Do any of your other teammates live in the neighborhood?"

I nod, my shoulders tensing. Up until this moment, I was thrilled to have three of my teammates living on the same street, but now that Nella and Amber are here...does this mean a steady stream of unexpected visitors? The thought, along with my mother's visit and Amber's impending surgery, makes my heart race. I roll my lips together and push a hand into the pocket of my shorts. I find my pocket empty, and remember the coin is up in my room. Another piece of my routine forgotten in the chaos.

Swallowing, I force my shoulders back, hoping to look relaxed. "Yeah, actually West recently bought a house down the street, and Mitch bought one around the corner. Mitch and Andie aren't moving in until after their wedding, though."

Colby chuckles. "Probably only a matter of time until Bruce joins us. But he's still enjoying the pleasures of penthouse life."

"Bruce is the goalie?" she asks, worrying her bottom lip as if trying to memorize all the names being thrown at her.

"Yep, that's him," Colby answers, then pulls out his phone and snaps a selfie of him and Nella. He looks down at his phone, typing something. "Noel is going to be so jealous I'm holding the baby." He sets his phone on the rug and tickles Nella's belly. "She's adorable, by the way."

Nella kicks her feet and coos.

Amber stands and takes a step toward them. "Thank you, I agree. I'm afraid I need to steal her from you though." She wrinkles her nose in apology. "If I don't feed her in the next five minutes, she's going to get really pissed off."

Colby's jaw drops, and he turns his attention to the smiling infant again. "These two keep talking shit about you. The audacity."

I clear my throat. "Language, Knight."

"Gah! Sorry."

CHAPTER
NINETEEN
AMBER

WHEN I START GETTING comfortable on the couch to feed Nella, Colby makes a quick exit. Ford following behind to walk him out. It's nice having people drop by. I never had that in Ohio. However, Ford looked pretty miffed the entire time.

When Ford walks back into the living room, he seems calmer and more relaxed. I don't think he appreciates surprise visitors as much as I do.

"You okay?" I ask as he settles down on the couch a few feet away from me.

He groans, leaning forward and running his hands through his hair. The messier Ford's hair is, the more stressed he is. This isn't a good sign.

"Was Nella difficult for you?" Suddenly, I feel horrible for taking a nap and leaving him to take care of her. He's already doing enough for us as it is.

His head comes up, those dark brows knitting together. "What? No." He scoots closer to us. "She was great. And I was happy to help." He pauses, but I know there's more he wants to say because those eyebrows of his give everything away, whether he realizes it or not. "It was just a wild morning. You know I like my routine; I won't deny it. But that doesn't mean I can't adjust to a new one, okay? Just…be patient with me."

I place my free hand on his knee. "I will. And it's okay for the newness to be difficult. Do you think I seamlessly fell into a rhythm of taking care of another human?" I scoff.

"Um, yes. I do, actually. You're amazing with her, Ambs." He covers my hand with his.

Warmth spreads through me, starting at my hand then moving into the rest of my body, at his words and the heat of his skin.

"Thank you. That means a lot to me."

He leans back, taking his hand with him. "Most of my stress today is due to my mother. Which is what I was coming to talk to you about this morning."

"Ahh, Nella really hijacked that conversation, huh?"

He nods slowly. "So, my mom is going to be here tomorrow. And she's bringing Farrah with her."

My eyes dart up to meet his gaze. "Oh, wow. My procedure isn't for three days, so I thought we'd have more time to get things prepared." I take a deep breath, realizing why Ford was tense during Colby's visit. We have a lot to do and a lot to talk about before family comes to stay.

Ford looks away from me. "We need to discuss…appearances. I think you should sleep in my room while they're here."

I inhale a sharp breath. I don't even know why I'm surprised; it makes sense for us to share a room. This week has been so insane, I haven't had time to think about it. "Right, yeah. That would make sense. What about Nella?"

He finally looks at me. "My house has five bedrooms, so she could have her own room. But if you like to keep her close, that works too. My master is plenty big enough for the three of us."

"She slept in her own room in my tiny apartment. I actually sleep better when I can't hear every move she makes, but I have a video monitor for peace of mind."

His face relaxes, those surprisingly full lips turning up in a smirk. "She's a noisy sleeper."

I laugh. "Don't I know it."

"She gets it from her mom." He leans back, settling into the couch.

My mouth gapes and I shove his shoulder with mine, causing Nella to lose her latch. She roots around until she latches again and slurps greedily, making obscene noises.

Ford's face reddens, but his head falls back on the couch with a loud laugh. I stare at him; I've always loved his laugh. Ford doesn't always connect with people's humor, and jokes sometimes don't make sense in his beautiful brain. Which makes his laughter all the more special when it appears.

He sighs, his laughter trailing off. "For such a small person, everything she does is so loud."

"You're not wrong." I smile down at my noisy girl, who now has milk dripping down her chubby cheek. "Okay, so besides sharing a room and acting like we're in love, what else is there?"

His jaw ticks, and very briefly, he looks frustrated. Before I can analyze the look, it's gone. "We probably need wedding rings," he admits, looking down sheepishly. He blows air into his cheeks as he stares at his lap. Like wedding rings are embarrassing to bring up. His body language reminds me of the boyish Ford from twenty years ago.

I smile. I'm not sure why he's embarrassed—because rings make this feel more real, or because he's ashamed there's something he didn't think of and prepare for. "Yeah, I guess we do. I hadn't thought of that. Is there a jewelry store we could stop at later today after Nella's morning nap?"

"Remember the shopping center we went to when you visited last? There's a jewelry store in there. I think it's where West bought Mel's rings, actually."

Snorting a laugh, I adjust Nella in my arms. She's sound asleep now, so I gently pull her away so I can snap my top back in place, then cuddle her against my shoulder so she can burp. "We don't need *real* rings."

"Yes," he says firmly. "We do."

My head snaps up to look at him, to see if he's teasing. He's not. "Ford, you're not buying me an expensive ring. You already got me a whole freaking truck."

"Amber," he starts, looking deep into my eyes. His eyes shift slightly, as if he wants to look away, but he stays focused on me. This gives me a chance to look at the deep brown color of his eyes and admire how pretty they are. Ford's eyes are almost so dark, they match his pupils. You have to get really close to see the contrast. "People are going to be watching you. They're going to ask questions and be nosy. It's the worst part of my life, the media…the attention." He groans. "Unfortunately, you'll have to deal with it now too. Which means you *have* to have a real ring. People will dig until they figure out the cut, clarity, and design of your ring. There will be articles about the ring Ford Remington purchased for his wife. It's really stupid, but for whatever reason, fans are fascinated by this stuff."

"Are you kidding me? I'm going to be awesome at being famous." I flip my pink tipped hair over my shoulder. "Besides, I'm pretty sure I'm the only red-headed NHL wife out there. We needed some distinction amongst the blondes." I'm teasing, but being in the public eye really doesn't scare me. I love dressing up and doing my makeup. So, photograph your hearts out, paparazzi.

"Why are most NHL wives blonde, by the way? Have you dated all blondes?" I ask, genuinely curious.

He quirks a brow. "I don't date."

"Ah, you're into hookups?"

"No." His head pulls back in offense. "I barely like touching the people I know. Why would I want to touch people I *don't* know?"

"True," I admit. "But there's no way you've been a monk for thirty-four years."

"Ambs, we're not going to talk about sex." His words are clipped and matter-of-fact.

"Why not? I'm your wife, after all."

He stands from his seat on the couch with a heavy sigh. "Conversation over."

"You're no fun!" I yell after him as he crosses the room and starts up the stairs.

I watch how the fabric of his t-shirt and shorts stretch against his muscled back and his well-developed back side as he ascends each step. There is absolutely no way this man has never been with a woman. He's a professional athlete. Admittedly, a smoking-hot professional athlete. He must get offers from women literally every day.

I shake my head, standing to carry my baby girl to her pack-and-play upstairs for her nap.

Yeah, there's no way.

CHAPTER TWENTY
FORD

WE ARRIVE at the jewelry store that afternoon and are led to a private room in the back, as I requested. The last thing I want to worry about while buying my wife a ring is people asking for photos or autographs. I realize the fans are a big part of my job, and I appreciate them…I do. But I don't enjoy it. I've gotten better at pretending to enjoy it, but making small talk with strangers, even if they're wearing a jersey with my number on it, is still painful.

Nella is strapped into her carrier, as per usual. I wonder if she'd like a stroller. I should buy her one.

The jewelry store owner, Mr. Vance, is the one who met us at the front and now opens a door leading to an office near the back of his store. He's wearing a simple grey suit and pale pink tie. His hair is salt-and-pepper grey, and his hand has a simple gold wedding band, despite owning a store full of fancy rings.

As we step inside, I note the glass display case lined with navy blue velvet sitting on a large cherry-wood desk. Behind the desk is a black office chair, and in front of the desk sit two matching chairs. The overhead lights in the office seem to pour light directly onto the jewels, probably placed to make the diamonds sparkle all the more.

Amber releases a small, barely noticeable gasp as her eyes take in the gleaming diamonds. I smile to myself. Amber is a girly-girl. Always has been. Spoiling her will be so easy. I might enjoy it just as much as her, seeing her pretty face light up, knowing I'm the one who did that. It will never get old.

"Have a seat," Mr. Vance says, stepping behind his desk.

Amber smiles at me, bouncing Nella. "Actually, I think I'll stand so she stays happy."

"Ah, yes, babies do like to be on the move." He looks at Nella with a fondness that only a father could, someone who knows how fun babies can be.

I notice the family photo on his desk. Mr. Vance with his wife and three daughters. All grown now.

A pang of sadness unexpectedly hits me. How wonderful and simultaneously heartbreaking it must be to watch your children transform from small babies to grown adults. I'd never thought about it before. No wonder Mom tears up every time she looks at old photo albums.

I follow Amber to stand in front of the glass case and watch as she studies each wedding set.

"There are endless ring styles in the shop, but I selected one of each shape to get us started, and we can go from there." Mr. Vance smiles, both of us watching Amber, who looks like a puppy with a new ball.

My eyes move away from Amber, briefly, to see the rings. They're all pretty, but none of them look like Amber. I try to control my eyebrows, I really do. But like Amber says, they have a mind of their own.

"What are you thinking?" Amber asks, her voice quiet, but not a whisper.

"This isn't about me. What do *you* think of the rings?"

She looks up at me, then over at Mr. Vance and then the rings. "They're all so beautiful."

I know that tone, and I know there's a but. And that she's too nice to voice her opinion, especially since she's uncomfortable with me spending money on her. Something she's going to have to get used to.

"But none of them are your style?" I ask.

She rolls her lips together.

Glancing up at Mr. Vance, I give him a knowing look. One I'm sure he can interpret somehow since he sells jewelry for a living and has a houseful of women.

"Mr. Vance, I think we need some more…organic looking options. Does that make sense? Something earthy and unique? One of a kind."

He grins. "Of course, I know just the collection for you. I'll be right back."

When the door snicks shut behind him, Amber laughs. "How do you read my mind like that?"

"Ambs, I've been watching you for twenty-six years." The words are out of my mouth before I can change them and make them sound less intense. So I follow it up with, "I mean, we've been friends for a long time. I know your tells."

She purses her lips, absently running one hand over her daughter's head. "I always hated the ring Theo gave me. It was ostentatious yet plain at the same time. Just one big diamond with a simple band. I should've known right then he didn't know me at all, but I ignored it, like all the other signs." She sighs. "So, I have to know. If you picked out a ring for me by yourself, what would it look like?"

I grit my teeth, shoving down a snide comment about Theo. How he was always trying to change her when she's perfect just the way she is. I school my features into a soft smile, changing my focus back to rings and what I'd get for her, if I was surprising her with a ring, I chose myself. "The band would curve around your finger, like a vine. It wouldn't be a straight band. And the vine would be encrusted with tiny diamonds, just enough to twinkle when the light hits. A diamond would sit on top of the band, and it would be a unique shape, maybe an oval?" Biting my bottom lip, I try to picture what I'm describing, and liking what I'm seeing. "Yeah, an oval. And it would be a pink diamond. Not bright pink, but a very pale pink. The ring would be delicate, and when it was on your small finger, it would almost look like the tiniest garden."

I nod my head, satisfied with the ring my brain came up with. Noticing Amber is deathly quiet, I glance at her and find her staring at me with wide eyes.

"What?" I ask. "Am I way off?" I can't tell if she's horrified by my description of the ring, or something else.

"Ford," she says slowly. "Do you have Pinterest?"

I quirk my head to the side, unable to tell if that's a serious question. "Um, no."

"You've never been on Pinterest? Do you swear it on your life?"

"I swear it."

Her voice lowers to a whisper, "I have a ring pinned to my wedding board that matches that exact description. It's the only ring I've ever pinned." She pulls her pink backpack off her back and removes her phone from a pocket, then starts frantically flipping and scrolling until she finds what she's looking for. She turns the screen so I can see.

My jaw drops when I take in a photo that's almost exactly what I just described. Except in the photo the vines have tiny green stones to look like real leaves. It's feminine, and ethereal, and perfect for Amber. "Ambs, we have to get you this ring."

"No," she argues. "I can't have my dream ring just to take

it off in two years and never get to wear it again. It's too heartbreaking."

My stomach is in my throat. Of course. Why didn't I think of that? Of course she doesn't want to waste any of her dreams on this fake marriage. She'll get all of that with her real love someday. And it won't be me. I feel my shoulders sagging and have to make an effort to straighten my spine and square my shoulders again. "Right. Well, maybe we can find something sort of similar?"

Mr. Vance opens the door, entering with a cart loaded up with dark blue velvet boxes. "Okay, we have options now." He grins.

When we leave the jewelry store, we're both wearing official wedding rings. Mine is a simple platinum band—I'll have to take it off for games anyway. But Amber's is a delicate vintage style with a large emerald-cut diamond. Still unique, but totally different from her dream ring. Something about that niggles, and I can't quite decide why it annoys me so much. Maybe the fact that she's already thinking about the future with another man?

I take a step toward the parking lot where Amber's shiny new pickup sits, but she stops me with a hand on my arm. "Actually, while we're over here, do you mind stopping in that cute salon with me? I wanted to see if they have any booths available to rent."

She starts walking that direction without waiting for me to respond. I quickly step in front of her, settling my hands on my waist. "You're about to have surgery."

She rolls her eyes and pushes past me. "I'm thinking about after the procedure, duh! I have to go back to work eventually, or I'll go crazy and start painting every surface of your house. I have to have a creative outlet, Ford."

I catch up to her, and she keeps talking. "And Luxurious Lather is so cute. I just want to check it out."

With a sigh, I walk beside her and open the salon door once we're in front of it. The bell above the door jingles, and my hair guy, Peter, grins when he sees me walking in.

"Ford!" he exclaims, moving toward us. He's dressed in stylish houndstooth trousers and a white button-down shirt. They obviously have a black and white dress code because all the stylists are wearing only those two colors. "How's my favorite client? How I've missed that gorgeous hair of yours."

"Peter." I nod my head in greeting. "I could use a trim, actually. You have time?"

He beams, his blue eyes twinkling. "I do. My last haircut was a no-show." His head swivels in Amber's direction and he smiles again. "And who's your guest?"

"This is Amber," I clear my throat. "My wife."

I watch Amber's face as I say the words and my heartbeat speeds up when her face turns bright red. I tell my heart to calm down—she's probably just embarrassed to claim me as her husband.

Peter dramatically brings a manicured hand to his chest, his nails painted a glossy black. "You got married? All the girls are going to be devastated." He winks when he adds, "And some of the guys too."

Now it's my turn to blush.

Thankfully, Amber moves in front of me, sticking her hand out for a handshake. "Nice to meet you."

He shakes her hand. "Likewise. My name is Peter by the way. Let's take this party over to my station, and I'll start on Ford's hair."

Amber chuckles. "You're right, by the way. He really does have great hair."

What? Amber likes my hair? This is news to me. It's just hair, but I'm here for anything she likes about me. She can run her fingers through my hair all she likes.

"I'm a hair stylist too," she adds. "I always appreciate great hair."

Peter's eyes widen as he pressed down on my shoulders, prompting me to sit in the spinny chair. "Ahh, I should've known from the pink tips. Super cute."

"Thank you." She smiles. "I just moved here, and I'm looking for a booth to rent. Is the salon owner here by chance?" Her tone is very professional, but the effect is shattered when Nella releases a loud wail. Amber unbuckles the baby carrier and turns her to face-out so she can see Peter and me. She calms down immediately, like she simply wanted to be a part of the conversation. "Is that better, baby girl?" Amber asks her before turning her focus back to Peter. "Sorry about that."

Peter takes a fresh, black cape out of a drawer at his station, swivels the chair so I'm facing the floor length mirror in front of us, and drapes the cape around my neck. He combs his fingers through my hair as he surveys Amber and Nella.

"Are you kidding? She's such a doll. Definitely your little twin." Amber's face softens at his complement. "I guess she didn't get any of daddy's features, hmm?" He leans over so I can see his face.

My mouth opens and closes like some kind of fish begging to be thrown back into the water. Peter changes the subject quickly, not because he notices my discomfort, but because he always talks really fast. "Our owner is out today, but I'd be happy to leave your name and number for her," Peter adds, grabbing a water bottle and spritzing my hair.

"That would be perfect!" Amber's eyes widen, and she looks so excited. I hope it works out for her to rent a booth here. "Would you mind holding her for a second while I grab a pen?" She asks me.

I open my mouth to answer, but Peter beats me to it. "Girl! You don't have to ask your baby daddy to hold his own kid."

I offer Amber an apologetic smirk, and she rolls her lips, trying not to laugh. Nella is hoisted into my arms, and she kicks happily in my lap. Peter continues wetting and combing my hair, not starting the cut yet, probably so he doesn't cover Nella in hair.

Amber finds a pencil and a pink notepad and neatly writes her name and number on it, leaving it on Peter's station before reaching for Nella again. She fusses when I hand her back to her mother, which makes me smile. Does it make me a mean person that I think it's cool Nella wants me instead of Amber to hold her?

I don't know, but it makes me feel a little special.

As soon as Nella is out of the way, Peter gets out the clippers, snaps on a number four guard, and starts the fade on my sides. Peter gives good, no-nonsense haircuts, with zero razzle-dazzle. And that's why I keep coming back to him. He strikes me as a person who loves the razzle-dazzle but can tell when his clients don't. He also doesn't try to give me any steamed towels or shoulder massages like some of the other stylists I tried.

I close my eyes and let him work. He quickly finishes the sides, back and neck, then pulls out his scissors for the hair on top of my head. Noticing the girls are quiet, I open one eyelid and peer at them. Nella is watching Peter's ministrations, her drool-covered lips open. Amber is watching the chunks of my hair slide down the cape, her pretty mouth turned down.

CHAPTER
TWENTY-ONE
AMBER

"YOU REALLY DO LIKE MY HAIR?" Ford asks.

My eyes snap up to meet his, not realizing he was watching me as I mourned each snip of those gorgeous locks that rested on his brow. His shiny brown eyes look directly into mine, so curious.

I smile slightly, hoping he won't notice I'm a little embarrassed that he caught me staring. "It's just so thick and shiny. You don't realize how envious girls are of it. And you cut it all off and keep it short. It's a pity, but I get it. I know how you hate it to touch your ears."

Ford shrugs, earning a glare from Peter. "Please hold still or I'll accidentally get your ear."

Ford snorts a laugh, then his eyes meet mine again. "All these years I've been marveling at your vibrant red hair, just for you to be doing the same to my boring brown."

My body warms. Memories of all Ford's comments about my hair over the years make me feel a little lighter. Ford was the first one who admired my hair, especially after hearing all of my mother's demeaning comments about how unfortunate it was that I was a ginger, taking after my scumbag of a father —her words, not mine.

But Ford's fascination with my hair color when we were kids, and his few but very honest compliments of the color, made me fall in love with having red hair. Made me realize how unique it was. Sometimes I'd catch him staring at my hair.

And now here I was, staring at his. Wishing I was the one giving the haircut, feeling the thick, smooth strands floating through my hands. Soaking in the warmth of his skin as my fingers ran along his neck, over his ears, and through his hair. When a shiver runs down my spine, I grit my teeth. What the hell, Amber? Don't be weird. You're becoming just like every other woman on the planet having fantasies about Ford Remington…your *best* friend. Your *only* friend.

Can I continue blaming these feelings on post-partum hormones? I glance down at Nella, and as if she can read my mind. She looks up at me and scrunches her nose. I'm pretty sure that was a *no*.

I'm so deep in my own thoughts, the jingle from the door makes me jolt in surprise.

Peter grins at the newcomer, a very stylish woman who's probably around sixty. Her black hair is styled in a pixie cut, which complements her shiny red earrings. She's wearing skinny black jeans and a flowy white top with little, black polka dots.

"Well, if it isn't the boss lady! I wasn't expecting you today, Darla."

Darla grins at him, dropping the large box she's carrying onto the floor then gracefully moving toward us.

"I had to restock some of our hair color," she tells him, her focus then turning to Ford's head. "This fade looks perfect." She admires the haircut, but not the man.

Something inside me eases that she's not ogling Ford. Even though she's old enough to be his mother. She's simply studying a great haircut, and I can respect that.

Peter nods his thanks. "Darla, this is Amber," Peter says, jutting his chin in my direction. "I believe she wanted to talk to you." He winks at me.

Her slim face turns toward me and I say a silent prayer that I age as well as she has. "Hi, Amber. Why don't you follow me to the back while I put the color away? Then we can chat."

"Of course," I agree, widening my eyes at Ford. He smiles at me and extends his arms to take Nella.

Peter must notice my hesitation and says, "I'm done with the cut now, sweetheart. I'm just going to style him up a bit."

That's all it takes to convince me to give my arms a break while I talk to the salon owner, and I hand her over. Nella, of course, kicks and coos. Happy to be back with her favorite guy.

I follow Darla to the back room. It's very organized, with a whole wall of tiny cubbies, dedicated to housing all the different hair color formulas. The opposite wall is full of more storage cubes. These are labeled with tabs, so everything is easy to find. I've never seen a salon so organized.

She hefts the box of color down and rubs her back before she gets to work restocking the color wall. "I'm getting too old for this." Darla chuckles.

I laugh, then bend and take some from the box and help her.

"So, I just moved here from Ohio. I worked at a salon there for fifteen years and loved the work. Your salon is gorgeous, and I'd love to rent a booth here, if you have anything available," I tell her, getting right to the point.

She pauses, resting a hand on her hip. "Amber, right?"

I nod.

"Amber, I'd love to hire you, but we don't have any free booths right now." She quirks a brow. "Unless you'd like to buy it, then I can finally retire."

Laughing, I shake my head. "Sadly, I'd make a terrible manager. I just like the creative side of the job."

She chuckles. "All right, why don't you leave me your number? I'll call you the moment a booth opens up."

Hiding my disappointment, I smile. "Yes, of course. That would be great."

"I love your hair, by the way. Did you do it yourself?" She asks, back to her task.

"I did," I say. "I love pink."

"You and me both, girl." Darla winks.

After Ford pays for his haircut, and we're in the truck driving home, he asks me how my talk with Darla went. By the set of his jaw, and the concern written all over his face, I think he already knows. But I tell him anyway.

"They don't have any booths available right now." I square my shoulders and offer him a smile. "But that's okay." My voice comes out a little squeaky. "I still need to transfer my cosmetology license, and you know, get my heart fixed."

The joke doesn't land, and he frowns, turning his head slightly so I can see him narrowing his eyes through his glasses.

As much as I miss the dark waves that rested on his forehead, the short cut really does suit him. Not every man has a good head shape, but Ford does. And with a jawline that looks like it was carved from marble by Michelangelo himself, the short haircut is devastating.

"Sorry, I was trying to keep things light. But honestly, I'd really love to work there. The owner was nice. She obviously runs the place well, and the location is perfect."

Ford nods. "Well, hopefully next month something will change, and they'll have an opening."

"Yeah, hopefully."

CHAPTER
TWENTY-TWO
AMBER: 8TH GRADE

WALKING down the beige hallway at school after my art class, I turn a corner and where my locker is and find Ford backed up against the lockers...which are also beige. Why's everything beige in this school? I'd paint the walls for them if they'd let me. Add some color, maybe a few flowers.

Ford stares straight ahead, not meeting the eyes of any of the three boys getting in his space. They're not putting their hands on him, so I stand still and just watch. Ford isn't a hot head, and his stony expressions usually bore the bullies enough that they give up quickly. Pestering someone isn't any fun when they're unflappable.

I hug the white canvas and paint brushes I'm holding a little closer to my chest as I watch, knowing Ford wouldn't want me jumping in to protect him. *We're not in elementary school anymore, and I don't need anyone fighting my battles for me*, is what he said last year.

When I see Justin, the leader of the middle school bullies, flip a gold coin into the air with a sinister chuckle, my body tenses. This isn't good.

"Oh, sorry...did you want your lucky coin back? You sweet

little baby," Justin says, his voice doing a baby voice that I know will drive Ford nuts.

"Please give it back," Ford says calmly, too calmly. "My dad gave it to me. If you need money, I can give you the five dollars in my backpack. Are you running short on cash today, Justin?"

His voice is steady, not giving even a hint of sarcasm. I bite my bottom lip, waiting to see what happens next, and trying to keep my feet glued where they are. Ford is almost fourteen. He wants to prove himself.

"No, you asshole," Justin says through gritted teeth, his two minions behind him snickering. "I have tons of money. Millions."

He's lying. His mom is a nurse, and his dad isn't in the picture. Something Justin and I have in common. I've never even met my dad, don't even know his name. He's one in a million in the lineup of boyfriends my mom has had.

"In that case, you don't really need my Cincinnati Tigers championship coin, do you?"

Justin snorts. "No, I don't need your stupid hockey coin. But I can still make sure everyone in school knows what a dork you are, carrying a coin with you every day. Like a security blankie." He says blankie in a baby voice.

Ford's jaw ticks. But the three school bullies still tower over him. Ford's probably stronger than they are, from years of playing hockey...but he's still a head shorter. Ford is going to be huge; I just know it. Ford's dad is the tallest man I've ever been around, and his hands are so big they engulf his coffee mug. But Ford's growth spurt hasn't hit just yet.

The bell rings, echoing down the hallways. Justin flips Ford's coin into the air and when it comes back down, Ford catches it easily in his palm. Justin gives him one big shove so Ford's back hits his locker, and then struts off down the hall.

His minions follow, purposely hitting Ford with their shoulders as they pass by him.

Several yards away, Justin turns back and says, "You lucked out today, Remington. Next time you won't be saved by the bell."

I roll my eyes. Justin is so lame.

Ford heaves a sigh, tucking his dad's hockey championship coin from college back into the pocket of his jeans. I come up beside him, smiling. We're the same height, eye to eye. Ford visibly relaxes when he sees me and gives me a hesitant smile.

"How much of that did you see?" He asks.

I wrinkle my nose. "Enough to know Justin is a jerk."

Ford's shoulders slump. "He's right, though. The coin is like a blankie. It's stupid."

Rushing to get in front of him, I stop, making him stop too. "It's not stupid. People carry things around all the time and collect random stuff. Grown adults who drive Jeeps collect rubber ducks, okay?" I huff a laugh, and he smirks. "A coin isn't even weird."

"You're right," he says, and we start walking again, almost to the door of our social studies class. "Ducks are way weirder."

I grin and watch my friend as he walks into the class and takes a seat. Ford is all cool confidence, not cocky or showy.

And I smile to myself, because I know something Justin doesn't know—that when Ford Remington finally hits his growth spurt, he will be the tallest guy in school. Justin, nor any of his stupid friends, will ever mess with him again.

CHAPTER
TWENTY-THREE
FORD

I'M STANDING in my kitchen, searing steaks in a cast iron skillet, the picture of domesticity. Amber is pacing around the kitchen, making sure everything is *perfect*. She said she wants to make a good impression for my mother's first glimpse of her as a housewife. But she's probably more nervous about convincing my mom that she's really in love with me. I know she's exhausted, too, since we've spent the last twenty-four hours moving her stuff into my room and setting up a real crib for Nella in the guest room across the hall.

"Please stop pacing. You're making me nervous," I tell her, aching to slip my hand in my jeans pocket and grasp the coin that rests there. I resist, knowing it's nothing more than a nervous habit after all these years.

Amber sighs dramatically. "Sorry." She moves around the large island to stand beside me, inhaling a deep breath with her eyes closed. Nella is taking a nap upstairs and the video monitor rests on the infinity island. We haven't had many moments with just the two of us, and I relish being alone with her.

"This smells amazing, Ford. I didn't realize you were such

a chef," she says before reaching for the fresh sprig of rosemary sitting on the countertop in front of her and sweeping the herbs across the buttery steak.

I watch in satisfaction as the ring on her hand glitters in the overhead kitchen lights. Knowing that I bought the ring and put it there does something to me. Even though there's a niggling feeling when I remember the ring she really wanted but refused to let me buy her.

"There, now it's perfect," she exclaims, leaving the rosemary on top of the steak and removing her hand.

Then she surprises me and takes a step closer, placing one of her hands on my shoulder and then resting her head against my arm.

"Is this okay?" she asks, her voice sounding nervous, hesitant even. "I thought I should get used to touching you more, but I don't want to make you uncomfortable." Her voice is barely above a whisper, and I hate that she's nervous to touch me...to be near to me.

Instead of answering her with words, I show her just how comfortable I am with her touches and reach a hand up to rest it on top of hers. She sighs in relief and allows more of her body weight to sink into me.

"This is kind of nice. You're always warm."

I chuckle. "Perks of the muscle I suppose. Extra body heat."

Amber sniffs my shirt. "I can't believe you still use the same body wash you used in high school."

"If it's not broke, don't fix it?"

She laughs, and I feel the vibration of it through my shirt and my skin, like it shoots straight to my heart, giving me a boost of serotonin.

"It smells good on you," she says, gently pushing herself away from me, her hand trailing across my back with the movement, making me suck in a sharp breath.

My skin breaks out in goosebumps with the lingering heat of her touch. I stand there with my back toward her, trying to wipe the stunned expression off my face. Did Amber Park just lean on me and tell me I smell good? Blinking rapidly, I attempt to clear the brain fog caused by her nearness and her comment. I remind myself that Amber gives compliments freely. She's a woman. Women compliment a lot. I have two sisters, after all, and I've heard them hyping their friends up for years. Saying things like, *girl, slay*, because their friend bought a new shirt or something. So, Amber liking the way I smell is just another thing that's completely not a big deal, and I shouldn't read anything into it.

When I finally fix my face and turn around, Amber is walking to the large window in the living room, where she has a view of my circular driveway. Her hips sway in a hypnotic way, but she's all relaxed now, obviously not affected in the same way I am, by the world-altering knowledge that I smell good. Her cool demeanor changes as soon as she reaches the window.

Amber gasps. "They're here! Ohmygosh, ohmygosh, ohmygosh." The woman starts spinning in circles like she doesn't know how to function any longer.

Too bad it's my mother who makes her lose her mind and not me.

I shake my head, turning off the stove top and meeting her in front of the window. Placing my hands on her shoulders to stop her from spinning, I say, "Everything is going to be fine. We can be affectionate with each other, like we just were in the kitchen, and my mom and sister won't think anything weird is going on."

She closes her eyes and blows out a deep breath. "Okay."

I spin her slowly, rotating so my hands are still on her

shoulders but I'm behind her, then push her toward the front door to greet our guests. *Our* guests...I like the sound of that.

She straightens her legs, trying to stop the procession, then turns her head towards the baby monitor. "Oh, I think that was Nella! I'd better go get her."

I glance at the screen. "Nice try. She's sound asleep."

Amber groans, finally relenting and allowing me to lead her to the front door. I release her shoulders and open it just as my mother and sister are about to knock.

"Hey, Mom." I step onto the front stoop and pull her in for a quick hug, then do the same with Farrah. When I pull away from my sister I notice her unkempt appearance, which is unusual for her. Her dark hair is usually down and sleek, but now it's in a mess of a bun on top of her head. It's secured with a scrunchie. I never realized she was a scrunchie person. Farrah is wearing an Eagles hoodie I gave her for Christmas years ago, with black leggings and fuzzy slippers.

"Hey, what's with the slippers?" I ask.

Farrah quirks a dark eyebrow, the same eyebrows I see in the mirror every day. "We were just in the car all day. I wanted to be comfy."

It's a perfectly reasonable explanation, but the way she avoids eye contact gives her away. I'm number one at avoiding both eye contact and subjects I don't want to talk about, and I can sense it in others from a mile away. But I let her walk past me and inside the house. I can talk to her about this later.

Mom and Farrah hug Amber, probably tighter and longer than they did me. Which is fine. Everyone knows brief hugs work better for me.

"Thank you both for coming. We really appreciate it," Amber says, moving to the side, allowing them farther into the house.

Mom and Farrah walk into the living room then both cross

their arms. "Are we just going to move past the fact you guys got married and didn't invite any of us?" Farrah asks, pursing her lips.

Mom smirks, glancing at her daughter. "I agree. I would've loved to come. But let's not pretend we didn't know these two would end up together."

Farrah laughs. "Okay, true. However, I always thought Ford held a candle for Amber, but I didn't think the feelings were reciprocated. Boy, was I wrong!" She sighs, uncrossing her arms. "You've always stared at Amber like she was the only girl on earth."

Heat moves up my neck and face. Amber takes it all in stride, looping an arm around my waist and looking up at me. She's so much shorter than me, barely coming to my shoulder. "It took me a while to see it, but I'm pretty lucky I finally realized this big hunk was the man for me."

Placing a hand at the small of her back, I softly move my hand up and down her spine. I've dreamt of touching her for ages, and I finally have an excuse to do it. "Yeah, I couldn't take it anymore, and finally told her how I've felt all these years," I lie. "And we just couldn't wait another minute to make it official."

Mom and Farrah's eyes are glossy now with tears. A few tears leak out and run down my mother's face. "It warms my heart to see you so happy, Ford."

Farrah sniffs then waves her hand in the air. "Okay, enough with the tears. Where's my cute little niece?"

Amber smiles and points to the video monitor. Mom and Farrah rush over to stare at the screen. Both of them *aww* and talk about how cute she is.

This time I hear a sniff from Amber. I've noticed she gets emotional when anyone is giving Nella attention, I'm not sure why. I should ask her about that tonight since we'll be sleeping in the same bed.

A squall comes from the video monitor, and Mom claps her hands together. "Oh, can I go get her?"

Amber nods, blinking back tears. Farrah follows my mom upstairs.

Lord, help me...four crying women in one house. What, exactly, did I sign up for?

CHAPTER
TWENTY-FOUR
AMBER

FORD and I ate our entire meal without holding Nella. *And Ford might not be a chef, but the man can sear a steak,* I think to myself as I clean up the kitchen and load the dishwasher. Ford worked so hard on our meal tonight and I know how he likes things to stay tidy, so it's the least I can do. He's upended his whole life for me, and even bought me a vehicle...and there's nothing I can give to him, nothing I can offer him, besides friendship and loading the stupid dishwasher. I hate how uneven our arrangement feels. But the man seems perfectly content, so maybe it really doesn't bother him.

I walked Sally and Farrah through Nella's bedtime routine before leaving them to it, and they've been upstairs for an hour now. I hope it's going okay. It's been nice to have his mom and sister here, better than I imagined.

But it's only been one evening, and I haven't had to share Ford's bedroom—and bed—with him yet.

Nella took to them just like she did on Thanksgiving. Good thing she's not a shy infant, even though she barely saw anyone but me for the first three months of her life. Farrah and

Grandma Sally happily took turns holding her, sitting with her beside her play mat, and even feeding her a bottle and then making sure she burped several times. I'm relieved she's taking bottles okay. I love nursing her, but it's really nice that other people can feed her too so I can have a break once in a while. It's weird to go from barely having help, to having Ford's family here. And it's hard to think about staying overnight at the hospital. Away from my daughter. I'm dreading being away from her that long.

A chill goes down my spine at the reminder of my impending procedure. I know everything will be okay, but the nerves are creeping in. Inhaling a deep breath, I remember that it's a simple procedure and hopefully I'll be back home the next day. No biggie. I turn the hot water off, remove a clean hand towel from the drawer beside the stove, and dry my hands.

"Sweetie, you look exhausted. Why don't you head to bed?" I jump at the sound of Sally's voice. I thought she was still upstairs. "Nella went right to sleep. She's such a good baby."

I smile at her comment, thankful I got the best girl. "I'll head to bed as soon as I finish cleaning up," I say, making excuses. Because the truth is, Ford went upstairs—to our room—to take a shower. And with the way my mind has been going lately, that's the last place I need to be.

What if he came out in nothing but a towel? And he was all damp, and glistening, and warm...and his layered abdominal muscles were more pronounced with the moisture.

There I go again! I *cannot* go upstairs yet.

I open the cabinet beneath the sink and remove the all-purpose cleaner, spritzing it all over the modern, cement countertop. I hope this is what I'm supposed to use on the infinity island... maybe there's a special cleaner for this fancy kitchen.

Ford's mom takes the spray from my hands and gives me a gentle push toward the steps. "I'll clean up the rest. That's what I'm here for." She winks. "Now go to bed, mother's orders."

I laugh, splaying my hands out in front of me. "Okay, okay. Thank you for finishing up."

"I know my son likes his house spick-and-span." She rolls her eyes. "You go get some sleep."

With a wave, I head toward the stairs. I glance back to make sure I'm out of her sight and move up the stairs with the speed of a snail that's been smoking weed. It's probably been about twenty minutes. Maybe he's already out of the shower and dressed? One can hope.

If I was being honest with myself, which I'm not, I'd admit I will be mildly disappointed if he's already dressed. There's some tiny piece of my messed-up heart that really, really wants to see him in his towel.

I mean, I *could* die Tuesday while under anesthesia, and at least I'd go out with that brilliant image in my head.

But I'm not going to die, and I'm not going to be a creep. What if roles were reversed and Ford was trying to see me in a towel? He's too much of a gentleman to even think about that, but still.

I will respect him as my friend, and not objectify him for being a very hot athlete.

And with that, I'm outside his bedroom door…our bedroom door. I squeeze my eyes shut, and open the door, jumping inside and closing it behind me before I can chicken out.

I hear Ford clear his throat, and my eyes snap open to find him studying me. He's sitting on his side of the bed, his back resting against the headboard, a book in his hands. He's wearing flannel pants and a fitted white tee.

Before I can be disappointed that he's wearing a shirt, I notice his distinguished reading glasses. I think the studious look on him is almost as panty-melting as the shirtless look. I swallow and it feels like I'm trying to choke down a rock.

"Why are you being weird?" he asks, setting his book back on the nightstand and using one hand to slide his glasses down his nose. "Your eyes were closed."

I manage to find my voice. "I wasn't sure if you'd be dressed."

One eyebrow and one side of his mouth quirk in unison. "And finding me undressed is scary enough that you squeezed your eyes shut like you were about to face a dragon?"

I straighten my spine, trying to come across breezy. "It's been a long time since I've seen a naked man. I'm practically re-virginized." My eyes widen. "I mean, my eyes…not other things."

He scoffs. "Did you have something strong to drink while I was showering?" His expression sobers, and his voice grows serious. "Because I read online you shouldn't drink until you're cleared by your cardiologist."

"Stop worrying. I haven't drunk alcohol in over a year. I'm going to jump in the shower now."

His mouth quirks to the side, like he wants to say something but isn't sure if he should. "What is it?" I ask.

"You shouldn't jump in the shower, it's not safe."

I burst out laughing, but Ford doesn't join me. Sometimes I forget that figures of speech aren't his thing. "I didn't mean literally. Don't worry, hubby. I won't get sloshed or *jump* in the shower."

His head tilts to the side, a light blush on his handsome face. "Oh, right. Sorry."

I sigh. "Don't be sorry, it feels good to laugh."

When I get out of the shower, I lotion my entire body and braid my hair back in a French braid. I've slept in the same bed as Ford before, even when I came to visit him a few weeks ago. But I feel suddenly shy. Maybe it's because we're married…or maybe it's this whole façade. But I've never slept beside a man while wearing a wedding ring. Something about sleeping next to him, in his grown-up bedroom, with his ring on my finger, feels a little more intimate than I'd like to admit. I even chose a black tank and pink pajama pants for tonight instead of my usual nightgown. Ford's body temperature runs very hot, so I have a feeling I'll regret the choice here in a few hours.

When I finally open the bathroom door and make to get into bed for the night, I avoid eye contact with my best friend—er, husband—until I'm completely immersed under the covers. A literal security blanket.

I can feel Ford's stare and then hear his book close, but he stays sitting up in bed, on top of the covers.

"So, what kind of non-fiction book are you reading?" I ask, breaking the silence, but still staring at the ceiling.

"How do you know it's non-fiction?"

Finally, I turn on my side and look up at him. "I've never seen you read a fiction book."

"I'm not the same person I was in high-school and college, Ambs," he says pointedly, then rolls his eyes. "But yes, it's non-fiction. It's a biography of a World War II vet."

I snort. "Just a little light reading before bed?"

A soft laugh escapes him, something about the sound puts me at ease, makes me feel like we're still Ford and Amber…not Mr. and Mrs. Remington.

"Yeah, I guess it's not the most relaxing read. Maybe that's why I'm an insomniac."

Ford slips under the covers and lies on his side so we're facing each other.

"You still don't sleep well?"

"Unfortunately, that part of me *hasn't* changed since I was a teen."

I allow myself to study him for a moment, taking in those bottomless eyes that make me feel like I can see straight into his soul. A soul so pure and so selfless and so beautiful, it almost makes my heart ache.

For years, I think the camaraderie we felt toward each other, both being underdogs, made me unable to see him as anything but a friend. But now? I just see a very handsome, very wonderful man. A man who has always taken care of me and made me happy. If only I'd seen it sooner—not that I'd change anything, since all my past decisions led to a little girl I love more than I thought I ever imagined I could.

But wow, what if I could've been with Ford for real, all this time? I think he might've cherished me…as more than a friend. Or maybe I'm just dreaming. Ford is untarnished, a gentle soul, and I've already given away so many pieces of my heart.

"What is going through that mind of yours?" Ford asks, his voice as soft as velvet, but as deep as those eyes of his. A voice I'd like to feel whispering against my mouth, my neck, my… everywhere.

I smile, hoping the emptiness of regret isn't written across my face. "Just thinking about you and what a good man you are."

His eyebrows raise in surprise. "Um, thank you."

Laughing softly, I pull the covers up to my chin, making myself comfortable. His mattress is firm, but also soft, just like the man who sleeps in it. It's the most comfortable mattress

I've ever laid my body on. I have a feeling I'll sleep like a baby in here. "Go to sleep. You have early practice tomorrow."

He groans, the sound doing something weird to my stomach. "All right. Goodnight, wife."

I know he said it in jest, but hearing the word wife come out of his mouth sends chills down my body. I tug the blankets closer again. "Goodnight, husband."

CHAPTER
TWENTY-FIVE
AMBER

THE NEXT MORNING, while Ford is at practice, I'm sitting on my bed—Ford's bed—just about to take a sip of coffee, when I receive a text from a random number.

Nella is down for her morning nap, Farrah is having a very intense phone conversation in the guest room down the hall from Nella's room, and Mrs. Remington—Sally—went with Ford to watch his practice.

I tap on the text, thinking it's probably confirming my pre-op appointment tomorrow morning, but I'm pleasantly surprised at what I find.

UNKNOWN NUMBER:

Hey Amber! This is Mel! (West's wife)
Welcome to the WAG CHAT!

UNKNOWN NUMBER:

Welcome Amber! Can't wait to hang with you.
This is Andie, Mitch's almost-wife.

UNKNOWN NUMBER:

> Welcome to the insanity, girl. (From Noel, Colby's fiancée.)

With a big smile on my face, I save their numbers to my phone, just as they introduced themselves.

AMBER

> Wow! I'm so honored. What does WAG mean?

ANDIE

> We have so much to teach you. *GIF of Patrick from SpongeBob rubbing his hands together*

NOEL

> WAG stands for wives and girlfriends (specifically ones attached to a professional athlete)

MEL

> Noel beat me to it! But yes. And I've been running the group, but now... technically, as the captain's wife, that job goes to you.

I bite my bottom lip. I don't know this woman at all, but something in the text makes me wonder if she's sad to relinquish her duties. And I'm not going to be the one to take it from her. I hate being in charge of stuff anyway. I prefer other people telling me what to do.

>   AMBER
>
> If you don't mind, I'd love it if you continued running things. With my procedure and everything. But I'm so excited to get to know you all! *Heart eye emoji*

MEL

> Okay! If you're sure.

ANDIE

> I'm snort-laughing over here! We all know Mel just breathed a huge sigh of relief. She loves organizing all this crap. And we love her for it. *Wink emoji*

NOEL

> I'm sitting next to her right now, and she literally sighed in relief when Amber sent that text.

MEL

> I did not!

MEL

> ANYWAY. Here's a spreadsheet where you can fill out your name and favorite color and favorite scent etc. We do a yearly donation/buy-in and then use that money for birthday gifts and fun WAG events!

Wow, this girl is organized. Glad she's not forcing me to take the job. I click on the link she sent and take a minute to fill it out.

>   AMBER
>
> Just filled out the form. When's the first WAG event?

MEL

I was hoping to host at my place next week, since it's right down the street from you. A girl's night in, if you're feeling up to it. We can also start a meal train and arrange dinners for you guys while you're recovering if you'd like.

NOEL

I apologize in advance for being a terrible cook.

ANDIE

Same.

MEL

Well, some of us will cook for you, and others will order something for you. *Tongue sticking out emoji*

MEL

The men will have a guys' night at your place while we have our WAG night. They're all excited to babysit Nella. Although, I feel like someone needs to babysit all the man-children too.

ANDIE

My thoughts exactly. But Remy is the dad of the group, so they're in good hands.

I smile at that. I can totally picture Ford being the dad of the group. The responsible one who quietly blends in while making sure everyone else is taken care of.

> AMBER
>
> You're all so kind. And a night in sounds perfect. I'm sure Ford won't mind letting the guys take over his house for an evening. And wow, Nella is going to have a blast with the guys!

> NOEL
>
> You mean YOUR house.

I grimace. I'm already bad at this acting thing.

> AMBER
>
> LOL right. I keep forgetting. I'm looking forward to it! Thank you for welcoming me into the fold.

Setting my phone down, I lean against the headboard and smile to myself. Friends. I already have friends here…a sort of family. A group that looks after each other. I haven't felt like I had that since I was a teen and could still hang with Ford at his family's house. I think I'll adjust to D.C. just fine.

Ford is seated beside me in one of the patient rooms at my new cardiologist's office, and he looks as tense as I feel as my surgeon goes over the pre-op instructions.

"Make sure you arrive at seven in the morning—that's one hour before the procedure. Like I explained, I will likely place the catheter in your left wrist, so you'll have a small incision there," Dr. Montgomery says, pointing to a large poster on the wall of the human body that shows all the major arteries and blood vessels.

"And no sex or physical activity for at least two weeks. After your two-week post-op appointment, I'll let you know if you're cleared for sexual activity." She pauses, taking in our expressions. "You two are married, right?"

Ford nods his head once.

Dr. Montgomery laughs, her dark skin crinkling around her mouth and eyes. She runs a hand nervously through her black hair and blows out a breath. "Whew, I thought I made things awkward." She turns her attention to me. "Do you have any questions?"

"How soon afterward can I nurse my baby?" I ask, unable to think of any other questions. She was very thorough in explaining everything during our appointment. If I'm honest, I like her much better than the doctor I was seeing in Ohio. She's warmer, almost motherly.

The doctor smiles. "I'd like you to be off any pain medication for a full day before you nurse. Everyone's pain level is different, so use the medication however long you feel you need it. I recommend taking it for a day or two. After that, you could try going without."

"Okay, that sounds doable." I offer her a smile, but it feels wobbly. This is really happening. Tomorrow. They'll just sedate me, and hopefully I'll wake up again.

"I know it's nerve wracking, but you're in good hands with our team here. I perform this procedure several times each week, along with other, more difficult ones."

I blow out a deep breath, but my heart is racing. And I don't think it's because there's a tiny hole in it. "You're right. I'll be okay, I've just never been under anesthesia before. It seems so weird to go to sleep and then wake up with a repaired heart."

"I always tell my patients to try and do something relaxing the day before surgery, do something to ease your mind and body. Maybe take a bubble bath or watch a good movie. And don't forget, no eating after midnight. I'll see you bright and early tomorrow morning, okay?"

I nod my head, unable to form words as the intensity of my nerves escalates so much I can barely think.

From my peripheral vision, I notice Ford standing and shaking the doctor's hand, then saying, "Thank you, Dr. Montgomery."

The door clicks, and the room becomes eerily quiet. Ford doesn't sit in the chair next to me again. Instead, he crouches in front of me. Placing his large, warm hands on my knees.

"You okay in there?" His deep voice croons, making my nerves calm down just a little. If only he'd keep talking to me in that deep, soothing tone.

He waits for me to answer, but I can't. I feel a hot tear drop down my face and onto my jeans.

"Hey, I'm right here, Ambs. You're going to be okay. I know it's scary, but you're going to be okay. I won't let anything happen to you. I promise." He says it so fervently, so intently, that I believe him.

He lets me sit there for a minute, tears streaming down my face, before he sits back down. Ford pauses, and I can feel his stare, then he effortlessly picks me up and settles me on his muscular thighs. I should be surprised, or maybe get off him and put some space between us.

But instead, I wrap my arms around his solid neck and burrow my face into his chest. Because this is the one man who has never, ever let me down. And everything about him—his masculine scent that hasn't changed in fifteen years, his muscular shoulders, his strong grip on me…everything about this man makes me feel calmer, safer, more content.

Ford holds me until my tears run dry, his hand rubbing gentle circles across my back as he waits patiently for me to calm myself.

But I find that even though my heart is no longer racing, I want to stay here, wrapped up in him.

CHAPTER
TWENTY-SIX
FORD

"SHE'S AWAKE MR. REMINGTON. You can come back and see her," a nurse says from the waiting room door.

I've been sitting in this chair at the hospital for over an hour, waiting to hear word that Amber's procedure is finished. It's a good thing I got a haircut the other day, otherwise it would look insane from how much I've been running my hands through it.

"Thank you," I reply, grabbing my overnight bag and standing.

As I reach the door between the waiting area and the recovery room, the nurse holds it open so I can pass through.

"The procedure went well, and Amber is doing great," she says.

I can't remember her name. I don't think I have the brain capacity today to learn any new names. The only name running through my head is *Amber*.

I nod and follow her down the hallway. We arrive in front of an open door, and the nurse steps aside, allowing me to enter first. Slowly, I walk toward the bed. Amber's sleepy eyes blink a few times, like she's trying to clear something from them.

She's still groggy and acting strange. She grins at me, looking goofy and adorable before she slurs, "Well, aren't you a big hunk of man."

I snort a laugh, even though I know I'm blushing. "Wow, someone got the good drugs."

The nurse giggles as she checks something on the monitor and makes notes on a tablet.

Amber sighs. "Ford Remington...captain of the D.C. Eagles hockey team," she says in a deep voice the way a sports announcer would.

I laugh, enjoying this more than I probably should. Amber's nose wrinkles, making her freckles shift. "Be honest," she whispers. "Do you think you're the hottest guy in the NHL?"

It's difficult, but I keep my face neutral. "No. The hottest player in the NHL is Colby Knight."

She nods, then her eyebrows draw together as if she's deep in thought. "Colby Knight *is* hot. But not as hot as you."

I have to roll my lips inside my mouth to keep from laughing. I know she's coming off anesthesia, but damn if her words don't make me stand a little taller. I can't wait to tell Colby about this conversation.

The nurse walks toward the door. "Press the button on your remote if you need me. I'll come check in every hour," she says to Amber. Then she turns to me and gestures toward the very small chair in the corner. "And make yourself comfortable, Mr. Remington. As comfortable as you can, anyway."

She leaves and I toss my backpack onto the stiff-looking chair. "How ya doing, Ambs?"

Amber smiles at me. "Better now. Could you hand me that water?"

I grab the water jug from the table and hold it up so she can take a sip.

She takes a few gulps then huffs a laugh. "I can hold my own water, Ford. But thank you."

Setting the jug back on the table, I sit in the small chair, moving my bag to the floor and hiding a cringe at how many germs are likely being transferred from the laminate floors to my bag.

I study Amber, noting how flushed and clammy her skin is. "Are you okay?"

Her brows scrunch together. "I feel…so dizzy. And cold."

Alarm has me up and pressing the nurse's call button before she can say another word.

Five seconds later the nurse is back. She takes in Amber's appearance and grabs the thermometer to take her temp. The screen shows she has a fever, but nothing crazy. "Sometimes the contrast—the dye—they inject during the heart catheterization can cause fever and chills, even nausea," the nurse tells us.

Amber shivers, despite having a low fever.

The nurse gives her an empathetic look. "Would you like a warm blanket?"

Amber nods, and the nurse is off to retrieve one.

I sit on the edge of the bed, taking her right hand in mine, trying to warm it.

"You're so warm," Amber says, opening her eyes.

The nurse returns with a blanket and spreads it over the lower half of Amber's body.

I hate how sick and pale she looks, even if it's a normal reaction to the dye. I want to see her skin full of color and her eyes bright with amusement. Seeing her sick and in a hospital bed is the worst thing I've experienced in life.

"I'll come back soon to check on her, okay?"

I nod and the nurse leaves us again.

Amber's teeth begin to chatter, and she removes her hand from mine, then uses it to pull the blanket higher on her neck.

"How can I help?" I ask, feeling desperate and useless.

"Can you warm me up?" she asks, her green eyes lifting to mine. "You're so warm, and your body heat is way warmer than this blanket."

My heartbeat speeds up at the thought of warming her up, of getting close to her. I bend down and slide my shoes off, then pull back her covers and scoot inside the bed beside her. She makes room for me, sliding as far as she can to the edge.

Being large is great for hockey, but not so much for hospital beds.

I adjust my body in the small bed until my side is pressed up against hers. "Is this okay?" I ask.

"I need more, get closer." Her request isn't sexual, not at all. But that doesn't keep my mind from wandering since I know she's practically naked under the hospital gown.

Rolling onto my side, I wrap an arm around her waist. Her light-blue gown is partially open in the back. I slide my hand into the opening, so my hand is pressed against the skin on her back. Her skin feels hot from the fever, but she's still shivering.

She brings her left hand to my chest, and I'm careful not to bump the bandage on her wrist as I pull the covers up around our shoulders.

Amber sighs. "That's better."

Silently, I agree. But for totally different reasons than she's probably thinking. I'm in a tiny bed, with my best friend—who's also my wife. The skin on my hand feels tingly where it's touching her body, and it's incredible. The sensation of being this close to her doesn't make me itch, or squirm. It just makes me want to get even closer. I knew it would be like this, knew it wouldn't be like touching anyone else. But the reality of being skin-to-skin, even this small amount, has surpassed my imagination.

I glance down at her face to find her sound asleep against my chest. Tightening my arm around her, I rest my chin on top of her head, the urge to protect this woman, at an all-time high.

But even that protective urge doesn't stop me from relaxing with my favorite person in my arms and falling asleep right along with her.

Early this morning, after an uneventful night in the hospital, Amber's cardiologist checked in and said her vitals were stable, and she discharged her. Amber was quiet during the drive, still groggy and not feeling a hundred percent. But the moment she was in the house, she wanted to see Nella.

Thankfully, Mom and Farrah meet us in the kitchen, happy Nella in hand.

Amber's face crumples, a sob breaking free, as she reaches for her daughter. I place a gentle hand on her back, guiding her to the sofa. "Why don't you sit down and then you can hold her all you want, okay?"

She nods, moving to the couch and making herself comfortable. Mom hands Nella to her mommy, and Amber's face lights up the moment she has her daughter in her arms. "Oh, Nella. Mommy's okay now. My heart is all fixed up."

My throat feels thick with emotion at her words. I knew she was nervous about the procedure—who wouldn't be?—but I didn't realize she was so scared that she might've worried she'd never see her daughter again if the procedure went wrong. If the cardiologist made a mistake.

I swallow, closing my eyes and willing the thought away. I can't stand even the thought of a world without Amber. And I don't have to because she's right here.

Mom and Farrah sit on the couch with Amber, and I come around and join them.

"How are you feeling sweetheart?" Mom asks Amber.

"Much better now," Amber admits, giving her daughter a squeeze.

Nella sighs, her eyes blinking slowly. She rests her head against her mother's shoulder and closes her eyes.

"Aw, sleepy girl," Farrah says. "We were just about to lay her down for a nap." She smiles.

Amber's eyes droop. "As much as I want to hold her all day, I don't think I can stay awake. Would you mind laying her down for me, Farrah?" Amber asks, and my sister looks delighted to get the baby back.

When Nella is out of Amber's arms, Amber moves to stand up but she's unsteady on her feet, still experiencing some vertigo from the dye. I'm there in an instant, one hand under her arm and the other sliding around her waist. "I got you; can you make it up the stairs with my help? I could carry you."

Amber turns her head in my direction, quirking a brow.

Mom snickers from where she's sitting on the couch. "Oh, Ford, watching you as a doting husband might be my favorite thing ever."

Amber doesn't look as amused as Mom. She sighs and says, "I can walk, but I might need your help."

I try not to be disappointed. I kind of wanted to carry her. "Okay. You got it."

She makes it up the stairs fine and I get her settled into bed, pulling the blankets up over her small body. Amber's smaller than me, of course, but something about seeing her in a state of recovery makes her seem even smaller.

She yawns, and I turn to leave so she can rest, but her voice stops me. "Will you stay with me?"

"Of course," I answer, toeing my shoes off then crawling into bed beside her. "You don't want me to get you any water or anything?"

"No. I just want you here with me." She yawns.

"I'm here," I tell her, reaching out to search for her hand under the blankets. Her small hand wraps around mine, and we both fall asleep.

When I wake up, I can barely remember where I am or what day it is. I know I had the easy job the past thirty-six hours, wasn't even the one being sedated, but the anxiety of the whole thing apparently wore me out. I also was sharing a hospital bed with Amber, a hospital bed that was *not* made for a 6'4 athlete. As great as it was cuddling with Amber, I didn't get the best sleep.

My eyes open to find Amber awake and watching me. The color of her skin has returned to normal, and she looks well-rested.

"So, did I say anything weird after the sedation wore off?" She asks.

My eyes shift to the side. "Nope."

"Liar." She laughs.

I find something interesting to study on her nightstand. A glass of water from the night before her surgery. Fascinating.

"Just tell me what I said."

"It wasn't that weird."

She raises her brows, and I groan, rubbing my eyes with my fists. "You said I was more handsome than Colby Knight."

Amber's eyes widen and she slaps a hand over her mouth. "No, I didn't," she mumbles through her hand.

I nod slowly.

Amber lets her hand fall away and starts giggling uncontrollably. The sound soothes me—it's nice to have her back to herself. As much as I enjoyed her half-asleep revelations of my hotness.

Her laughter fades when she moves to get up, grunting in pain when she puts weight on her left hand. "I might need some help."

I smile. "I got you."

CHAPTER
TWENTY-SEVEN
AMBER

FORD'S three days off fly by faster than I want them to. I'm lucky we even got those three family emergency days with him though, considering it's the middle of the season.

I thought I'd be okay on my own after few days, but I'm so grateful his mom and sister are here for another week. Especially since Ford leaves for a week of games on the West coast tomorrow. I've been married to him for one week, and I'm already spoiled and don't want to give him back to the NHL just yet.

My bedroom door is open, but a knock comes from the doorway. I look over from where I'm resting on the bed to see Sally holding Nella, always the doting grandma. I'm so happy Nella has her. Sally uses her hand to make Nella wave at me. "Someone wants some snuggles with her mommy. Are you feeling up to it?"

I laugh, and the sound makes Nella grin. Ford's mom brings Nella into the room and very gently hands her into my arms. I hold her with my right arm, avoiding the small incisions on my left wrist.

"How are you today? Missing that husband of yours?"

I answer honestly, not needing to act. "Yes, so much. I loved having him here."

Her face goes soft. "Seeing you two together after all this time has been so, so special. Me and Gordon used to talk about how Ford looked at you like you were the only girl in the world, but you two just never seemed to be in the right place at the right time, you know?"

I contemplate her words. What she said is so similar to what Farrah said the other day. About how Ford has been in love with me all this time. "Do you really think Ford had a crush on me when we were younger?"

Her eyebrows shoot up, obviously surprised by my question. "You really didn't see it?"

I huff a laugh. "No. I always thought he was too good for me."

"Oh Amber. You're the only girl for him. The only one who understands him. I can't remember a time when Ford didn't love you."

Love me. I look down at Nella, trying to focus on anything other than that word.

Sally glances at the gold watch on her wrist. "It's almost five. Do you need any more pain medicine?"

"I'm okay. I stopped taking them this morning so I can nurse Nella tomorrow."

She smiles down at me and Nella. "You're such a wonderful mother, Amber. It's a joy to watch you with her."

Her words mean so much to me, but there's a pang of sadness somewhere inside me, something telling me it should be my own mother bonding with my daughter and telling me I'm a good mom. But that will never happen. I appreciate the kind words, though, and nod my thanks while trying not to let the tears creep up. I've cried enough in the last week to last a lifetime.

"Thank you. I learned from watching you, I think. All those afternoons spent at your house."

Ford's mother shoots me a look that's full of sympathy. "Has your mom met Nella?"

With a sigh, I shake my head. "She hasn't spoken to me since I got pregnant and Theo broke off our engagement. Her last words were something like, *You ended up making the same mistakes I did, and I want no part of it.*"

Sally tsks. "I'm sorry. It's her loss because you're both amazing." She reaches over and runs a finger across Nella's soft red curls. "She's the cutest thing ever, with all that red hair."

"I agree."

We laugh together, and Nella smiles, as if she knows we're talking about how adorable she is.

Farrah peeks into the room. "Am I missing all the fun?" Her gorgeous, dark hair is pulled back in a Dutch braid and she's wearing black leggings with a lavender athletic top.

"We were just talking about how cute my daughter is," I admit.

Farrah strides into the room, curvy and confident as always. Her deep blue eyes twinkle as she sits on the end of the bed. "Ah, my favorite subject! I love being an aunt." Her words are honest, but there's an underlying sadness to them. I'm not sure why. Maybe I'm not what she pictured for her brother. I wouldn't blame her. Ford deserves the best.

"I was just making dinner," Farrah says, her eyes bright again. She loves cooking, especially baking, I've learned. And with all the fresh homemade treats in the house, I'm not going to fit in my pre-pregnancy pants anytime soon.

"We're having chicken pot pie," she adds. "With French bread."

Sally and I both groan at the same time, then laugh.

"Your cooking is terrible for my waistline, Farrah," Ford's mom says.

I laugh. "Yeah, I'm going to need to use Ford's gym at this rate."

"Sorry." She grimaces. "But hey, the chicken pot pie has veggies, so it's fine."

"True! More bread for us," I say with a shrug.

Nella turns her head and begins rooting around for a nipple. She whimpers as she searches. My chest tightens, I wish I could nurse her. I miss those sweet moments.

Ford's mom chuckles. "Oh, dear, someone's hungry. Do you want me to bring a bottle up here so you can feed her? Or I can feed her, whatever you'd like. I do love the snuggles."

I smile and allow Sally to take Nella since my incision is feeling sore.

Sally gently pulls her out of my arms and moves off the bed, smiling once more before she heads downstairs with Nella in hand.

Farrah lingers behind. "Any snack requests while we watch the game tonight?" she asks.

I bite my bottom lip. "Actually, I always eat popcorn while watching his games. I swear it's good luck."

She grins. "Popcorn it is."

It's almost midnight when Ford slips into our room. I can hear the opening of a drawer and then his footsteps padding to the bathroom. I'm sure he showered in the changing room after the game, but he's likely still in his game day suit.

The bathroom door opens and then more footsteps, until he pulls back the covers. The bed dips with the weight of his body, and a sigh escapes him. Not a content one, a frustrated one.

"Sorry about the loss," I whisper, not wanting to startle him.

He seems unsurprised I'm awake. "Something's off, but I can't put my finger on what it is. This is our third loss in a row."

I nod, even though he can't see me. Losses are expected, every team has them. But three in a row is bad for morale. Especially for a team captain.

The bed dips again, and he's rolled over on his side to face me. "I feel like I'm failing the guys, like I should know how to fix the issue. Our chemistry is all wrong, but I don't know what to do."

Reaching out, I lay a hand on his arm. "You're the captain for a reason. I have no doubt you'll figure it out. Maybe the coach has some ideas?"

Ford brings a hand up and rests it on top of mine. His hand is large and warm and comforting. I want to roll closer to him, let him pull me into his big arms—the way he did in the hospital.

"Yeah, I'm hoping to sit down with Coach Young soon and troubleshoot this. We should have time to discuss it during our flight to California."

His thumb gently moves up and down across the back of my hand, sending a tingle down my spine. "Anyway, how are you? Sorry I was gone all day—and that I have to leave again tomorrow."

"Don't worry about me. Your mom and sister are spoiling me to death…and Nella too." I smile into the darkness. "I've missed Nella the last few days, but I'm still sore, so it's been a godsend having them here."

He hums. "My mom is a little obsessed with her. Understandably so. How's your wrist?"

"I'm just sore where my incision is, but as long as I'm careful it's not too bad."

"Glad you're feeling better. I hated seeing you so tired and not like yourself. I need my spunky best friend." His thumb continues its path along the back of my hand, and I shiver at the warmth of the caress.

"You cold?" he asks.

I'm not. I'm plenty warm, especially with his nearness. But it's okay to lie sometimes, right? "A little."

Ford, ever the caretaker, scoots all the way over until his body meets mine. He scoots close enough that my body is pressed against his, then he ever so gently wraps an arm around my waist. It's not a provocative touch, but caring and tender. Everything I'd expect from Ford Remington.

And it's just what I need to fall fast asleep and never want to get out of this bed.

CHAPTER
TWENTY-EIGHT
FORD

ON THE FLIGHT from Virginia to Anaheim, California, I *try* to sit near Coach Young. The Eagles charter a small plane, just large enough to hold our players and the people who work closely with us. Coaches, general manager, Jeff the equipment manager, etc.

Tom, our general manager, beat me to the open seat next to Coach Young. The two of them obviously had things to talk about and dove right into a hushed conversation.

There are only two large seats per row, so I couldn't squeeze in and interrupt even if I wanted to. Bruce or Colby probably would, but the thought gives me that itchy feeling. Confidence on the ice is one thing, but confidence in social situations, I'm lacking. I would just make everything awkward.

I can find another time to speak with coach. Hopefully before our game tomorrow night. Meanwhile, I pull out my iPad to watch game footage from our last few games and see if I can pick out the issue.

Until Bruce slumps down in the seat beside me with an exaggerated sigh.

I ignore him, then he sighs loudly again a minute later. Closing my eyes, I remind myself that building relationships with my teammates is part of my job as captain. And if our chemistry on the ice is off, maybe the first step is working on off-ice relationships.

Opening my eyes again, I look up at Bruce and offer him a smile. "How's it going?"

Bruce blows out a breath, sending his long blond waves flying upward. "Fine. How's married life, Cap'n?"

I smile, trying not to let the fact I already miss Amber and Nella show on my face. "Great. Amber's healing well from her procedure, and Nella is sleeping like champ."

Bruce smiles back, then looks away. "I'm the only one alone now."

My eyebrows shoot up. Bruce always seemed content to do his own thing, dating and all that. "You're not alone. You have all of us." I gesture toward the seats around us, the plane filled with his teammates.

"Mitch and Andie get married in a few weeks, then Colby and Noel tie the knot after playoffs. And I'll be the only unmarried guy in our group," he whispers like he's embarrassed... as if he's telling me he has herpes or he can't pronounce the word *espresso* correctly.

"It's nothing to be embarrassed about," I whisper back. "I thought you liked being single."

He scoffs. "Nobody likes being single. We're all looking for *the one,* aren't we?"

Leaning my head to the side, I study him. He appears very serious, more serious than I've ever seen him before.

"I'm sorry it's bothering you," I say, trying to remember the comforting things that are socially normal to tell someone. Things people have said to me over the years. "But you do have all of us. We have your back. And you're a charmer, Bruce. You'll meet the *one* soon enough, I'm sure of it."

He perks up in his seat. "You really think so?" he asks, his voice still hushed. "I think it'd be kind of cool to have a wife waiting for me back home."

I chuckle. "Yeah, I really think so."

He finally looks down at my iPad screen and notices the paused video of our last game. "What are you looking at?"

I slide my tongue along my front teeth, thinking before answering. "Our season started so strong. We won against some of the toughest teams. Honestly, I really thought this might be our year to go all the way, to win the cup. But now, we've lost three games in a row, it's not one person's fault, but all of us, I think." I pause, scratching my chin. "Every team has losses, but it's something more than that. There's something bigger going on, but I can't put my finger on what it is. And I'm desperate to figure it out."

What I don't add is that I'm terrified I'm the problem. I've completely changed my life, which I'd choose again and again, but I'm not great with change. It upsets the delicate balance I've created for myself to thrive. What if that's all out of whack now, and I can't get the balance back? What if my autism finally ruins my career.

No. I refuse to believe that. If I found balance once, I can find it again, this time with Amber and Nella.

Bruce nods. "Play the footage. I'll help."

The following evening, we win our game in Anaheim, but it's not a satisfying win. Anaheim is not a top-tier team, and we didn't even win in overtime—we went to a shootout. But it's a win, so I'll take it.

As I step onto the jet for our flight from Anaheim to San Francisco, I quickly take the seat next to Coach Young. Tom always sits next to him, so he gives me a funny look when he walks past this row and takes a seat in the row in front of us instead. Bruce sits beside him, so I hope he's ready for a chatty two-hour flight.

"Hey, Remy," Coach Young says when he finally looks up and notices it's not Tom in the seat beside him.

"Coach," I say, nodding my head. "We need to talk."

The engine of the plane whirs to life and we take off down the runway.

Coach Young waits for the plane to level out before speaking. "You're right, I've been meaning to pick your brain, but our schedule is so hectic while traveling. I assume you want to talk about our losses?"

I nod again. "I know we won last night, but—"

"I hear you. I wasn't satisfied with that win either."

"I've been watching game footage, and I think we need to switch up our first line."

His expression turns thoughtful. "Really? The first line? Why?"

The first line includes me as center, Colby as right-winger, West as left-winger, then Mitch and Rasmussen, two of our best defensemen. So, I understand his confusion. Our first line is solid. Why would I pick it apart? The five of us have played together forever. We know each other's moves and tricks. We move like a well-oiled machine.

But just because you've done one thing for a while, doesn't mean it's the *best* thing. That's something I've learned tenfold these past few weeks. "We've got a good thing going, but I think changing it up would spice it up. Make us more alert, more aware. And we have the rookie…" I trail off, trying to remember his name.

Coach Young smiles. He knows I don't forget names because I think I'm better than anyone else. He probably thinks it's a personality quirk or something. He doesn't know it's just that my brain gets overwhelmed and shuts down.

"Thomas," Coach Young offers. "You wanna give him a try on first line? Rasmussen might not be thrilled with this change."

"Rasmussen has great energy, and he's been with the Eagles for five years now. I think he'd do well on second line, and it would give him the chance to lead and work with some of the younger guys."

Coach Young brings a hand up and rubs the back of his neck. His eyebrows are drawn like he's deep in thought. "I don't think it's a terrible idea, maybe worth trying. I'll talk to Tom and see what he thinks too. I appreciate your input. This is what makes you a great captain, you know?" He smirks. "Not every captain would take the time to troubleshoot an issue like this or be willing to switch up his own line."

I huff a laugh, not wanting to accept the compliment. Half the time, I think West would make a better captain than me. He's confident and charismatic, and everyone loves him. He's great at public appearances, and in interviews. Also, he probably never has to watch what everyone else is doing to know how he should act in social settings.

Maybe I'm too distracted by trying to be normal to have the focus it takes to lead an NHL team.

And now I have two brand new, totally wonderful distractions on top of that.

"Hey, I heard you got married?" Coach's comment draws me out of my own head. "What the hell? You didn't even tell us."

"Sorry." I grimace. "It happened kind of fast."

He frowns at that; he knows me well enough to know I never jump into things without thinking.

"But it's a good thing," I say, hoping to reassure him. "Amber and I have been best friends since second grade. I can't imagine being married to anyone but her."

He grins. "Happy to hear it. And she has a baby?"

"Nella." I smile.

"You look happy." He sighs. "But you should know that Knight is planning a very large, very ostentatious party for you guys."

I roll my eyes. "I'm not surprised, but thanks for the heads up."

CHAPTER TWENTY-NINE
AMBER

I'M SITTING on the large white sectional downstairs with Farrah and Sally while we watch Ford's game. I've got my sketch book and some pencils, needing to do something creative after sitting so much. The Eagles are playing against the San Francisco Lions. Nella is lying on her pink playmat on the floor and batting at the toys that dangle above her face. The teams are tied 2-2 in the second period, and I'm hoping it's not a repeat of the Anaheim game. I can't stay up that late again. Especially since we're Eastern time and these games are at 7pm Pacific time.

I also hated how bummed Ford sounded on the phone today. For someone who won a game the night before, it was obvious he still feels something is off with the team and wants to fix it. I wanted to be there beside him, to wrap my arms around his big body.

A week and a half of fake marriage, and I don't know how I went months without seeing him in person. All we had was phone conversations from September when pre-season started to November when I came to visit him, and it was fine. But now I miss him so much, I feel wholly unsettled. I wonder if I need another heart procedure, or if this is just what it feels like to miss someone so desperately your chest aches. And we still have three days to go.

Farrah squints at the screen where Ford, West, Mitch, Colby, and a guy I don't recognize are on the ice. "Did they change the first line?" She asks, turning toward me and her mother.

Both of our eyes snap to the screen, studying the players.

"You're right," Sally says. "Rasmussen is usually on the first line, but now it's Thomas. The new kid."

I feel my lips move up in a smile. I just know Ford did this, trying to mix things up and see if it helps them get their mojo back. And I adore him for giving the rookie a chance. That's so Ford.

"I bet they're mixing it up to get out of the funk they've been in," I say, and the other two women on the sofa nod, agreeing with me.

Farrah leans her head to the side, focusing on the screen again. "It doesn't appear to be working, but it'll take more than one game for them to adjust to the change, I'm sure."

"Yeah, give it some time," Ford's mom offers, fully in support of her son's decision, which makes me smile.

Nella fusses from her mat, and Sally pops up from the couch to get her. She pauses mid-step and turns back to look at me. "Sorry, I don't mean to keep stepping in! Do you want to put her to bed?"

I chuckle. "You're fine, I appreciate the help." I put her down for her nap earlier and got lots of good snuggles, plus I really want to finish watching the game and see what happens. "You're welcome to put her to bed. She adores you."

Sally grins then rushes to pick her up.

Once she disappears up the steps with my daughter, Farrah's phone pings with a text. She looks down at the phone where it sits on the couch next to her thigh and frowns, then turns it over so the screen is facing down.

"Everything okay?" I ask.

She glances toward the stairs, then at her phone, and finally at me. "It's my husband." She sighs and lowers her voice to a whisper. "We've been separated for ten months, and I haven't told anyone."

My eyes want to widen, and my mouth wants to gape open, but I school my features into what I hope is a comforting and empathetic expression. "I'm sorry, are you okay?"

She slumps back into the couch, letting her head fall back against the cushion. "I'm getting there. It's just that I thought we'd work things out and everything would be fine, so I never bothered telling my family. But now he's asking me to sign divorce papers, and I know everyone's going to react...badly."

"That sucks, Farrah. I'm sure your family will want to support you and be there for you though. They'll be there to help, and so will I."

"Duh, you're family now." She gives me a watery smile.

"Why did you guys separate?" I ask, then add, "You don't have to talk about it if you don't want to."

She sighs, facing me and crossing her legs. "We were trying to have a baby, but after a year, I still wasn't pregnant. I went to the doctor and found out I have polycystic ovarian syndrome...PCOS. And it can be difficult to conceive because of it. Connor always wanted to be a dad, so he had a really hard time with the news."

I blink. "*He* had a hard time with the news?"

Farrah laughs, but there's no humor in it. She looks away from me, playing with the end of her long braid. "Yeah, I think his lack of concern for me during the whole process was my first realization he wasn't the man I thought I married. Then he started blowing up at me for stupid little things, like forgetting to put the laundry in the dryer. He told me one day he didn't know if he could be with someone who might not be able to give him children."

One lone tear falls down her cheek, and I reach over and place my hand on top of hers.

Farrah sniffs. "I was crushed, of course. But I held out hope he'd feel differently once he experienced life without me, you know? Well, it turns out he loves life without me. And this whole experience has made me less than loving toward him too."

I shake my head from side to side. "Farrah, he's an asshole. Like the worst kind of human." I fill my cheeks with air, then blow out a deep breath. "I can't picture Ford getting into a fight, but when he finds out about this, I think he'll come pretty close."

She huffs a laugh. "Yeah, which is another reason I haven't mentioned it."

I chew the inside of my cheek, thinking about the whole thing. "It's crazy how many people are out there waving nothing but red flags. Your relationship ended because you couldn't get pregnant, and mine ended because I *did* get pregnant."

She gasps. "You're kidding."

"Nope. Theo, my ex-fiancé, broke off our engagement the day after I told him I was pregnant."

"Wow. Do men even like women?"

I laugh. "Right? It's okay, though. Everything turned out the way it was supposed to. And it will for you too. You're a wonderful person, Farrah. I just know things will look up soon."

I mean every word, even the part about things turning out

for me the way they were supposed to. I know I'm supposed to be acting, pretending I'm really in love with her brother… but I'm not acting. I should be guarding my heart, keeping my emotions in check. But I'm finding it harder and harder to suppress anything when it comes to Ford Remington. My best friend. And maybe more.

CHAPTER THIRTY
FORD

WE LOST our game against San Fran last night, but it felt like a small win. Thomas played well on first line. I think we just need more time. We need to build the chemistry and rapport that makes a seamless line. But the way he played last night gave me hope.

Our game tomorrow is in Sacramento, against the Fire Cats. The flight was so short we already took our pre-game naps and had some time to kill. Colby somehow got me, West, and even Mitch to go with him to a local shopping center. The pretty outdoor shopping area that reminds me of the one Amber likes back home, but this one has palm trees everywhere, and the buildings are stucco. It's all very *California*.

While Amber is on my mind, I pull up my phone and shoot her a text.

FORD
Hey, what are you upto?

AMBER
I'm bored out of my mind.

I smile down at my phone. Amber is not one to sit around and rest. She's always enjoyed being busy, especially doing something creative. I bet she misses working.

> FORD
> Sorry you're bored. Wish I was home to watch some Bob Ross with you.

> AMBER
> Remember when we tried to paint like him?

> FORD
> I remember my "painting" being mostly happy little birds. Aka mistakes.

> AMBER
> Well, at least you're good at hockey.

> AMBER
> I miss you.

My heart stutters, instantly delighted she misses me too. I take a deep breath and remind myself she's told me that before, and it didn't mean anything romantic.

> FORD
> I miss you too, Ambs.

While I'm thinking of her, I tap on my Google app and order a dozen Pink Piano roses for her from a shop in Virginia. I even pay the extra fee to have them delivered today. I just want her to know that I wish I was there with her, so that's exactly what I request the card to say. Hopefully it sounds friendly, and not like *I'm in love with you.*

"What's got you smiling like that, Remy?" Colby asks as the four of us come to a stop in front of a vending machine.

We all look stupid with our ball caps and sunglasses, an attempt to conceal our identities and be left alone. Being hockey players, we're not always recognized—unless we're in Canada. Hockey isn't as big in the states as football or baseball, but you never know when fans will pop up, and today we just want to hang out and enjoy our privacy.

"Just thinking about my wife," I answer honestly.

Colby whistles, West claps me on the back, and Mitch tries to hide his grin.

I surge ahead, not wanting to invite anymore questions. The guys pick up their pace and catch up with me quickly. We already went into a few of the shops, West got Mel a California t-shirt, and Mitch bought some new headphones. The excursion up to now has been uneventful, until we pass a shop with a black door and a glittery doorknob. West stops right in front of the shiny door, the rest of us almost colliding into him from his sudden halt.

Looking up, I see the shiny black sign above the door says *Naughty Nothings*. I huff a laugh and make to start walking again.

"Wait, I wanna stop in here," West says from behind me.

I turn to see him staring at the window display where two mannequins are posed in lacey pink lingerie.

Colby stares into the shop, rubbing his palms together. "Oh yeah! I want to get Noel something for our honeymoon."

West opens the door to the shop. "Come on guys."

"Um, no thanks, I'm good," I say, pulling on the brim of my hat just for something to do with my hands. Thank goodness my face is disguised by these sunglasses, because I'm certainly as red as a tomato right now.

"You don't want to look for something for Amber? She'd love it! Women like when they know we're thinking about them, especially when we're away," West says, smirking. "Don't be shy. We're grown adults, Remy."

I glance over at Mitch, whose been quiet this entire time.

I'm hoping he'll side with me. Colby and West head into the shop, leaving me and Mitch behind.

Finally, Mitch shrugs a shoulder and takes a step toward the door.

"Really?" I ask, feeling unamused.

"I'm getting married in a few weeks. I like the idea seeing my girl in lingerie as much as the next guy. Sue me." With that, he walks inside Naughty Nothings, leaving me staring at the sparkly door handle.

I close my eyes and grit my teeth. If I don't go in and shop, they'll think it's weird. I'm supposedly a frisky newlywed after all. But if I do go inside the store, I'll be awkward and embarrassed, and then they'll wonder why I'm so shy about buying lingerie for my wife.

I'm damned if I do, damned if I don't.

With an exaggerated groan, I yank open the stupid shiny door and step inside.

Looking around the place, the first thing I notice is that everything is pink, black, glittery…or all three. The floors, the walls, the light fixtures. It's overwhelming to my senses, but I continue walking to catch up to the guys. They're shopping with purpose, eyeing the delicate lace ensembles, and waggling their eyebrows. Except Mitch. He's separated from the pack and is shopping alone. Typical.

Colby looks up from where he's holding a pair of underwear that's basically just a string. "You look lost, Remy. Don't worry, I'll help."

Before I can refuse, he drops the panties and drapes an arm around my shoulders. "All right, what's Amber's favorite color? That's a good place to start."

"Um," I stutter. "Pink, but…"

"Ahh, so she likes pink, but *you* prefer her in a different color?"

I squeeze my eyes shut, not knowing how to answer.

"So, what's *your* favorite color?" he asks, putting his arm around me to steer me around the shop.

"Red," I say, then decide that sounds too made up since it's our team color. "Black."

"Ahh," he muses. "A simple man. Black is a classic choice, my guy." He ushers me to a section of black silk.

One garment catches my eyes immediately, smooth black silk trimmed in ornate, white lace. The very deep v at the front is lined with the same white lace, and the edges of the bottom too. It looks so silky, and before I can stop myself, I reach up and glide one hand over the fabric. My rough hand, calloused from lifting weights doesn't even snag on the fabric. It's as soft as Amber's skin, and the vision of her wearing this sexy yet sophisticated little number has my blood boiling. I can feel the heat all the way from my toes to my face.

I sense Colby's stare and glance over to find him smirking at me, arching one eyebrow. "Yep, I think you found the one, Captain."

Trying not to be humiliated about blushing like a schoolboy in the middle of a lingerie store, I roll my eyes at him. But I also grab the nightie off the rack and head to the check-out counter before the guys coerce me into looking at anything else.

I tell myself I'm buying the negligee to be a good actor. To show the guys this marriage is real, and to pretend like I will totally see my wife in this tiny scrap of fabric. But deep, deep down, there's that fantasy of some miracle happening, getting to see it come true.

The girl at the front desk asks if I found everything okay. I try—and fail—not to blush again. After I pay, she wraps the nightie in pink tissue paper then slides it inside a black shiny bag. With the bag in hand, I high-tail it out of the store and inhale a deep breath as soon as the fresh air hits my face. Winter in California isn't that cold, but the cool breeze still calms the wild blush that was burning me alive.

Looking down, I remember the bag in my hand and my head swivels to take in my surroundings. What if someone recognizes me and I'm photographed with a Naughty Nothings bag? I drag a hand down my face, the one that's not clutching a bag that contains a lifetime of fantasies.

"Damn it," I growl to myself.

"You okay, Remy?" West is outside now, his sudden presence startling me. "Sorry man, didn't mean to sneak up on you."

I attempt an easy smile, but surprise, it's not easy. Instead, I calmly stick my hand in my jeans pocket and feel that familiar cool coin. The one that soothes me but makes me feel childish and stupid. Because I shouldn't need it. A comment Amber made years ago pops into my head, and I smile, my shoulders relaxing just an inch. We were in the hallway at school, and I admitted that I thought it was dumb I needed the coin, and she didn't even pause before reminding me that grown adults keep rubber ducks in their vehicles. I bite the insides of my cheeks to keep from laughing.

Feeling more myself now, I glance over at West, who's staring at me with concern. He's holding his own Naughty Nothings bag. Actually…make that several bags. This is the bad thing about teammates. We know each other a little too well for my comfort.

My eyes snap back up to his face, and he grins.

"That was a great stop. I see you found something too." He winks.

"Yep. Can we go now? I'm done shopping."

West just chuckles.

A second later, Mitch and Colby join us. I don't look to see how many bags they're holding. That's information I do not need to know.

"Well guys," Mitch starts, his voice laced with amusement. "Our captain has everything he needs now, and he's ready to go."

"Ready to go back to our hotel...or back home to Amber?" Colby teases.

Mitch smirks and I narrow my eyes at him. He's going rogue today, apparently.

Giving up on my teammates being mature, I stride ahead of them, relishing the silence. The truth is, I'd give anything to leave California right now and head back to Amber. To hug her, to sleep beside her.

And yeah, to see her in that little nightgown. Which I likely never will.

CHAPTER
THIRTY-ONE

AMBER: SOPHOMORE YEAR OF
HIGH SCHOOL

FIRST DAY OF SOPHOMORE YEAR, and I'm saving a seat in math class for Ford. He struggles with math, a lot. But I'm here to help him. I prefer art and English, but math isn't horrible. Someone stops right in front of my desk, and I grin as I look up, thinking it's Ford. My smile drops when I see Justin, the school bully, sneering down at me instead.

"Waiting for your loser boyfriend?"

I glare back at him, not standing down. "Ford's not my boyfriend. He's my friend."

Justin holds his hands in the air, and his two minions flanking him snicker. "He's not your boyfriend, but he sure wants to be. In his dreams," Justin's voice is mocking and annoying.

His two buddies high-five him. "That pip-squeak will never have a girlfriend. He'll just wind up married to that stupid coin he carries." Justin bursts into laughter at his own comment and his buddies join him.

Justin takes one step toward me, crowding so close to my desk, I have to look straight up to meet his gaze. His eyes are brown like Ford's, but they're a cold, muddy brown. They're not warm and bright the way Ford's are. "You know, I could take you out, Amber. Show you what it's like to hang out with a real man."

Ew. Gross. I don't want Justin to *show* me anything. "No thanks. Not interested."

He leans down, placing both of his hands on my desk, his mousy brown hair flopping into his eyes with the movement. "I know you're just trying to save his feelings. You want me. I can see it all over your face."

He's probably talking about how red my face is. But it's red with anger, not with a blush. Why is it the very worst teenage boys who have all the confidence?

"The lady said she's not interested," a deep, deadly voice echoes around the room. Justin eases away from my desk, and he and his friends turn to look behind them.

Ford stands there, towering over all of them. Yeah, I'm guessing Justin hasn't seen Ford since he finally hit his growth spurt—and voice change—this summer.

Justin blinks a few times, unable to speak as he looks *up* at the man he referred to as a pipsqueak.

I bite my bottom lip to keep from smiling.

"Ford?" Justin asks in disbelief.

"Justin," Ford responds, crossing his arms.

Justin's minions have disappeared, and Justin is still staring at my best friend. Ford hasn't threatened him or thrown punches. All he had to do was be his usual strong, steady self. My chest fills with pride at how awesome he is.

"I think you should find your seat, Justin. Class is about to start." Ford blinks slowly before sliding into the seat I was saving for him, his long legs barely fitting beneath the desk.

Wordlessly, Justin turns and heads to the back of the class to take his seat.

I snicker. "That was amazing."

Ford is unamused. "Are you okay?"

"I'm fine." I huff a laugh at his concern.

The bell rings, and our teacher passes out an algebra packet and tells us we will work through the new material as a class this week.

Ford stares down at his paper, his entire body tense. His face starts to pale, and I know he's holding his breath.

I place my hand on his desk, not touching him but letting him know I'm there. He exhales the breath he was holding and glances over at me. "This looks like hieroglyphics," he whispers.

I offer what I hope is a reassuring smile. "We'll get through it together."

His throat works as he swallows, and he looks doubtful. "I read an article the other day that said people with autism are usually really good at math and science. I'm apparently the only dumb person with high-functioning autism." His deep baritone is hushed, not wanting to draw the teacher's attention.

"That's ridiculous." I roll my eyes. Ford *is* smart. Just not in the typical sense. He's smart in the way he thinks before acting, in how he cares for others, in how his brain processes hockey strategy, and in how much effort he puts into taking care of others. Intelligence isn't always about grades.

But I can't tell him that now because the teacher is narrowing his eyes in our direction.

CHAPTER THIRTY-TWO
AMBER

FORD FINALLY COMES HOME this evening, and thank heaven my heart is fixed, otherwise I'm not sure it could withstand the excitement. My heart is fluttering today even more than it did when I received the most gorgeous bouquet of Pink Piano roses I've ever seen. Along with a sweet note from the man who seems to be the cause of all the fluttering.

I've been jittery all day, waiting for his SUV to pull into the garage. I even washed and curled my hair. My incision is still slightly sore but not enough to keep me from looking good today. I slipped on some cute black joggers and a fitted white, V-neck tee. I feel comfortable but put together.

Even though Ford has been away for half of our two-week marriage, I've grown accustomed to sleeping next to his big, warm body. Something about knowing he was there with me made me feel extra safe and cared for. Sleep hasn't come as easily since he's been away, especially last night when I was so excited, anticipating his return today.

"Amber, you're wound tighter than a twister this evening." Ford's mom chuckles as she pours herself a glass of water from the filter by the sink.

Farrah joins in her laughter. "It's honestly really cute."

I smile at Ford's sister. I feel like we're closer now, after our conversation a few nights ago. We bonded. "Doesn't it feel like he's been away more than a week?"

Both of them burst into giggles again.

"You're a woman in love," Sally says with a wistful sigh. She takes her glass into the living room and smiles down at Nella on her playmat before peering out the window. She gasps. "I think your wait is over, sweetheart!"

My stomach does a goofy flip at the knowledge that Ford's Land Rover is pulling up the driveway—and also at the word *love*. Sure, I've always loved Ford, and I think he feels the same. But the love she's referring to is a totally different type, and I'm not quite ready to think about.

I run to the side door that leads to the garage. Ford parks his vehicle then opens the driver's side door. I rush, barefoot, to greet him. I'm sure I have the dumbest smile on my face, but I can't seem to suppress it.

His brow is furrowed, and his glasses are sliding down his nose. He opens the passenger door and grabs his suitcase, but as soon as he turns and sees me, his expression softens. His mouth pulls up into a smile, and if I didn't know better, I'd think he looked unsure.

Ford has always been confident on the ice but not so much in every other aspect of his life, so I make the first move and step into his space, wrapping my arms around his trim waist. I hear the suitcase drop onto the cement floor as his arms wrap me up tight. I've never really felt at home anywhere unless I was with Ford. But the muscular arms attached to this man feel a lot like home too.

He lays his head on top of mine, and we rest in each other's embrace for a full minute. He smells so good, the way he always does—a scent so enveloping that it drowns out the smell of dust and gasoline from the garage. The scent I've missed all week. And his grey suit is smooth to the touch, pressed to perfection. One of his hands moves up my back and folds gently around the back of my head. I'm not as slim as I was before having a baby, but the sheer mass of Ford's hands makes me feel so small and dainty.

Ford's head lifts away from mine and I can practically feel his gaze. I pull away from his chest and look up at him. Our mouths are only a few inches apart, the way we are holding each other, and I take a second to appreciate how plump and soft his lips look. When I lift my eyes to meet his, I find his beautiful brown eyes on my lips as well, and a current of heat shoots down my spine.

His eyes finally move up to find mine, and those warm brown eyes are aflame, molten-hot. He's looking at me like he's seeing me for the first time. He's looking at me like he's never looked at me before...with desire. With want. With yearning.

Ford Remington is looking at me like he missed me as much as I missed him. And maybe he did. Maybe those flowers he sent were to show me just how much he missed me.

I've never been the shy one here, so I lift my chin in invitation, a silent decree: *here I am, kiss me.*

I don't expect him to take advantage of my boldness. Ford doesn't act on impulses...outside of hockey. But to my delighted shock, he leans toward my mouth, just one inch. Our mouths are so close, I can feel his breath on my lips. This man that's been right in front of me since second grade, is literally a breath away. His hot breath is minty, and I want to feel it all over. I must be a glutton, because I don't just want to feel his lips on mine, I want to feel all of him with all of me.

Never in my life did I think I could feel annoyed to hear my daughter's happy coos, but right now? Yeah, maybe a little. Nella's little sounds echo through the garage, and Ford jumps away from me like he's a match and I'm a drop of gasoline. The man can't get away from me fast enough.

I sigh and glance toward the garage door to find Ford's mom, who's holding Nella, and Farrah is beside them with her arms crossed. They're watching us with knowing smirks. Except they don't know because they don't know this marriage is fake. Something that I also need to be reminded of, apparently.

Ford grabs his suitcase from the floor and smiles up at them, his cheeks are pink from embarrassment. And I try not to let it hurt that he's embarrassed to have been caught almost kissing me. His wife. *Fake* wife, I remind myself.

"Hey, how's my Nella?" he asks, his voice soft which makes me melt just a little more. He moves away from me and closer to my daughter. She kicks her feet happily at the sight of her favorite person.

Farrah and Sally scoot out of the way so Ford can enter the utility room and let go of his suitcase.

We make our way into the kitchen, the setting sun filtering through the large windows from the open living room and making the whole house shine. Sally hands Nella into Ford's outstretched arms, and he holds her close. I swear I see him sniff the top of her head, very briefly. His mom boops Nella's nose and talks to her. Joy hits me like an arrow through the chest. Everything happening is what I've dreamed of my whole life. A healthy baby in the arms of a perfect husband. Family surrounding us, making even this mansion feel like a cozy little home.

It's everything I've always wanted, and all the things I've never allowed myself to envision.

And here I am, all of it unfolding before my very eyes...but none of it is real. I'm here on borrowed time.

They say it's better to have loved and lost, than to never have loved at all. But is it? For all this joy and happiness to just…expire?

I shake my head, forcing away the negative thoughts. Because I've been looking forward to this day all week, and I won't let these thoughts sour it. For two years, I get to embrace this life. And for two years, I'm going to wring every last joyous drop from it.

Ford turns to me, a big smile on his face. Looking just as happy as I felt a moment ago, before those intrusive thoughts entered my brain.

He bounces Nella slightly to keep her happy, already knowing what she likes after only a few weeks. "It feels good to be back home with my girls," he says, offering me the softest smile.

My girls. *Don't swoon, don't swoon, don't swoon.*

I smile back, knowing I'm already falling for Ford in a way I hadn't thought possible for me and him. And even though I didn't mean to, it happened.

He kisses the top of my daughter's head, still smiling.

But how could I not fall?

How could I have ever thought it was possible not to?

CHAPTER THIRTY-THREE
FORD

I MIGHT HAVE trouble reading social situations, but I'm 95% sure Amber wanted me to kiss her. Actually, I'm 99% sure.

The happiness in her eyes when I arrived home earlier today about made my heart burst. And then seeing Nella was equally happy to see me? The best feeling in the whole world. Arriving home after an away stint has always been comforting to me, being in my own home, my own bed, taking a shower in my waterfall steam shower. I'm most comfortable in my own space.

But this was different. This was special. Coming home to my girls was inexplicably wonderful.

Farrah made a delicious dinner for us all—beef enchiladas, and a homemade two-layer, vanilla cake for dessert. Her cooking is impeccable, as always. And the company is great. But all I want to do is crawl in bed beside Amber and get the first restful night of sleep in a week.

The first few nights Amber slept in my bed, I slept like a rock. I thought it was due to how busy and tiring things had been, but once I was in a hotel room alone on the road, I realized it was all Amber. She's like a comforting bedtime story as a child, but the grown-up version.

Amber went upstairs to nurse Nella and put her to bed for the night, so it's just me, Mom and Farrah left at the dining room table. I can tell my house has been full of women because there's a nice tablecloth covering my table, with the bouquet of roses I sent Amber in the center with two of my favorite Sweet Tobacco candles I had in a storage cabinet in the utility room.

I'm minding my own business, totally at peace, popping the last bite of an enchilada in my gullet when Mom pipes up with words that make me internally cringe.

"Let's stay up and play a board game!"

You know that meme from The Office where Michael Scott is screaming *no*? That's where my brain is. I stare at my mother, and she stares back, eyes narrowing.

"I know board games aren't your favorite, but we've barely gotten to see you since we've been here. How about a game of cards instead?"

One of my eyebrows arches. She knows I don't like card games any better. But she and Farrah have been here all week helping Amber, so how can I say no?

I clear my throat, plastering a smile on my face. "Yeah, sure."

Farrah chuckles. "He probably wants to spend time with his wife, Mom."

I offer her a silent look of thanks. Because that's exactly what I want to do.

"Okay, I get it." Mom smiles. "No card games tonight."

Amber chooses that moment to enter the room. "Did somebody say card games?"

I stare blankly into the distance. The very woman I want to be alone with is ruining my chances of being alone with her.

Perhaps my 99% certainty that she wanted me to kiss her was a little overly confident.

My mother's face lights up. "Do you like cards?"

"I love Uno!" Amber takes her seat beside me. She glances at me once she's seated and wrinkles her nose. Probably because my inner turmoil is broadcasted across my face.

"You okay?" she whispers, leaning close to my ear, so close I can smell her hair. I close my eyes and allow myself to revel in her nearness.

"Yes," I croak, my voice sounding as unsure as I feel. Surprisingly, I actually have a set of Uno cards. They're the collector's NHL version that Coach Young gave all of us for Christmas a few years ago, and I've never opened them. I'm not much of a frivolous game player.

Begrudgingly, I scoot my chair back and head toward the drawer where I keep the unopened deck in.

When I bring them back to the table and sit down, Amber shoots me an amused glance.

"You've never opened them." It's a statement, not a question.

"Nope."

Mom takes the package from my hands and opens it, shuffling the large deck, then dealing each of us six cards.

Farrah organizes her cards in her hands then gasps. "Ford is on the reverse card!"

"You're kidding!" Amber squeals, riffling through her own cards to see if she has a Ford Remington reverse card.

I roll my eyes when Mom gasps. "I have one too! Oh Ford, this is too cool."

You know what would be cool? Lying in bed beside my wife as I try to count her freckles and stare into my favorite pair of vibrant green eyes.

Glancing at the clock on the stove, I see it's only seven and hold in another groan.

Two hours later, I'm finally following Amber upstairs to bed. As soon as the door clicks shut behind us, I remember that Mom and Farrah will leave next week. Amber and I will no longer need to sleep in the same room.

The thought makes me deflate, all illusions of romance shattered. Amber is sleeping with me because it's a necessity, an act. Even if she looked at me earlier like she wanted a kiss, that doesn't make this marriage real. Maybe that was her pretending to be my adoring wife.

Amber takes her pajamas from one of the dresser drawers I cleared out for her. Three drawers. Just for her. I don't want to put my stuff back inside those drawers. I'm not sure I can bear it. Maybe I'll just leave them empty once she moves out of my room. Or maybe I'll just keep clearing out more drawers and see if she stays and keeps filling the drawers with her things.

With a smile I can only describe as shy, she walks past me and into the master bathroom. While she's in there, I hang up the suit I never changed out of and slip on a fresh pair of boxer briefs. I glance at myself in the large mirror that takes up a wall of my closet. I'm fit, abs on point—despite having eaten my weight in cake and enchiladas earlier. My haircut still looks decent too, and although my eyes look tired from traveling and not sleeping well, I'd say I look good. Conventionally attractive, even.

Staring at my physique, I make sure my small hip tattoo is covered, it is. And I silently contemplate going to bed shirtless tonight. Maybe then she'd look at me like something more than a best friend. Maybe she'd want to trail her hands across my pectorals...or rub my back, which is also very muscular. I've heard women like muscles.

I wouldn't know from personal experience, since Amber is the only woman I've allowed this close to me. Something I've never told anyone—that not a single woman has ever been in my bed before Amber. And I like it that way.

I look myself over once more and lose my confidence, throwing a black tee over my torso and stomping out of the closet.

"You okay?" Amber's sweet voice draws my gaze toward the bed. She's sitting at the foot of the bed with one leg folded beneath her, her nightgown hiked up to expose the creamy freckled skin of her thigh.

Interesting. Since moving into my room, she's worn pajama pants and tank tops instead of her little nightgowns. Maybe her other pajamas are dirty. Yeah, that's probably it.

The thought of Amber's pajamas leads my brain down a rabbit hole, and suddenly I remember the lingerie in the glossy bag that I stuck inside my closet when I got home earlier. I hid it behind a box of skates Bauer Hockey sent me and I haven't used yet.

My eyes scan Amber from her toes, painted a pretty pink, to her red hair, which she put up in a messy bun while she was in the bathroom changing. A few curled pieces look like they've fallen out of the bun and now dance gracefully around her face, almost on purpose.

I allow the devil on my shoulder to win this one, and picture her in the silky, low-cut black teddy that's currently stashed behind my skates. There's no way in this world that she wouldn't look even better in the black silk than the mannequin did, with her soft curves, made softer with motherhood, and her vibrant red hair standing out against the black fabric.

I shiver, and Amber notices. "You're cold."

Wordlessly, I walk to the bed and sit down next to her. The mattress shifts with my weight, and she slides into me. She catches herself with her hands on my chest, and I regret my choice to put a shirt on. What I wouldn't give to feel her hands on my bare skin.

With a hand on her back, I steady her, and she looks up at me with those shiny green eyes, unique to this woman alone. Never have I seen another set of green eyes so bright. Sometimes I think I might be able to see right through them.

Her warm skin warms my hand, even through the cotton fabric of her nightgown, making heat trickle from my hand and into the rest of my body. Touching her is like getting into your car on a hot summer day in Virginia—so hot you don't know how you'll ever cool down again.

Her hands don't move from my chest, and her eyes hold mine. I swallow, and my throat feels thick with the motion because she's looking at me like she did in the garage earlier... like she wants me to kiss her.

No, devour her.

But this time, there's no audience around to watch. No show to put on. It's just her and me, and we've never allowed ourselves to be this close, to look at each other so intensely.

"Earlier," she whispers, so quiet it's barely audible. "In the garage...I thought you might—"

"Kiss you?" I finish her sentence.

She pulls her bottom lip into her mouth, and my eyes track the movement. Amber pauses for a second before tilting her chin up like she did earlier. A movement so subtle I thought my eyes were tricking me then, and I wonder again now. This time, she closes her eyes.

For a moment, I miss the green color that has always made my heart race, but then her beautiful lips part and I realize this is an invitation. An invitation to enjoy each other in a new way. An invitation to change our friendship forever.

Because there's no going back after this.

If I choose to accept this kiss.

And that's when I realize I'm a very, very selfish man. Because I want this kiss, no matter the cost.

Leaning forward, I brush my mouth against hers, testing the water, seeing what lies beneath. Amber inhales a sharp breath with the contact, but keeps her eyes shut tight like she's dreaming.

There's something about her closing her eyes and allowing me to control the kiss that makes this even hotter. Because I think we both know I'm not experienced, and yet, she trusts me completely.

And Amber's trust in me makes me almost as hot as thinking about that teddy in the closet. Okay, not quite *that* hot.

I brush my lips against hers one more time before fully pressing my lips against hers, craving the pressure of her mouth. She meets the movement and gently pulls my bottom lip into her mouth. The groan I've been holding in all evening finally releases, and I feel Amber smiling against my lips.

She pulls back slightly, and I think she's ending the kiss, but instead she tenderly runs the tip of her nose down the center of mine. It's not something I'd ever imagined being sexy, but it's so sweet, so intimate. Coming from anyone else I might not think so, but from this woman? I'd let her nuzzle my nose all night.

Amber moves down to my lips again, doing that thing where she tugs on my bottom lip. She's exploring my mouth with hers, and then her hands begin exploring as well. Yeah, the shirt was a really stupid idea.

She slides her hands up my chest and then my neck,

bringing them to rest on the sides of my face, her thumbs softly grazing my jaw on both sides. One hand pulls away, and I feel the tip of her fingers dip into the dimple on my chin.

I chuckle against her mouth. The sound is raspy, almost unrecognizable to my own ears. Nothing like my usual laugh. But I can't even think clearly, with all the things she's doing with her mouth, and her hands. Speaking of her hands, they're dragging back down my pecs now, and I'm relishing the touch. I flex my abdominal muscles, wanting to impress her.

"Can I ask you to take your shirt off without sounding like a fan girl?" Amber whispers, her hands stopping right on the hem of my shirt.

I grin at her, pulling away just enough to grab the back of my tee and yank it over my head. It lands somewhere on my bedroom floor.

She studies my chest unabashedly before lacing her arms around my waist, and resting her head on my chest. I wrap one arm around her, and with the other, I run the backs of my fingers along the impossibly soft skin of her arm. To my delight, her skin breaks into goosebumps beneath my caress.

Tonight, I kissed a woman…and not just any woman.

The woman.

My wife.

CHAPTER
THIRTY-FOUR
AMBER: SENIOR YEAR OF HIGH SCHOOL

IT'S A BEAUTIFUL, chilly evening as I walk from Ford's house to my apartment. It's August 22nd, my birthday. And it was the best day, thanks to my best friend.

Ford brought me flowers at school like he always does, the Pink Piano roses from his mom's garden I admired all those years ago. They're still my favorites, the prettiest color of pink.

After school, we went to his house, where his mom had baked me a birthday cake. Angel food cake with strawberries and whipped cream. Last year I told Ford it was the yummiest kind of cake, and of course, he remembered and requested it from his mom.

Ford has grown up these past few years, and it's hard not to notice the muscle he's packed on, the facial hair he can now grow. He's become a man, with his deep voice and rugged good looks. And better than all that, his heart is so kind.

I hope someday I'll end up with someone as great as him. But he doesn't look at me that way—he never has. I'm not sure he looks at any of the girls at school with interest…but maybe that's just because he hates eye contact?

I hum thoughtfully as I open the door to the apartment.

When I see my mother sitting in our tiny living room, her face pinched in irritation, I nearly drop my small purse.

"Where have you been?" she demands, not bothering to introduce me to the man sitting next to her whom I've never seen before.

He looks away, probably feeling uncomfortable that my mom is upset with me.

"I was at the Remingtons'," I answer with a smile, not wanting to let her ruin my birthday.

She scoffs. "You're still hanging out with him?" Her nose wrinkles in disgust. "Why bother with that Remington boy? Despite the freckles, you're pretty! You could do so much better."

I swallow back an angry response. "Ford and I aren't dating, Mom. But I'd be lucky to be his girlfriend—any girl would."

Mom rolls her blue eyes and tosses her blonde hair over her shoulder. I'm reminded again that I look nothing like her—and hopefully I act nothing like her either. "The Remingtons don't have any money, Amber. Don't waste your time."

She obviously missed my comment about how Ford and I aren't dating. And I'd never be with a guy just for his money. I don't want to be like my mother. The guy sitting on our sofa, dressed in a black suit, like he just got off work, gapes at my mom.

"Is that why you're with me? For my money?"

Mom's eyes widen, and she backpedals. "Of course not, Stuart! Don't be ridiculous. I'm with you because you're such a gentleman."

He narrows his eyes. "A gentleman who buys you expensive gifts?" My mom's flavor of the week, Stuart, rises from his seat and makes toward the door. It's a very short walk in our

900 square-foot apartment. "I'm out of here. You can mooch off someone else."

Mom chases after him, latching onto his arm. "Stuart, baby! Stop!"

They continue their fight outside in the hallway. I close the door behind them, so I don't have to listen to it. This is nothing new, coming from my mom. I used to make excuses for her behavior, thinking she must be really lonely or something. But now I'm old enough to realize she's just selfish and miserable. Some rich guy could finally wife her up tomorrow, and she'd still be this way.

She didn't even tell me happy birthday.

Walking into the kitchen, I spin in a circle, looking for any sign that she remembered the day of my birth. Some years she does, usually the years she's between boyfriends and has time to think about someone besides herself.

The kitchen is bare, save for an empty bottle of red wine and the two glasses she and Stuart must have used. No cake, no streamers, no card, no present.

The Remingtons might not have a lot of money—although they definitely have more than we do—or a fancy house. But judging by their happiness, and joy in being with each other, you'd think they were the richest people on the planet.

Ford's mom made me feel special today by making a cake for me. It probably cost her ten dollars. Ford makes me smile on my birthday every year by bringing me free flowers from the garden in his backyard.

Mom is focused on money when that's the last thing that matters.

CHAPTER
THIRTY-FIVE
AMBER

I WAKE up to find my best friend watching me. His brown eyes are thoughtful, and when my eyes meet his, his lips tug up in a smile. He reaches out and runs a hand down my exposed arm.

The touch makes me want to do more than kiss him, but I'm not sure either of us is ready for that. We already went from best friends to husband and wife, to…? I'm not sure what this is.

Has he always had feelings for me like his mom and sister said, or am I just convenient because I'm here in his bed?

And is that how he thinks *I* feel too?

"So, we kissed." I say, thinking we should talk this out before going on about our day.

"We did." His rough morning voice has me considering throwing this conversation out the window. "You look shy," Ford says, reaching up and tucking a strand of hair behind my ear. "You weren't shy when we were kissing."

It's not meant to sound sexy; he's stating a fact. I wasn't shy then, and I am now. His furrowed brows are saying, *Tell me why.*

"I guess I'm not sure what this means."

He nods, scooting a little closer to me.

I put a hand over my mouth. "Don't come any closer. Morning breath."

Ford rolls onto his back laughing, and I cherish the sound. The normalcy. *See? We can kiss and still be fine. I can feel up his entire torso without anything being amiss. Just best friends over here!*

He rolls back toward me, still with a smile on his face. "Amber, I know I'm hard to read, so maybe you genuinely never noticed. But I've pretty much always wanted to kiss you."

My heart rate speeds up. "Really? Why didn't you say anything until now?"

Ford sighs. "You never looked at me like you did yesterday. In the years I've known you, I never got the impression you wanted me to kiss you. Or wanted us to be more than what we were."

"I did think about it once, before I pushed it out of my head."

"When?"

"After my eighteenth birthday. You brought me flowers at school like you always did. But then you made sure your mom made my favorite cake. It was so thoughtful." My hand lifts and strokes over the stubble on his cheek. An innocent touch, really. But intimate, a way I've never touched Ford before. It feels so natural to reach for him, to be with him like this. "That day I thought about how lucky someone would be to be with you. But you'd never expressed interest, so I shoved that thought very deep down."

Ford's mouth quirks to the side, he looks annoyed and a little pouty. "We could've saved a lot of time if you had just told me that when we were eighteen."

I shove him playfully and he smiles. "You never said anything either! How old were you when you thought about us as more than friends?"

His expression grows serious, those bottomless brown eyes drilling straight through mine and right into my soul. "Amber, I can't remember what it feels like to *not* have a crush on you."

I blink back tears, his honest admission making it difficult to hold them back. "You didn't just kiss me because I was here and it was convenient?" As soon as the question leaves my mouth, I know how ridiculous it sounds. Ford would never treat me like that. He'd never treat anyone like that.

Ford closes the distance between us and wraps me in his arms. His mouth brushes against my ear as he whispers, so sweetly, "I kissed you because I've wanted to kiss you since you sat with me under that desk in second grade."

"Oh, Ford," I sob into his black tee, the one he put back on last night before we crawled under the covers. It's soft and it smells like him, and I might steal it and keep it forever once he takes it off. I'll never wash it. Too much happened when he was wearing this shirt.

"We've wasted so much time." My words are muffled with my face pressed against his solid chest.

Ford pulls back so he can look at me. He takes my face in those big hands, his eyes glossy like he's about to cry. "Don't say that. We're here now, and we have Nella. Everything happened exactly the way it was supposed to." He pauses, his eyes searching my face. "No regrets, okay?"

I nod, knowing he's right. I wouldn't change a thing since life gave me my daughter. "No regrets. Except maybe not kissing sooner."

Ford winks and I commit the moment to memory, because it's adorable.

"Yeah, we definitely should've kissed sooner."

The video monitor on my nightstand comes to life with whimpers from my precious daughter. Ford grins and jumps out of bed, coming over to my side and pulling me up with him. After this conversation, I think we're both anxious to be near her, to hold her and acknowledge how happy we are she's here. That neither of us would change the path that got us to the moment we're in right now.

I grab a hoodie from a hook on the bathroom door and slide it over my head in case anyone else is up, while Ford slips on some black joggers.

When I open the door across the hallway to Nella's room, her cries escalate. Ford steps past me, glancing at me as if asking for permission to pick her up. I nod and he gently picks her up, cradling the back of her head. He bends his neck and kisses her chubby cheek.

Her crying quiets and she looks up at him intently. He looks like a giant in this room with all the baby items. And his hand almost wraps around her whole head. Ford is the definition of a gentle giant.

The giant himself smiles down at my daughter, looking the happiest I've ever seen him. His brown eyes meet mine.

"I missed you two so much," he says, walking closer to the doorframe where I'm standing and watching.

He cradles Nella with one arm and uses the other to cup my face, the rough calluses of his hands feeling so enticing against my skin. Ford leans down and plants a soft kiss on my lips. I close my eyes and savor the moment, all thoughts of morning breath forgotten.

CHAPTER THIRTY-SIX
FORD

AFTER GETTING THE COFFEE GOING, I run back upstairs to grab my tennis shoes. I'm off today, but I'll still workout on my own in my garage gym. Entering my bedroom, I walk straight to the closet for my shoes and socks, but when I hear Amber's phone go off—pinging not once, but five times—I turn and walk toward her phone instead.

What if it's her doctor? I decide to peek so I can run her phone across the hall if it's urgent.

But the name on the screen makes me stop in my tracks, and I nearly drop her phone.

> **THEO**
>
> Did you stalk my mom? How did you know where she would be?
>
> **THEO**
>
> My life was going great, and now my mom is practically begging me to take you back. She wants to know her grandchild.

> **THEO**
>
> If you had just left me and my family alone, my mother wouldn't even know about the baby.
>
> **THEO**
>
> But no. That was too easy for you, wasn't it?
>
> **THEO**
>
> My mom wants a relationship with her grandchild. I hope you're happy now.

She obviously doesn't have a passcode on her phone because all these texts are up on the lock screen. I know it would bother me—a lot—to have my privacy invaded. So despite wanting to play detective and see if she's been communicating with her ex before today, I set the phone down and traipse back to my closet. My mind is reeling with possibilities and playing out the ways Amber might react to these texts. I'm moving back and forth between anger at how Theo is speaking to Amber, and frustration that his mom met Nella and Amber never mentioned it to me.

There's a third feeling coiling around my stomach, too. I can't quite name what it is, but the gist is this: if Theo changed his mind, and he did want Amber back, if he wanted to build a family with her...I'd have to back down. I'd have to give her up.

I could never tear a family apart, and he's Nella's father by blood. They have a genetic bond I will never have with her, even though she already feels like mine. Which is scary after reading those texts.

Also, I remember Amber mentioning that Theo's family has

money—lots of it. How far are they willing to go to be in Nella's life?

This is all too much. I sit on the edge of the bed and rest my head in my hands, rubbing my temples.

"You're not a kid anymore. Get it together," I tell myself, jumping back to my feet and taking a deep breath to calm my racing thoughts.

I need to work out, *need* the physical activity to settle myself. Quickly, I lace up my tennis shoes and make for the bedroom door. But I pause and walk back to my nightstand. Grabbing my stupid coin, I study it for a moment. It's worn now, my dad's college hockey team logo in the center—the Cincinnati Tiger's—in the center is almost completely rubbed smooth from all the time I spent running my fingers over it as a kid. Now I mostly just like the weight of it in my pocket and knowing it's there. I guess that's progress, that I don't need to play with it and hold it anymore? With a groan, I thrust it into the pocket of my workout shorts and head to the garage.

Mom and Farrah are up, sitting at the island in my kitchen and partaking of the fresh coffee, when I walk by.

A terse nod is all I can manage as I pass by them. They stop their conversation and concern etches their expressions. I ignore it, not slowing my stride until I open the door between the garage and my home gym. They probably think I'm angry, but I'm not. A lot of my emotions have been translated as repressed anger over the years, but usually I'm just frustrated and too overwhelmed to talk about whatever is bothering me. Amber was always the person I could confide in, but what happens when my confidant is the reason for my dizzy, swirling brain?

I connect my phone to the speakers in the gym and select a classical music station. Now's not the time for heavy metal. I want to calm down, not amp up.

A text pops up on my phone, and it's not from any of them women inside my house, so I open it.

BRUCE
Hey, man. You working out today? And can I join you?

I close my eyes and release a sigh. Bruce would be the perfect distraction since he never shuts up.

FORD
Sure, I just got out here, actually. The side door to the garage is unlocked.

BRUCE
Great! See you in a few, Cap'n.

He must've been near my neighborhood already, because ten minutes later Bruce waltzes into my gym with his signature grin, and his hair cut into a modernized version of a mullet. My eyes widen at the new cut. It's shorter around the ears than I'm used to seeing on him. Bruce has completed the new look with short black workout shorts that are stretched to the max by his powerful legs, and a D.C. Eagles tee that he's cut the neck and sleeves out of. I can almost see his nipples since the cutouts are so big. With his goofy personality and Swedish features, he somehow pulls the look off.

"Nice haircut," I offer dryly, already feeling calmer with Bruce here to distract my brain.

He winks. "Thanks. I went to your man, Peter. Cool dude."

The salon. I nearly forgot the call I made on the road last week and make a mental note to follow up on that.

"I thought you never cut your hair because it's bad luck?" I ask, knowing how superstitious he is. "And we have a home game tomorrow night."

He shrugs, setting up his weights for chest presses. "You were brave enough to change up the first line, so I figured I could embrace change too. Sometimes change is a good thing, right? Keeps things fresh."

I grab a fifty-pound plate and slide it onto the bar on the squat rack. "Good point. How do you think the rookie did?"

Bruce shifts his head back and forth. "So-so. But it's only been a few games. I think he has the instincts but just needs to adapt to working with you guys."

I nod, agreeing with him. "He's a powerhouse, even though he's one of the smaller guys."

Bruce chuckles, laying on the bench and getting his hands in position on the bar. I don't spot him since he's got a doable load on the bar, nothing too crazy. "Right? He's tiny compared to Mitch the Machine."

I smile at Mitch's nickname, given to him because of his defensive skills, and all the fights he used to get in…before therapy taught him how to channel his anger.

Bruce does eight reps of chest presses, groaning as he lifts the bar one last time, then sits up. "How's married life? Is Amber healing okay?"

Running my tongue along my front teeth, I think on how to answer. An hour ago, I would've been shouting from the rooftops about how amazing life is, and I still feel that way. But now there's this looming dread in my gut. And its name is Theo.

"Married life has been busy," I answer honestly. I'm not going to wax poetic about how amazing it is because I'm a terrible liar, and our marriage so far has been a wild ride. And I've been gone for most of it. However, having Nella and Amber here to come home to was pretty amazing. "It was nice having people to come home to. And Amber is feeling great."

He quirks a brow at my bare-minimum responses. "All right. Good."

"How have you been? Still looking for a wife?" I ask, turning the conversation on him instead.

Bruce's thunderous laugh fills the gym. "I was doing okay until I heard you all went lingerie shopping for your wives and didn't invite me."

I busy myself with the squat bar, completing my reps, desperately trying not to blush. "It was West and Colby's idea," I mutter.

Bruce gives me a disbelieving stare, one that says, *right... I'm sure you hate lingerie.*

We finish the rest of our workout in amicable silence, him doing upper body, and me doing lower, so we stayed out of each other's way.

"You want some coffee before you head out?" I ask once we put the weights away.

"Sure! And I haven't met your wife yet, so you can introduce us."

At my nervous expression, he claps my back with his hand. "Dude, don't worry. I'll keep the charm at a minimum. I'm not trying to make her fall in love with me."

I shrug his hand off my back and roll my eyes. I'll let him think that's what was worrying me and not the fact that this will be the first time Bruce will see me and Amber together as a married couple—and he might be the most perceptive one in the bunch.

Bruce follows me through the garage and into the kitchen where Farrah is pulling a fresh batch of muffins out of the oven. How early did she wake up this morning? She's still in her pink plaid pajama shorts and an oversized tee. Farrah's long, dark hair is tossed up in a messy bun, which seems to be her new thing.

She smiles at me, and her eyes go round and wide when she notices Bruce trailing behind me. Probably because she didn't realize anyone had joined me for my workout.

Amber comes down the stairs holding Nella and smiles at us. Thankfully, she changed into navy blue leggings and a floral top that flows around her as she walks.

"Do we have company?" she asks, pausing to give Nella a kiss on her head. Nella coos, in a better mood now that she's been fed.

"Yeah," I say, my voice coming out breathy from how pretty she looks. Calming down before talking to her about the texts was a good plan. I feel levelheaded now and realize Amber is trustworthy and wouldn't do anything to put Nella at risk. I have no clue what Theo was talking about, but there has to be a reasonable explanation. "Amber, this is Bruce, our starting goalie."

She smirks, raising her eyebrows and flicking her eyes to the man behind me. I turn to see what she's looking at and I find Bruce, in a trance. I follow his line of sight to see he's either staring at my sister, or the muffins she's holding.

My sister is flustered, probably because a strange man is staring at her. I wave my hand in front of Bruce's face, and he shakes his head. "Sorry, what?"

"I was just introducing you to my wife, Amber."

He finally turns in her direction. His mouth widens in a grin as soon as he sees Nella. "Oh, my, she's so cute. Can I hold her?"

"I hope you're talking about the baby."

He snorts a laugh. "Yes, of course. Although, you're cute too, Amber." He winks, and ambles over, holding both hands out to Nella. She kicks her feet and Amber lets him take her out of her hands.

Bruce looks natural with a baby, being an overgrown child himself. I can't help but smile at the joy on his face as he cradles her, baby-talking and making faces until she smiles up at him.

Amber laughs at his antics. "It's nice to meet you, Bruce." Then she turns her attention to me. "Looks like we found a new babysitter."

"I will absolutely babysit," he says. Bruce walks with Nella back toward the kitchen—and my sister. "And what's your name? I'm Bruce. Starting goalie for the D.C. Eagles."

My sister rolls her lips, trying not to laugh.

"That's my *married* sister, Farrah," I respond for her.

He glances down at her hands, causing me to do the same…and that's when I notice she's not wearing her wedding ring. What the hell.

"Farrah," he says, like he's testing her name on his tongue.

I glare at him, but he's not paying attention to me.

My mother chooses that moment to come down the stairs as well. She beams at Bruce and rushes toward him, pulling him and Nella into an embrace. "Bruce!"

"Mrs. Remington, long time no see! How ya doing, babe?"

I groan. "Would you leave my mom and sister alone?"

Mom waves me off. "I see you met my adorable granddaughter."

My eyes move to Amber, wondering how she feels about my mom referring to Nella as her granddaughter. Her face is soft as she looks at my mom. For the first time since reading those texts earlier, my heart leaps with hope. Surely she wouldn't want Theo's mom in Nella's life when she already has a doting grandmother.

And even if Theo or his mom do want to be in our lives, that's okay, I tell myself. It's just more people to love Nella.

Farrah turns off the oven and puts the oven mitts away in the drawer nearest the oven. She dusts the flour from the front of her pajama shorts, then messes with her bun.

I take a step closer to her. Bruce and Mom are distracted, fussing over the baby.

"You okay, Farrah?" I ask, keeping my voice low.

"Of course," she whispers. "Does your, um, friend, want a banana nut muffin?"

My eyebrows scrunch together, unable to decipher why she's acting so nervous. "No. He's not staying," I answer. Something inside me is telling me I need to get Bruce out of this house and away from my sister as soon as possible.

I clap my hands together. "Well, thanks for coming over to workout Bruce. I'll see you at practice in the morning."

He looks up at me, his bottom lip sticking out. "But I'm not done holding the baby. And I haven't had coffee yet."

Mom gives me a look full of motherly reprimand and moves toward the coffee pot, pulling a mug out of the cabinet above it and pouring it full of steaming coffee for Bruce.

Giving up, I walk into the kitchen and grab a mug and fill it with coffee for myself. Apparently, Bruce is the only one getting served in this house. He grins at me as Mom hands him his mug.

Not trusting Bruce to hold Nella *and* a mug of coffee, I set mine on the countertop and take her from him.

As she's sliding out of his arms and into mine, he whispers, "You're super territorial, I'm seeing a new side of you."

I heave an exasperated sigh. Amber comes up behind me, looping her arms around my waist. I'm still sweaty from my workout, but she doesn't seem to mind and rests her head on my bicep.

"Wow, you guys are adorable," Bruce says, removing his phone from his shorts pocket and pointing it at us. "Cutest family ever. Let me take a pic to show the guys." He sticks his tongue out in concentration, tapping on his iPhone screen to capture shots of us. "Remy, could you smile? You have a house full of beautiful women. Smiling should come easy, man!"

My mom playfully shoves his shoulder. "Oh, Bruce! You rogue!"

I glance at Farrah to see if she's as charmed as our mother, but she's gawking at Bruce like he's a cartoon character come to life. Honestly, I've looked at him the same way once or twice.

My sisters made me watch Disney's Frozen last Christmas, and the blond guy in that movie who sells ice looked eerily like Bruce. I think he had a moose? Or a deer?

I smile at the camera, and he's right—it is easy to smile when my girls are with me. Speaking of Amber and Nella, of course. As much as I love my mom and sister, they're not *my* girls.

Bruce flips through the photos he took with a satisfied smile, then puts his phone away and resumes drinking the mug of coffee Mom gave him.

My house is chaos.

Not for the first time since getting married, I crave normalcy. Not the normal I had before Amber married me, but the new normal we can hopefully find once we don't have a house full of people.

I want Mom and Farrah to head back to Ohio, I want Bruce to go back to his own damn house, and I want the woman filling all my thoughts to have a successful follow-up appointment with her cardiologist.

But despite the chaos whirling through my usually very

calm, very quiet home, I must find a moment to talk to Amber about Theo's texts.

CHAPTER
THIRTY-SEVEN
AMBER

BY THE TIME BRUCE LEAVES, it's well after lunch. He's quite the character, and he talks a lot. I know Ford loves his teammates, but he seemed irritated during the entire visit. Like a big angry bird ruffling his feathers.

After I've put Nella down for her afternoon nap, I head to our room to check my phone. It's been such a busy morning, and I didn't give it a second thought. Until I enter the room, and Ford is sitting on my side of the bed, looking like a child about to be chastised. I've seen that look before—when he was a boy. But it's always been for teachers, or his parents. Never me. I don't like it.

"I looked at your phone," he blurts, telling on himself. Ford runs a hand through his short hair. "I picked it up to give it to you, but saw texts from Theo. I'm sorry for invading your privacy."

My eyebrows shoot up. Not at Ford for reading my messages—I couldn't care less about that. He can dig through my whole phone if he wants to, but he's just going to find a bunch of balayage hair color videos I've saved.

What alarms me is that Theo texted me. My blood turns

cold at that name. I have zero feelings for the man anymore, but what if this is something about Nella?

I rush toward my phone and tap the screen to pull up the texts and take a moment to read them. I gasp at his comments, covering my hand with my mouth.

Ford stands, his face as dreary as a sad puppy. Realizing I never responded to his apology, I place a hand on his forearm. "Ford, it's okay. I have nothing to hide. I'm just in shock that Theo texted after a year of silence." I shake my head, dropping my hand and letting it fall at my side.

Ford exhales a breath, probably relieved that I'm not mad at him, then he asks, "You saw his mom?"

"After Thanksgiving," I admit. "I'd completely forgotten about it. I ran into her in the grocery store, and she was pretty stunned to see Nella. It looked like she was doing the math in her head. But then she rushed off and I never heard another thing from her—or Theo." I slump down on the bed. "Until now."

Ford sits down beside me, but he doesn't crowd me. He's good at giving people space, since he needs space himself. "He's still a prick."

I huff a humorless laugh. "Yep."

"What do you want to do? Do you want Nella to know them?" he asks softly, and I look up, meeting his eyes. There's no judgment on his face. I know he'd support me either way.

I groan. "I don't know. I'd hate for her to not know them if she wants to, but she's not old enough to tell me, obviously. Selfishly, I want nothing to do with them. His mother wasn't very friendly to me, and Theo left me." Tossing my phone onto the bed, I lean forward with my elbows on my knees. "I need some time to think about it. His tone doesn't make me want to hurry to respond."

"I could throttle him for talking to you like that." Ford's

voice is rough. I glance at his profile and see he's clenching his jaw.

I place my hand on his thigh and offer him a sad smile. This is my issue to deal with, and I don't want my drama affecting him. That wouldn't be fair.

His jaw flexes, but he rests his warm hand on top of mine.

"I'm sorry. I feel like we've turned your life into a living, breathing tornado."

He looks at me, his brown eyes locking with mine. "Thankfully, I've always liked storms."

Unable to hold back, I throw my arms around his neck and hold on tight. If there's going to be a storm, I wouldn't want to weather it with anyone else.

Two days later, I have a follow-up appointment with my cardiologist. Ford had to be at practice, and Sally stayed home with Nella. So, it's just Farrah and me in the waiting room. She came along because someone had to drive me here since I'm not cleared to drive yet. Hopefully, today I'll be cleared for all normal activities and can start seriously looking for a job and childcare.

A nurse opens the door to the waiting room and studies her clipboard. "Mrs. Remington?"

My heart flutters at the name, and I stand. "That's me."

Farrah winks at me, grabbing a cooking magazine and making herself comfortable in the waiting room chair.

The nurse leads me to the same room where I had my preop appointment. She takes my vitals and asks me some questions. Her questions make me nervous, but after listening to my heart rate she smiles and says it sounds great.

She leaves and my cardiologist, Dr. Montgomery, enters

shortly after. "You're looking great, Amber. Healthy and happy," she says, tugging her stethoscope up to her ears. She gets right to work listening to my heart and nodding her approval at what she hears.

I release a deep breath. I didn't realize I was even holding my breath, and Dr. Montgomery chuckles at the sound.

A nurse comes in and hooks me up for an EKG, just to make sure everything is good to go. Dr. Montgomery stays in the room with the nurse, and they seem pleased with whatever the EKG is showing.

"You're recovering well, and your heart rate sounds perfect. You can rest easy now, okay?" She smiles, draping her stethoscope across the back of her neck. "Have you experienced any dizziness or blurred vision?"

"Nope," I answer. "I've felt great except for the soreness where the incision is."

She nods. "Yes, that's to be expected. Do you need more pain medication?"

"No, I'm doing okay with Tylenol."

She takes a seat on her roller-stool, the one they seem to have in every doctor's office. "I think you're free to resume regular activities. Driving, working, sex."

I blink and I know my cheeks must be bright red.

She looks away, probably noting my embarrassment. Dr. Montgomery types some notes on the computer resting on the small desk.

Finally, she turns back to me. "Do you have any questions or concerns?"

I shrug. "Not really."

"Well, stop at the front desk to schedule a three-month checkup, and don't hesitate to call if you're having dizzy spells or chest pain, okay?"

I nod quickly. "All right. Well, thanks for fixing my heart," I say, not knowing how to leave this appointment. It feels oddly anticlimactic to see the doctor who fixed my heart a week ago, just to be told I'm healthy now and to call if I think I might be dying or whatever.

Dr. Montgomery chuckles. "Just doing my job."

Once Farrah and I walk outside to the parking lot, I hold out my hand for the keys. She reluctantly hands them over—she's a big fan of my fancy new truck. But she can't park it any better than I can. I hold back a laugh when said truck comes into view, and it's nearly taking up two parking spots.

I unlock the large vehicle, and the built-in step stool folds out like magic. I step up and into the truck and Farrah bursts into laughter. I grin, loving the sound. Her laugh sounds like the more feminine version of Ford's.

"You're so tiny. It looks hilarious to watch you get in the driver's seat of this thing. Like a toddler wearing their parent's shoes."

I shoot her a mock glare when she slides into the passenger seat. She's taller than me by a few inches, but not nearly as tall as Colby's fiancée, Noel. "I'll have you know I'm the average height for a female."

She snickers. "With heels on?"

My jaw drops. "I liked you better when I was still healing and you felt sorry for me. Now I'm cleared for driving, and you're meaner than a chihuahua chasing a delivery man."

"How dare you compare me to a chihuahua! Are they even real dogs? Or do they qualify as cats?"

"I think that question is offensive to cats everywhere," I retort, starting the truck and backing out of the parking spot.

Driving feels natural, even though it's been a few weeks. The skin on my wrist that's still tender pulls a little when I turn the steering wheel, but it's not bad. "That reminds me. I want to get Ford a dog."

"I'd love to see him with another dog. He loved Moose so much."

"I remember watching them together and thinking about how calm Ford was around him. I know he doesn't need that kind of support anymore, but I still think he'd enjoy having a dog around."

"You're his Moose now." She glances at me as I drive. "You calm him, make him better. I think you always have."

I preen at her compliment. I don't think Ford needs me like that, but it's nice to hear all the same.

"He said we could talk about a dog once I had recovered. I want to find a job and start working again first—one thing at a time." I sigh. "I'd hate to get a puppy just to have to kennel the poor thing while I'm at work."

Farrah crosses her legs then steeples her hands on her knee, looking thoughtful. A light turns red, and I bring the truck to a stop, giving Farrah my full attention. "What?"

She bites her bottom lip, like she's unsure she wants to say what's on her mind. "When you go back to work, you'll have a nanny?"

I nod, turning my gaze back to the light, which turns green. I gently press the gas pedal, and the engine roars to life again. "Yes, I need to sit down with your brother and discuss all that."

"What if I was Nella's nanny?"

My eyes widen, and I look at her briefly before turning back toward the road. "What about your job in Ohio?"

She grimaces. "I quit right before I came out here with Mom."

"Farrah Remington, you're full of secrets."

She groans. "Ugh. I know. I need to come clean to Mom and Ford—to everyone. But everything's been so busy, and I haven't found the right time."

I offer her a soft smile. "Sometimes we have to *make* the right time. I'd love for you to be Nella's nanny, but I can't say yes or no without Ford knowing about any of it."

"Okay, I'll tell everyone, I promise." She hedges, toying with a hole in her jeans. "But if I was the nanny, I could take care of the puppy too."

"Farrah," I warn. "Talk to your brother."

"Fine."

CHAPTER
THIRTY-EIGHT
FORD

I'M STEPPING out of the showers in our dressing room after our game. We won tonight, and Thomas scored two of the five goals we made. I'm relieved this line mix-up thing is actually working.

Securing a fresh white towel around my waist, I slide on my shower shoes and head back out to my cubby. Our dressing room isn't just a locker room. It has all the bells and whistles appropriate for professional athletes who make millions of dollars.

Built-in cubbies—made from mahogany and polished to perfection—line the large rectangular space. A giant rug covers the center of the floor, featuring an eagle, of course. And the light that covers almost the entire ceiling is a huge Eagles logo. It's one of the cooler dressing rooms I've seen in the NHL. And I appreciate how clean the staff keeps it for us. I should bring by some of the bread Farrah has made as a gift to the staff. Lord knows we have enough baked goods at home.

When I arrive at my cubby, I see the guys huddled together. Bruce is still in his pads and he's whispering to West and Colby. Mitch is ignoring them, already showered, dressed, and making his way out of the dressing room and home to his fiancée.

Their heads pop up at the sound of my shower slides thwacking against my heels. Bruce stops talking instantly.

"What's going on?" I ask, not used to being the one left out of conversations. I'm always the one the guys come to to spill their secrets and ask for advice. I'm just now realizing how much I like being in the know. A prickle of annoyance moves down my spine that they're discussing something good without me.

Do I like drama? Hmm. Something to dissect later.

West and Colby smirk as their heads swivel in my direction.

"Why are you looking at me like that?" My shoulders tense. I really don't like this.

Colby shrugs. "I find it interesting that you never introduced *me* to your sisters."

I narrow my eyes at him. Colby has calmed down his roguish ways in the past few years and has become a whole new man since meeting his fiancée, but before, there wasn't a chance in hell I would've let him anywhere near my sisters.

"I wasn't purposefully keeping you all from meeting them, they just don't come down here much. One is married and the other just got engaged."

Bruce looks down at his pads, and West wallops him in the back of the head. "Dude. You can't be talking about married women."

Bruce throws up his hands. "She wasn't wearing a ring!"

I arch a brow because he's right—I noticed that as well. Farrah has always worn her ring, and until yesterday morning, I can't remember ever seeing her without it since her wedding. Add that to the fact that I haven't seen—or barely heard mention her husband—in almost a year? Very interesting.

"She was baking," I answer, thinking that's a pretty good excuse. What with the flour and dough and all that.

"I wasn't trying to be a creep; I was just telling the guys I met your sister. And no disrespect, but she is the most beautiful woman I've ever seen."

I nod. Men are allowed to notice a woman being physically attractive. But is it weird that he's talking about *my* sister in that regard? Yes.

"Okay. Fair." I finish drying myself off and reach for my duffel bag. "But I think we can all agree that no matter how attractive, sisters are off-limits. Yeah?"

Bruce nods frantically, like he thinks I'm about to pummel his ass. Which is laughable because I'm not one of the fighters on the team. Now, if Mitch had a sister, this conversation would be going much differently.

West rolls his lips. "I mean, I married my best friends' sister."

Grabbing my clean clothes out of my bag, I slide on my underthings before unzipping the suit bag hanging in my cubby. "But Farrah is already married." *I think she is.* "And heading back to Ohio tomorrow. So, it's a moot point."

Colby nods at my point. "True. Brucey, you can't be admiring married women."

Bruce sighs heavily, sitting on the bench in front of the cubby labelled with his name and un-velcroing his leg pads. "Point taken." He glances up from his pads to me. "You don't have any single sisters, do you?"

"No." I roll my eyes.

"Bummer."

―――

The following morning, I'm exhausted. Game nights go late, and I had to be up at eight because Mom and Farrah head out today. Mom wants to get an early start; I think she and Dad are really missing each other.

When I come down the stairs, Amber, Farrah, and Mom are already seated at the table. Nella must still be asleep. The three women are all eating—you guessed it—fresh homemade bread with butter and honey slathered on top. But even the bread doesn't look as scrumptious as Amber in the morning light. Her red hair is down and wavy, and the pink on the tips has faded over time. She's dressed already, wearing a white tee under pink slouchy overalls. The overalls look soft, though, like pajama fabric. My mouth waters at the sight of her. All I can think about is the kisses we shared a few nights ago. But with practice and a game the following day, I've barely seen her. She texted yesterday that her doctor cleared her for normal activities, and she got to drive her truck. But by the time I got home from the game last night, she was fast asleep, and my dream of more kisses was pushed back.

I shoot her a secret smile, one that promises more kisses later, as soon as Mom and Farrah have left and it's just our little family left here. *Our little family.* Wow, I love the sound of that. And Nella is clueless, which means I can kiss my wife anytime I want.

Amber raises an eyebrow at the look I'm giving her, and she smirks. Her green eyes shift to my sister, who's fidgeting with her bread, breaking it into small pieces instead of eating it.

She looks nervous. Really nervous. And Amber looks like she knows why.

Why is everyone in my life keeping secrets from me lately?

Mom swallows a bite of bread then notices my presence.

"Ford! Good morning. Have a seat, because your sister wants to talk to us, and my curiosity is killing me."

As I sit in the open seat beside my wife, the smell of her hair hits me like a slap in the face. Except her scent is sweet and perfect, so more like a caress to cheek. I want to burrow my face in her hair and pull the smell of her skin into my marrow. Instead, I place my hand on her thigh. She looks over at me and winks. I want to whimper, and make Mom and Farrah leave ASAP.

Farrah clears her throat, and our attention snaps to her face. Her hands are laced together on the table, and she's not wearing her wedding ring. Again. Her eyes stay on her hands, not looking at any of us.

"So, there's no easy way to say this. But Connor and I have been separated for a while."

My mom gasps. "What?"

Farrah ignores her and continues, "It's a long story, one that I can go into more on our drive home, but basically, it will be difficult for me to have children. He was grieving, I think, but instead of grieving with me...he wanted space. And the separation made it obvious to him that he wants a divorce. I need to go home and pack my stuff so we can sell the house, but I'd like to come back here in a few weeks, once everything in Ohio is squared away."

She finally looks up, directly at me. Familiar blue eyes—the same color as mom's—don't leave mine, as if she's expecting a reaction.

"I'd like to stay here, Ford. If it's okay. I could be Nella's nanny when Amber goes back to work."

Stunned, I blink my eyes a few times. The room is silent for what feels like a whole minute. On one hand, I want my wife all to myself. I want to explore more of that kissing, more of her. On the other hand, Amber does want to go back to work.

And she should get a call from Luxurious Lather any day now, according to my calculations. And Farrah would be a very trustworthy nanny, of course. But having her in the same house means less privacy for Amber and me.

"What about your job?" I ask, finally able to speak. Farrah makes good money as the event coordinator for a marketing firm.

"Actually," she says, her eyes snaking to our mother, "I quit right before I came here."

Mom gasps again. "Oh, Farrah. Why didn't you tell us sooner? I'm so sorry."

"I wanted to, but I genuinely thought Connor and I would work things out and no one would be the wiser. But we've been separated for ten months, and he wants out of the marriage. And honestly, I'm not thrilled at the idea of being with someone who considers me damaged."

Mom stands from her chair and moves behind her daughter, wrapping her arms around her shoulders. "You're not damaged. And that man is a fool for letting you go."

A few tears fall from Farrah's eyes. "Thanks, Mom."

I glance at Amber to find her already looking at me. She's studies my face intently then raises her eyebrows in silent question.

Quirking a brow, I silently ask, *Is it okay with you?*

She tips her chin—it's barely perceptible, but I know it's a resounding *yes*.

"You can stay here," I announce. At least I'll have two weeks alone with Amber.

Farrah jumps out of her chair, almost knocking mom over in the process, then rushes over and hugs me. It's awkward since I'm sitting and she's standing.

"Thank you, thank you, thank you!" Farrah hugs Amber next.

"So, I'm only going to have one kiddo left in Ohio?" Mom asks with one hand on her hips. "It's going to be so strange not to have you close." Her voice cracks.

"I'm sorry, Mom. I just don't want to live there anymore. I'd run into him in the grocery store or see him on dates with other women. I want a whole new start, you know?"

Mom nods. "I get it, I do." She sits back down in her chair, and Farrah does too. "You'll tell me more about this during the drive?"

Farrah sighs, her eyes filling with tears again. "I promise. Connor obviously didn't love me enough to be patient. He'll probably make a dating profile that says he's looking for someone with optimum ovarian health." She laughs through her nose, but there's no humor in it, and we all stare at her with concerned expressions.

Amber moves to put an arm around Farrah. "We'll be here waiting for you."

When I move in to hug my mother goodbye, I notice her jaw works like she's grinding her teeth. I'm positive she's holding back scathing words about the man we once welcomed into the Remington family, despite the calm façade she's putting on for my sister. Connor was a man they trusted to take care of their daughter. Forever. In sickness *and* in health. And he failed miserably.

I feel angry too, but I don't have time to be getting into fights.

Hell, I can't even find a moment to kiss my own damn wife.

CHAPTER
THIRTY-NINE
AMBER

AFTER SAYING goodbye to Farrah and Sally, there's a beat of awkwardness between Ford and me. And I hate it. It feels like neither of us knows how to act, now that we're alone again. Especially after that kiss.

A kiss I definitely want to repeat, but I don't know how he feels about it. Does he regret it? Does he want space?

We're standing at the front window, side by side, watching his mother and sister drive away down the street lined with tasteful mansions similar to Ford's. I can't stand the uncomfortable tension between us another minute and move to walk back into the kitchen for more coffee. But Ford's reflexes are fast, and he reaches out to grip my wrist—the one that doesn't have a small still-healing scar.

"Please don't go." He looks at me, and I see the urgency in his eyes. He looks down at where his hand gently grasps my arm and moves his hand down, lacing our fingers together.

By some miracle, our hands fit perfectly together despite the size difference. The way his hand envelops mine is a small comfort. Like a miniature hug. Ford's eyes look down to where our hands are joined.

Reaching up, I place a finger in that handsome chin dimple. The one I used to tease him about. I use my finger to urge his head back up so I can look into his eyes. When our eyes lock, I see the torment there, and my whole body heats.

There are no regrets in those warm, brown depths. Only longing. And perhaps a little fear? Maybe it scares him how much he wants this…how much he wants us. A feeling I can relate to. Ford isn't one to express his feelings, to put into words what he's thinking. But that's what I need.

I can see on his face what he wants, but I *need* him to say it.

"Hey, Ford?"

"Yes," he whispers.

"You're doing that thing where you're thinking on the inside, but I need to hear those thoughts…out here." I move my hand from his chin to his cheek, enjoying the way his morning stubble brushes against the palm of my hand.

He breathes a soft laugh, barely audible. "Sorry." He smirks. "It's just that, I'm thinking I really want to kiss you again. And I'm thinking that I'm scared you might not want me to. And I'm also thinking that my feelings for you are much stronger than yours are for me." He pauses. "And that's okay, but I just need you to know that I do feel strongly about you. And I have for a long time."

I hold his gaze. Shocked at his honesty, at how vulnerable he is being with his feelings.

His throat moves as he swallows. "And now I'm worried I said way more than I should have."

Moving up to my tippy-toes, I throw my arms around his neck and press myself against him. His arms wrap around me in the most intoxicating embrace. My mouth brushes against his neck and I place a kiss there. His skin is hot beneath my lips, his familiar scent warm and comforting as it wraps around me.

"I've thought of nothing but that kiss for days," I whisper against the strong column of his neck. Ford is strong everywhere, as solid as the oak tree we played under as children.

Ford continues holding me, and I don't take the touch for granted. Because I know he doesn't enjoy affection from everyone. This is special, this lingering physical contact. Testing the water, I tilt my head up, running the tip of my nose along his earlobe. I notice his hair has grown enough to touch the tops of his ears again, and I make a mental note to give him a haircut later.

I place a gentle kiss on his earlobe, and Ford inhales a sharp breath, his fingers digging into my back where he's holding me. It's not painful, just a firm pressure that makes my blood go from hot to boiling.

One of his hands moves up and threads into my hair, cradling the back of my head. He's in control of my movements now, and I'm perfectly okay with that. Ford uses his hand to angle my head back, and then surges forward.

When his hot mouth lands on mine, I melt into him. And I love that he's strong enough to support my body so I can go limp in his arms. The kiss is dreamlike, almost too perfect.

One of his hands moves down my back a little farther, resting right above the curve of my ass. I smile against his mouth, knowing he wants to move his hand lower, but he's too much of a gentleman.

"What's so amusing?" he whispers against my lips.

"Your self-control is admirable, but we *are* married, you know."

He huffs a laugh, closing his eyes and resting his forehead against mine. I glance up to see his eyes are closed, savoring the closeness between us. Then his hand moves a little farther down, resting on my backside.

A low sound rumbles through his chest, and I know he's

still holding back. "Make me feel good, husband," I whisper, half a dare, half a request.

And with that, his control snaps, and he hoists me up. My legs involuntarily wrap around him, and he carries me all the way up the stairs. I'm not even a little nervous he can't handle my weight, or that he'll drop me. I know that I'm completely safe in this man's arms.

Ford carries me into his room. Correction...*our* room. He gently lays me on the bed and hovers over me. The way his eyes dip down my body, then come back up, feels like the most intimate thing I've ever experienced. Because even before we had a physical connection, we loved each other.

"I've never..." he whispers, pausing and breaking eye contact. He's unsure of himself, and I hate it. This beautiful man. "But I want you...so much."

"I want you too," I tell him, reaching up and pulling his face down to mine. "We can take it as slow as you want."

He nods, pulling back to look at me, his eyes searing mine. His pupils are so dark, so large, I can't tell anymore where his irises begin, his eyes are just molten pools of desire.

Then he kisses me and finally let's go.

CHAPTER FORTY
FORD

WOW. That's the only thought in my brain.

What do you do when all your dreams come true after a lifetime of pining? Where do we go from here? How will I ever use brain cells again?

My brain is muddy, scrambled, relaxed. Since Amber has been sleeping in my room, I've slept better than ever before. I don't even have to do my usual bedtime routine, trying to will my body to sleep like it's supposed to. But this is different. It's like my entire body is in a state of relaxation.

I could get used to this. No wonder all the guys are in such a hurry to get home to their ladies.

Wow.

"What are you thinking about?" Amber is lying beside me. The early morning light streaming in through my bedroom window illuminates the red strands of her hair like flames.

I grab her hand and bring it to my mouth, taking the time to kiss each fingertip and noting the pale pink polish on her nails.

"Ambs, my mind is mush. I'm thinking nothing. I'm just… happy."

She smiles, her pretty pink lips separating. "I'm happy too. Really happy." Amber sighs, scooting closer and burrowing her head into my chest. "You told me earlier that you have strong feelings for me and that mine are probably not as strong." Her emerald eyes search my face. "Ford, my feelings might be new, but they're no less strong. I promise you that."

She pauses, bringing her hand to my chest. "Your feelings for me started when we were young and grew for a long time. They're sturdy and steadfast…like you."

I smile, loving the feel of her soft skin and loving even more the way she's looking at me. The trust and adoration there. "But my feelings are wild and unreserved…like me."

The love inside my chest seems to swirl and erupt inside me. My stomach flutters wildly, and my skin erupts with heat. Wanting to be closer to her, I move an arm around her waist and draw her into my chest. I pull her forward until she's completely pressed against me, her arms moving around my neck.

I kiss her neck, remembering the feverish way it made me feel when she kissed me there earlier. I relish the feel of her soft skin against my lips, I savor the sweet taste of her skin, I inhale the hypnotic scent of her, a scent now mingled with my own to make something new. Something exciting and full of hope.

"My wife," I whisper into her ear.

She hums softly, and I note that the area of skin right under her ear is extra sensitive. I want to explore that spot for a while.

A wail from the baby monitor startles me. I chuckle against Amber's ear, unable to help it. Honestly, it's a miracle Nella has slept this late. That we've had this precious time together. But I'm also anxious to see Nella, to hold her. To watch Amber in her role as a mother.

Amber laughs too. It's low and husky and makes me want to ignore the baby monitor...for just a few minutes. But I remove my arm, knowing Nella needs Amber right now more than I do.

"Do you want me to get her?" I ask as Amber slides out of bed.

She grabs the hoodie hanging on the peg by the bathroom door, turning and looking at me over her shoulder. I admire the view, until she winks and tugs the hoodie over her head, covering her body. "That's okay, I'll nurse her."

I watch as she walks out the door, then turn on my back and lace my hands behind my head. As I stare at the vaulted ceiling in my room, the texts from Theo come flooding back, souring my mood a little. I try to push the thought away, but the unanswered questions continue to torment me.

When Amber comes downstairs with a fed and happy Nella, I stride toward her, holding my arms out to take the baby. "I'll hold her. You go get ready."

She quirks a brow but hands Nella over. Nella grins the moment she's in my arms. "She likes me."

Amber laughs. "I think she likes you better than me. She's such a traitor."

I move Nella to one arm and use my free hand to gently push Amber toward the stairs again. "That's not possible. Now go. Get ready."

She tries, and fails, to dig her heels into the tile. "What for? What am I supposed to wear?"

I step back, giving her a satisfied smile. "Wear whatever makes you feel good. I'm taking my girls on a date."

Amber squeals and rushes toward the steps. Halfway up,

she pauses and turns back to look at me. "You know, *I* like you too, almost as much as Nella does." She rushes the rest of the way upstairs and leaves me grinning like a fool.

While she's upstairs, I sit on the sofa, holding Nella on my lap in a sitting position. She babbles and blows bubbles with her mouth. "Nella," I say seriously. "You and I need to have a chat."

She coos, then grins.

"You see, I never asked your permission to marry your mom."

Nella splutters.

"So, I'd like your permission to *stay* married to her. I'd like your stamp of approval, because as much as I'd like you two to be mine forever, I want my girls to choose me too."

She grins, and I smile back.

"Good. I'm glad we agree on the matter." I clear my throat. "Now, how do I look?" I glance down at my dark jeans and white polo. Nella burps loudly and my eyes widen. "Wow. That seems harsh. Is it really that bad?"

CHAPTER
FORTY-ONE
AMBER

FORD REMINGTON MARRYING me to save me from extreme medical debt was heroic. And having him kiss me was hypnotic. But having him ask my daughter's permission to stay married to me forever? That was just the cutest thing I've ever heard in my life.

Standing at the top of the steps to eavesdrop on their conversation was probably a little shady of me, but it was too adorable for me to step away.

I glance in the floor length mirror of Ford's closet and do a spin. I braided my hair back in a Dutch braid and pulled out a few strands around my face. I threw on some mascara as well, then donned my prettiest sweater—pink with white daises—and a pair of wide-leg boyfriend jeans. Deciding I look pretty cute but probably not as hot as Ford, I waltz back downstairs, excited for this date.

When I'm downstairs, Ford has Nella secured in her infant car seat and is being meticulous with packing the diaper bag. I can practically see the internal script he's running. *Diapers, check. Wipes, check. Bottles, check.*

I clear my throat, and he glances up. His eyes widen and

trail down my body, a slow perusal. He swallows. "You're beautiful."

Feeling suddenly shy, and unused to my best friend complimenting my looks so freely, I offer a quiet, "Thank you."

"You ready to go?"

"Yeah, but can you please drive?"

He rolls his eyes. "Still paranoid you can't park the truck?"

"I *know* I can't park the truck. From real-life experience."

Ford blows out an annoyed breath. "I got you the truck because it has—"

"Amazing safety ratings." I finish his sentence.

He laughs, then pauses like he's thinking. "Now we're finishing each other's sandwiches?" The joke comes out of his mouth awkwardly, as if he's unsure I'd think it was funny.

And a week ago, I might not have understood it, but Farrah made me watch Frozen with her a few days ago. Apparently, she and Felicity are obsessed with it.

"That's what I was gonna say," I sing it, just like Princess Anna does in the movie.

Ford chuckles, grabbing the car seat and the truck keys. I rush forward and take the diaper bag before he can load himself up like a pack mule. His big muscles are rather useful, but there's a lot of other fun ways I'd rather put them to use.

"Farrah made you watch *Frozen*, didn't she?"

"Yep."

Once we're in the car and on our way to wherever Ford is taking us, he reaches across the center console and places a hand on my thigh. It's comforting and intimate in a different way than holding my hand or kissing me. I love it. And it makes me wish this truck wasn't so large so I could sit closer to him. He has his glasses on, and I stare unabashedly, admiring his profile.

Nella babbles happily in the backseat, I glance in the small mirror secured above her rear-facing car seat and smile at her adorable face.

"So, where are you taking us for this spontaneous date?"

His hand tightens on the steering wheel. Knowing him, he's probably itching to tell me since he hates keeping secrets. "We're going to lunch at a café West told me about." He looks over at me and smiles. "Then, I thought we could pick out some real furniture for Nella's room. She's growing. I'd like her to have a dresser, some wall art, and maybe a rocking chair."

I laugh. "That's very thoughtful of you, but you really don't have to spend your money on that."

Abruptly, Ford slows the truck, turning on the blinker and pulling into a random parking lot. He stops the truck and puts it in park before turning his big body to look at me. Being the focus of all this man's attention is new and thrilling, but this look isn't a heated, sexy one. No, I said something to upset him, maybe even anger him.

"Amber," he starts. It's not a good sign he used my full name instead of Ambs. "You need to understand something."

He pauses, and I nod. "What's happening between us, not the fake marriage stuff, but the real stuff. It means something to me. I take this seriously. It's my honor to take care of you both—it's a privilege. And I plan to take care of you very, very well. For as long as you'll let me."

Okay, forget that I said the way he was looking at me wasn't heated or sexy. Everything he just said is very hot. Probably the hottest thing I've ever heard.

"I understand," I tell him, unbuckling my seatbelt so I can lean across the console and place my hands on his square jaw. A jaw that's been tense for too long—for a lifetime. And if he's going to take care of me, I'm going to take care of him too. Starting with getting that gorgeous jaw to relax as much as possible. "I take this seriously too. What's happening between us—it feels like a dream. You feel like a dream."

He leans in and kisses me. "Well, I'm real. And I'm not going anywhere."

"Good."

He pulls back, leveling me with a stern look through his dark-rimmed glasses. "Now put your seatbelt back on."

"Yes, sir." I mock-salute him.

When he pulls back onto the road, busy with D.C. lunch-hour traffic, he's wearing a smug smile on his face. But as long as that jaw is relaxed, I'll allow it.

Twenty minutes into the drive, my phone rings. It's not a number I recognize, but Ford tips his chin, like he's telling me to answer it, so I do.

"Um, hello?"

"Amber! This is Peter from Luxurious Lather. How are you girl? And how's that hunk you're married to?"

I chuckle. "Hey, Peter. He's great, actually. Sitting here right next to me."

"Wonderful. Well, I'm calling to let you know I'm the new manager here at the salon—about time they promoted me." I can hear the sarcasm in his voice, and picture him winking as he says the words. "And we have an open booth for you, if you're still interested."

I hold in the excited squeak that wants to come out of me. Instead, I widen my eyes at the man next to me and mouth the words, *I got a job.*

Ford's mouth widens into a handsome grin, and he gives me a thumbs up.

"That's great news! I'd still love to work there."

"Fabulous!" Peter says, and I hear the salon door jingle in the background. "Well, babe, I gotta go, my twelve o'clock is here. Why don't you stop by later and we can talk more?"

"That sounds perfect! Thank you so much." I hang up the phone and finally let out the scream I've been holding in. "That was Peter from the salon! He said there's a booth for me to rent. Maybe I can start as soon as Farrah comes back to nanny!"

"Congratulations. You deserve it." Ford smiles, and it warms my heart. "Oddly enough, the lunch place we're going to is right by the salon. So, this works out perfectly."

"No way! Everything is falling into place." I sink into my seat with a happy sigh.

CHAPTER
FORTY-TWO
FORD

AFTER EATING lunch at the cute little café with black and white striped awnings, the one right across from the salon, we walk right over to meet with Peter. I smile to myself. Peter called right when I asked him to, and I appreciate his punctuality.

The salon is as clean and lovely as always, even though it's under new ownership…from a silent owner. Peter will run it, and I, as the silent owner, will simply pay for maintenance on the building etc.

Nella is curled into my arm as we walk, Amber glances back at us and grins. She stops and pulls her phone out of her bag and snaps a photo of us. "Ford, I hope this doesn't sound weird, but you look really sexy holding a baby."

My face feels like it's on fire. I'm not used to Amber telling me I'm sexy. I love it, but it's still unexpected. I clear my throat. "Thank you."

She laughs. "Sorry, I didn't mean to embarrass you. It's just…you're so big and muscular, then watching you be so gentle with my tiny girl. It's really sweet." Amber smirks, her eyes twinkling. "I love it when you talk to her too, like a whole adult conversation. It's my favorite thing."

I chuckle. I hadn't realized she'd been listening in on any of my therapy sessions with Nella. "She's a surprisingly good listener."

Amber laughs, the sound a balm to my soul. She unzips the diaper bag, sticking her phone inside and pulling out the baby carrier.

"Here, let me," I say, reaching out a hand. She stares at me like I'm insane. I quirk a brow. "Real men wear pink. I can wear Nells while you get your tour of the salon and talk to Peter about your job."

"Really?" She's still hesitant as she drops the carrier in my hand.

I hand Nella over and strap the pink carrier on, the way I've seen Amber do it. I have to adjust the straps for my much larger body, then Amber helps me get Nella situated and we're on our way again.

Reaching down, I slide my hand into hers, intertwining our fingers. "This hands-free thing has its perks."

Amber's head falls back as she laughs.

We make it to the salon and the bell rings when we step inside. Peter greets us eagerly, his arms outstretched to give my wife a big hug. I happen to know he cleared his afternoon for this.

"Amber Remington! What a pleasure." He hugs Amber and while he does, he shoots me a wink. I roll my eyes.

Amber pulls back, grinning wide. "I'm so excited to work here."

Peter gets an ornery look on his face. We discussed how this was going to go, but something tells me he's going rogue. "So, we actually require a live haircut before we can officially hire someone. Your husband is looking a little shaggy. Maybe he could be your test subject?"

"Oh, sure." She glances back at me, checking if that's okay.

I nod. This isn't something I planned, but I won't shy away from having Amber's hands in my hair. Or *anywhere* on me.

Peter points to a tidy station. It looks just like his, with a large gold mirror and a pale pink salon chair. "This is your station, and it's right next to mine. You're a lucky girl, indeed."

He points again, this time across the salon. "And our shampoo bowls are over there. Ford always likes a shampoo before his haircut."

That's a load of crap, and he knows it. He tried to shampoo me the first time he cut my hair and I declined. I've gotten better about people touching me, but someone shampooing my hair seemed like a little much. Until now.

"I'll hold the baby while you show off your skills," Peter says. "If that's okay."

"She's pretty friendly, so that should be fine."

Amber unfastens Nella, and she kicks her feet as she's handed off to Peter. She smiles at him and his face melts. "Oh wow. Now I have baby fever."

Amber takes my hand and leads me toward the shampoo bowl. "All right, sir. Time for your shampoo." She waggles her eyebrows.

"I could get used to the sir thing," I whisper, keeping my voice low.

"I heard that!" Peter yells from his station several yards away.

Amber and I glance at each other, and I know we're both wondering how he heard me.

She shakes her head, still smiling at Peter's antics, then brings her hands to my shoulders and gently pushes me into the plush leather chair. There's a row of five washing stations, all with leather chairs that compliment the ones at each stylist's station. We're the only ones in the salon right now—one of the perks of being a silent owner. I'll tell Amber about it eventually, but not today.

Once I'm seated, she turns on the water. While it's warming up, she finds a towel in the cabinet below the sink and selects the shampoo she wants to use on me. She places a hand on my shoulder, urging me to lean back and relax while she washes my hair.

She smiles down at me, the red strands coming free from her updo are dangling down, nearly touching my face. I want to pull her down and kiss her senseless, but I refrain and let her get to work.

Amber wets my hair with the sprayer, and the warm water feels nice, and I relax into the seat a little more, allowing my legs to stretch out in front of me.

Amber turns off the water, and replaced it with her hands. Her brilliant magical hands. I close my eyes as she massages shampoo—spearmint-scented—into my scalp. The pressure of her fingers is firm as they run small circles along my scalp and nape. I think I could fall asleep here, with her massaging her hands through my hair.

"I'd give anything to trade hair with you," she whispers. "It's so pretty."

From anyone else, I wouldn't take pretty hair as a compliment. But I just like that she thinks nice things about my hair.

"I wouldn't let you," I whisper back. "I love your red hair too much."

I open my eyes to find her blushing. I wink at her, and she giggles. Giggling is a new thing, and I'd like to get her to make that sound again and again.

Amber continues massaging my scalp, and I wonder if she

shampoos everyone this thoroughly. I'm not sure I love the idea of some other guy getting to experience her hands like this. Her fingernails lightly scrape against my scalp, moving up so the pads of her thumbs glide over my temples.

A sigh escapes me, and for a moment I'm self-conscious, worried it was too loud. But Amber makes no comment about it.

Finally, she rinses out the shampoo, and I expect it to be over. But she holds up a bottle of conditioner—I never use conditioner, but I remember seeing it in my sisters' bathroom growing up. She squirts it into her hands and starts the massage over again. Conditioner is my new favorite thing.

By the time she's finished and wrapping my head in a white, fluffy towel, my knees are wobbly. Her shampoo has put me in a trance, like my brain was asleep the entire time, but my body was fully awake and feeling everything.

She raises the chair so I'm sitting upright again, and I have to blink a few times for the salon to come back into focus.

Somehow, I stand up and follow Amber back to her station.

Peter is sitting in his swivel chair and makes a show of glancing at his watch. "Good work on the relaxation techniques, but you might have to speed up the washing process in the future if you want to fit more than one client into your schedule."

Amber grins, draping me with a black cape. "Oh, don't worry. That was the husband special."

I want to breathe a sigh of relief that not everyone will get the husband special, but I hold it in.

Amber continues showing off her skills, and I end up with the best fade of my life. I study the haircut in the mirror, running my hands through the short strands on top, which she has styled with mousse. "Wow."

Peter heaves a heavy sigh. "Thanks a lot, Amber. Now Ford

will never let me at those gorgeous locks of his again. The haircut looks amazing, girl."

She beams at his praise. "Thank you!"

"So, when can you start?" He asks, reaching down and tickling Nella's feet.

CHAPTER
FORTY-THREE
AMBER

I'M tired after our full day of eating, my tour of the salon, and then shopping for nursery furniture. But I'm excited for my first WAG night and had an iced coffee on the way home to perk up.

I change out of my jeans into leggings and a pink sweatshirt. Mel said it was casual, and I'm all about comfort.

I tie on white tennis shoes and head downstairs where Ford is feeding Nella her bottle. Ford and Nella are studying each other intently while she eats, and I take a moment to watch the sweetness of their quiet moment.

When I walk into the living room, they both look up. Nella grins around the nipple of her bottle, making milk drip all over her chin.

I snort a laugh. "Babies are kind of disgusting."

He wrinkles his nose and nods. "Have fun with the girls tonight."

"Are you sure you'll be okay taking care of Nella?"

His eyebrows raise slightly. "We'll be fine. Have a safe walk," he teases, knowing Mel and West live just down the street.

I step forward, first kissing him on the cheek, then Nella. "Text me if you need anything."

He waves me off, and I leave through the front door to find four giant hockey players on the front stoop. "Hey, guys."

One at a time, the guys say hi. I recognize the foursome as Colby Knight, Weston Kershaw, Bruce McBride, and standing at the very back is Mitch Anderson.

"I'm so excited to babysit," Bruce says, grinning.

"Me too!" Colby shoves him out of the way and rushes through the front door.

Bruce gapes for a moment, then runs after him, yelling, "Don't hog the baby!"

West laughs and follows them inside.

Mitch lingers for a second, his hands in his pockets. "It's been nice to see Remy so happy these past few weeks," he says. Then, as if he's self-conscious about his own comment, he grunts. "I only came for the pizza." Without another word, he walks inside and shuts the door behind him.

I laugh to myself and head down the street. I don't need the house number to find West and Melanie's house because all the girls are huddled by the front door, grinning and waiting for me.

"Amber!" Mel yells, waving me forward like she's paranoid I'll run away.

"Hey, ladies!" I wave back.

They pull me into the warm home. I expect to find moving boxes and materials still scattered about, but there's no sign they just moved in a few weeks ago. Pictures are hung on the wall, furniture and rugs are in place, there's even a dry-erase calendar on the wall that's filled in and color coordinated. It looks like they've lived here for years.

"Wow, you didn't waste any time unpacking."

Noel scoffs and elbows Mel playfully. "This one's a bit of an organizer."

Andie laughs. "That's an understatement."

Mel rolls her eyes. "Oh, stop! Keeping my hands busy helps my anxiety," she explains.

"Fair enough," I say. "You're welcome to put together Nella's nursery, if you need something to do." I'm joking, but the way her face lights up tells me she would go over there right now and put it all together. And she'd have a blast doing it.

"You can have her after she plans my wedding," Noel teases. "I didn't hire her; she just took over."

"And you love it," Mel says with a harumph.

Mel guides us through the foyer and kitchen, into a formal living room. It's not attached to the kitchen like Ford's. I like that all the houses in this neighborhood look different, and are not all the same layouts.

Mel and West have tasteful tufted suede couches, in a medium brown. The earthy color contrasts beautifully with the indigo paint color and white stone fireplace.

A round wooden coffee table sits in the center of the room, and it's covered with chopping-block cutting boards and lined with meticulously plated charcuterie. There are four champagne flutes filled with Prosecco, and Mel hands one of them to me.

"Wow, you girls know how to throw a party. Ford just ordered pizza and called it a day."

Andie giggles. "Can we talk about how cute it is that you're the only person who calls him Ford?"

I take a sip of my Prosecco and snatch a piece of dark chocolate from one of the charcuterie boards. "I always forget the rest of the world knows him as Remy."

"It's so sweet," Noel says, picking up one of the champagne flutes. "It shows you know him on a more personal level."

Andie waggles her eyebrows. "Very personal."

Noel sighs. "How do you turn everything dirty?"

Andie shrugs, grabbing a crystal plate and loading it up with meats and cheeses.

Mel takes a plate and fills—no, organizes—her plate. Meat on one side, cheese on the other. Macadamia nuts in the center. Nothing touching. "So, the guys got Nella tonight, but do we get her next time?"

"It sounds like you want partial custody of Amber's baby," Noel jokes.

The comment reminds me of Theo's text. I thought he'd give up easily if I just ignored him, but then he tried to call twice today. I'm so happy here with Ford, starting a new life. And I hate that he's dragging me down, making me worry. Can't he just let me be happy? He already made his choice, and he *didn't* choose me and Nella. And although a year ago I was crushed by that, I'm grateful he didn't. He showed me he wasn't the man for me. And in turn, I learned how great Ford and I are together. I might have never had the chance to discover this had he stayed with me just to do the honorable thing. There's a part of me that's sad for my daughter, of course. I know she'll have questions about her father someday.

But Ford has stepped up as her dad, and he's done a damn good job of it.

"You okay?" Noel asks, looking regretful about the joke she made.

"Yeah, sorry." I shake my head. "Nella's dad keeps contacting me, and it's kind of stressing me out."

"You want to talk about it?" Andie asks, looking supportive but not trying to pressure me.

I smile. "Yeah, it's nice to have girls to talk to. I didn't have this back in Ohio."

"You have a whole slew of us now, girl." Mel pulls me into a quick side hug.

"I love it." I hug her back, then sigh. "I'm so happy with Ford. And it feels like my ex, Theo, waited until I was happy to try to have a relationship with Nella. Like he can't just let me live my life in peace."

"Ugh, what a prick," Andie's face scrunches in annoyance.

"Right?" I groan. "But someday, Nella might want to know her father. Even if he's not the man who acted as her dad. If that makes sense."

Mel nods and sits on one of the couches with her plate in hand. "I see how that could be complicated. Trying to make the best choice for her without her being old enough to have an opinion."

"What does Remy—sorry, Ford—say about it?" Noel asks.

I hedge, not knowing how to answer. So, I opt for the truth. "We've barely had time to talk about it, honestly. But I know he'll support me no matter what."

Our relationship is new and wonderful and blooming. This whole situation feels like a lot of pressure to add to something so delicate. Like a butterfly trying to pry itself out of a cocoon too soon. We need time to grow and thrive before the outside elements get us down.

But at the same time, I know Ford is a sturdy place to land. That his big shoulders can handle more than I'm giving him credit for. And I want to talk to him about all of this, but every time I try, we get interrupted with something else. Or he kisses me, and I forget anyone else exists.

I resist the urge to fan myself. Just thinking about Ford Remington has me dizzy in the head.

"Oh, girl. You're smitten." Andie rolls her lips, trying not to laugh.

Noel grins. "She's a woman in love."

"Madly in love." Mel sighs.

CHAPTER
FORTY-FOUR
FORD

NELLA IS SCREAMING. She's always, always happy. I don't know what I did wrong. Mitch is covering his ears, West is searching his music app for soothing baby noises, Bruce is bouncing Nella up and down—something she usually likes—and Colby is playing peek-a-boo with her using her favorite blanket.

I've fed her, burped her, and changed her. Still screaming. Now, I'm in the kitchen warming up another bottle. Maybe she's still hungry?

When I turn and see the remnants of our pizza night spread across my kitchen island, I itch all over. My long-sleeved tee seems to coil tightly around my arms and torso. I take a deep breath. I can get to the mess later, after Nella calms down.

I cannot, under any circumstances, call Amber. She needs to trust that I can take care of Nella. I want her to go out and relax and know that me and Nella are good.

Except right now we are not good.

Rushing back into the living room, I find a baby girl whose face is an angry red, nearly as red as her hair. I gently pull her out of Bruce's arms, and he heaves a sigh and bends at the waist to rest his hands on his knees. Like he just ran five miles and he's out of breath.

As soon as the bottle is in Nella's mouth, she's gulping it down like she hasn't been fed all day, even though I know she's enjoyed her regular feeding schedule.

"Holy shit," Colby says, running a hand through his dark hair. "She gets even madder than Noel when I coerce her into doing something she doesn't wanna do."

"She's usually so sweet," I say in defense of Nella. Surprising even myself at how protective I feel.

West, who has classical music playing on his phone now, sticks one finger in the air. He reads out loud to us as he scrolls on his phone. "Aha! Here's an article on whattoexpect.com that says babies go through a growth spurt around three or four months and may be unusually grouchy and want to cluster-feed."

Mitch slumps down on the sofa next to me, eyeing Nella like she might explode any moment. "Cluster what?"

"Cluster feeding," West repeats. "It's when they want to eat over and over again."

"Oh, so she has Colby's appetite?" Bruce teases, earning a shove that almost sends him into my television.

I close my eyes and try to take a few, deep steadying breaths. It's not working. The mess, the noise, the stress, the guys shoving each other. I hand Nella to a very confused Mitch and sit with my head between my legs. It feels like all the chaos and stress and drama of the last three weeks is hitting me all at once. Internally I'm panicking, feeling like I'm failing Amber and Nella by being so overwhelmed. Why can't I pull it together? If there was just less noise, or less... something.

I feel a broad hand on my back, and West's voice asks, "You okay, man? What do you need?"

I don't respond—I can't. I can't open my eyes or get the words to form in my mouth. If there was a desk to climb under, I'd probably be under there. I've reverted back to my childhood self. Everything is too loud and too tight and too much. Slowly, I stick one hand into the pocket of the joggers I changed into before the guys came over. I run my fingers across the familiar, stupid coin that rests there. It doesn't bring me the solace it once did. And I know exactly why. Because all I want right now is Amber. I want her to caress my back with her soothing touch, I want her to kiss my temple with her pillow-soft lips, and I want her sweet voice to tell me I'm okay in her sweet voice. None of these big, ugly dudes can do what she can. Not even my coin has the same effect as my wife.

My wife. I want my wife. I want her to talk to me until I forget what's going on outside of the two of us, just like she did all those years ago, like she's always done.

But I can't be codependent, and she deserves better than that. She needs me to be the steady presence in this constant storm of life. I'm her proverbial tornado shelter. With a few more deep breaths, I feel calmer. My clothing is starting to feel normal again, and the noises are quieting around me.

The guys are still, waiting for me to speak. Waiting for me to act like a damn adult.

A cool glass of water is thrust in front of my face by one of the lovable dumbasses standing in my living room. I take the glass and chug it, finally feeling level-headed and like my head isn't detaching from my body.

"Guys, I'm sorry. My brain just got overwhelmed."

I hear a soft pounding sound and glance over to see Nella propped up on Mitch's shoulder, he's patting her back to burp her.

At my surprised expression, he shrugs. "What? I listened to an audiobook about parenting, and it said babies should be burped halfway through their feeding."

Colby arches a brow. "We're definitely coming back to that in a second." He turns to me. "Can you tell us what just happened? Or what's going on?"

I inhale a deep breath and exhale it out of my mouth. "The past month has been…insane. I learned about Amber's heart, then we got married, and she had her procedure. My mom and sister were here helping. A-a-and it's just been a lot. It's been constant change, which I'm not great at handling. But I put on a brave face for Amber. Because I love her, and I'd do anything for her, you know?" I'm panting, breathless from talking so fast. And I realize I've never spoken those words out loud…*I love her.*

Suddenly, I recall my conversation with Amber and her encouragement to tell my teammates about my autism. That I could trust them with it. This is the perfect time to tell them, to be honest. And it would help them understand why I was so overwhelmed just now.

I bite my bottom lip, thinking of what I want to say then I stand up, my legs no longer feeling shaky. "There's more. There's something I've been keeping from you all. I haven't been completely honest about myself."

Looking down at my feet, I contemplate my words. But Colby chuckles and comes up beside me.

He slaps me on the back, hard. "I knew it! I could tell by the way you ogle me in the locker room. I mean, who wouldn't though?"

I shove him—away from the television, not toward it. "I'm not gay, you dumbass."

Colby dusts off the front of his shirt. "I was joking, anyway."

We all roll our eyes, knowing he's only half-kidding.

"I have high-functioning autism—er, Aspergers—whatever they're calling it these days."

West takes a step toward me. "Why didn't you tell us before now? We wouldn't judge you, man."

"I know." I hang my head, ashamed for having not trusted my closest friends with this. "It's just that the NHL was this big opportunity to create a new identity for myself, and when people hear the word *autism*, they treat me differently."

I hear a muddled burp from Nella and turn my head toward her. Mitch appears pleased by the burp, switches her to his other arm and uncleaned unceremoniously plops the bottle back in her mouth. She sucks contentedly, not caring who's holding her as long as there's milk.

Mitch looks up at me like there's nothing strange about this whole situation. "How did they treat you differently?"

Shuffling on my feet, I think back to college, when my teammates found out I received special tutoring because I have autism. They weren't mean, necessarily, just fascinated.

"Back in college my teammates discovered I have autism, and they immediately found a box of pencils and threw them on the floor. Probably a hundred pencils scattered in every direction." I drag a hand down my face. Still embarrassed by the debacle. "They all stared at me, expecting something. And when I asked them why the hell they threw pencils everywhere, they said in the movie *Rain Man*, someone drops a box of matches and the character who has autism counts them in like a half a second or something."

West's jaw drops in horror. "They didn't"

I nod wearily. "They did."

Mitch huffs a laugh through his nose. "I get why you'd want to keep it to yourself, but I'm also glad you finally trusted us enough to share it with us. Sharing hurtful things about our pasts helps us heal."

We all turn to stare at Mitch, our usually broody and quiet teammate.

"What? I learned that in therapy," he says, turning his attention back to Nella, who has pulled off the bottle and is now smiling at Mitch like he's the best thing she's ever seen. He grunts. "Hey, kid."

"Mitch is right." Colby nods his head. "This helps us understand you too, and now when you need space, we'll get it. And we won't pester you."

I quirk an eyebrow, and he shrugs. "Okay, we'll probably still pester you."

Sitting back down, I lean my elbows on my knees. "I feel like a fraud. I act like this competent NHL captain when really, I'm watching you guys to pick up on social cues so I'm not awkward."

West laughs. "Dude. You don't need to be Mr. Congeniality to be an amazing captain. Most captains would've never put a brand-new player on the first line. They wouldn't have given him the chance. But you look at skills and how people work together on the ice. You lead us well, Remy."

Bruce nods. "Agreed. Can you imagine if Colby was team captain? He'd just try to get more camera time."

Colby narrows his eyes at him. "I don't have to *try* to get more camera time. The camera guys love me."

Bruce rolls his eyes and walks over to where Mitch is sitting and holding Nella. "Can I have her back now?"

Mitch growls. "No."

"You're the only real adult out of all of us, man. I'm afraid you have no choice but to lead us. And we wouldn't have it any other way. Social cues be damned." Colby playfully punches my shoulder.

"Thanks, guys. Sometimes I feel like I don't deserve such incredible teammates. Then other times I want to convince Coach and Tom to trade all of you." I smirk so they know I'm joking.

Bruce grins, planting his hands on his hips in a superman pose. "Guys, I think we need to hug it out."

Mitch and I say *no* at the same time.

CHAPTER
FORTY-FIVE

FORD: THE SUMMER AFTER
FRESHMAN YEAR OF COLLEGE

LAST NIGHT WAS the NHL draft in Nashville, Tennessee. Although having the spotlight on me was overwhelming, my dream of being drafted drowned out the chaos. I was chosen by the D.C. Eagles and will report for training camp in a month. It was a late night, celebrating with my parents and the general manager of the team. But the only person on my mind is Amber Park. We drove back from Nashville this morning, and the first thing I did was pick a bundle of the Pink Piano roses from Mom's garden for her. Her favorites.

I'll be moving to a new city, and for the first time since second grade, I won't be with her for her birthday. Sure, I can send her roses from a flower shop. But it's not the same as seeing her in person and handing them to her. It's the one time her fingers graze mine—and it's a touch I look forward to every single year.

When I arrive in front of Amber's apartment door, I knock. To my surprise, her mother answers the door...and to my surprise, she appears happy to see me. That's new.

"Ford Remington! Off to the NHL! We are so proud of you," she says, pulling me inside and closing the door.

Amber is standing behind her mom, looking bewildered. She spots the flowers I'm holding and gives me my favorite smile in the world. She scoots past her mom, her arms wide like she's going to embrace me, and I find myself anticipating being enveloped in her arms. But she pauses, and something crosses her pretty face—I'm not sure what. But she drops her arms down, her fists squeezing at her sides. She's holding herself back from touching me.

I swallow, hating how my throat feels thick and my face is hot. Amber knows I don't avoid being touched by people, especially soft touches that can make my skin itch. Having someone tap on my shoulder or pat me on the back grates on me. It's different from a hockey hit—a hockey hit is a powerful, full body experience. And there's no skin-to-skin contact involved.

But she has to realize I'd love to be touched by her. Embraced by her. Kissed by her.

I don't even mind when my parents hug me, really. She's seen me hug them. So, does she not *want* to touch me? Or is she holding back, thinking *I* don't want to touch her?

It seems absurd, but then people have told me before I'm not great at conveying my emotions. In a rare moment of confidence, I decide to reach for her. I make eye contact and hold my arms out. Amber smiles, looking hesitant, and moves toward me.

But her mother steps into my arms instead. What the hell?

"Oh, Fordy! Congratulations. You're going to be one wealthy young man!" She giggles as she steps away.

Amber's eyebrows scrunch. "Mom, Ford and I are going for a walk, okay?"

Her mother sweeps a clump of blonde hair-sprayed hair over her bony shoulder. "Of course." She winks. "Take as much time as you need, Amber."

Amber turns her back on her mom and rolls her eyes. I have no clue what that was all about.

The moment we're out in the quiet hallway, Amber runs a hand through her red hair. It's curled in loose waves today—she's been experimenting with new looks. She's always busy making things beautiful, wether it's hair, makeup, or paint on a canvas.

I know she'll do amazing at cosmetology school this fall. But I hate that her dreams are keeping her in Ohio and mine are taking me farther away from her.

"Sorry my mom is so over the top." Her hand relaxes, one finger toying with a rose petal as we walk down the stairs of the apartment building and out into the balmy air. It's twilight now, the summer air cooling down as the sun disappears beyond the horizon. The perfect temperature to be outside. But I wish it was colder so I'd have an excuse to put my around Amber's shoulders.

Unfortunately, she seems perfectly comfortable in her cut-off shorts and pink tank top. I glance over to see if there's even a single goosebump on her arm, but she hands me the bouquet of roses and uses the hair tie on her wrist to put up her hair. Her slim neck is exposed now, and I'm distracted by the skin there that looks so, so soft.

"Can I have my pretty flowers back now?" she asks, smiling at me.

I shake my head, willing myself out of my stupor. "Yeah, of course. I thought I'd bring you flowers now since I won't be able to on your birthday."

Her eyes droop, and the sadness there makes my heart flutter. That probably means I'm a jerk, but Amber being sad that I'm leaving means she likes having me around. And I really like being around her.

"Ford," she says, stopping in front of me and looking up at

me with those big green eyes. Eyes that are prettier than any gemstone I've ever seen. "I'm so proud of you. I know you've worked so hard. But I'm going to miss you like crazy."

I hold her gaze, even though I want to look away, because it feels too personal to look into her eyes and have her look into mine. What if she looks too long and sees the way I feel about her? She'd never feel the same. Not about some loser who keeps a coin in his pocket, NHL or no.

"I'm going to miss you too, Ambs. But I don't leave for another month. So we have time."

Her eyes light up. "Really?" she brings a hand to her chest and breathes a sigh of relief, making me laugh. She does that a lot—makes me laugh. She makes my smiles and laughter come easy, like I do it all the time, which I don't.

"We should make a list of things to do together before you leave."

I huff a laugh through my nose. "You know, I'll still see you. It's only six hours away."

"I know, I know." She waves a hand in the air. "But six hours seems so far after we've lived just two blocks away from each other. And you're going to meet all kinds of new friends, and girls...and you'll forget all about me." She smirks, and I know she's teasing. But she doesn't know how wrong she is.

"You'll always be my best friend. No one understands me like you do. You'll see."

Amber laughs again, the sound swirling around me like fairy dust, filling all the cracks that seem to pry me open and make me feel like I'm broken somehow. Being around Amber Park makes me feel like I'm normal, whole, complete.

Every step closer to her feels like a step closer to safety.

A step closer to forever.

She's worried about me forgetting her, while I'm wondering how I will possibly function without her.

CHAPTER
FORTY-SIX
AMBER

THE DAY after my first WAG night, I'm in the kitchen making lunch. Andie kept talking about her favorite sub sandwich place last night, so I decided to use some of the homemade bread from Farrah's bake-a-thon to make subs. Ford just walked through the door, finally home from practice. He looks like a dream, with his damp hair, black joggers, and long-sleeved red athletic tee, molding to his body and to show off every dip and valley of muscle on his torso.

My mouth waters, and it has nothing to do with the subs.

Nella is down for a nap, and he throws his gym bag on the floor and rushes into the kitchen. I know he'll pick his bag up soon and put it away. But for now, he settles behind me and wraps an arm around my waist. His large hand is splayed across my stomach, and I resist the urge to suck in. Ford has made it obvious he's really into my body. The extra skin on my stomach from pregnancy doesn't bother him, and neither do the stretch marks or my c-section scar.

The gorgeous man, who sometimes I can't believe is real, kisses my neck. His kisses are soft and slow and hit every sensitive spot. I drop the butter knife I was using to spread mayo on the bread and lean into his touch.

"Nella will be napping for a while," I say, my voice breathy and low.

He hums against my neck, holding me a little tighter. "I've dreamt of this, you know? Having you in my kitchen, coming home to you."

Lifting my hand to the back of his head, I twine my fingers into his thick hair, arching to get closer to him.

I open my mouth to tell him to forget the subs and take me upstairs, but the doorbell rings.

Ford groans behind me like a wild animal whose prey just escaped. "Not now," he says through gritted teeth. "If it's one of my teammates, I'm going to be so pissed."

Turning, I pat his chest. He's all wound up, so I gesture at the sandwiches. "You finish here, and I'll get the door."

One side of his mouth tugs up in a smile, and I kiss the side that's still pouting.

I'm walking to the door—barefoot and happy—ready to sign for a package or whatever it is then get back to my man. But when I open the door, my whole body stills. My mouth is open, but I can't form words.

Because my daughter's father—my ex-fiancé—is standing before me, and he looks annoyed.

"Theo?"

"Wow, I can't believe you still remember my name. Considering you won't respond to any of my calls or texts." His words are clipped.

His mother, who I hadn't noticed was behind him until now, steps forward. "Calm down Theo. Let's do this properly."

Theo takes a deep breath, straightening his shoulders, then forcing a smile on his face. "I'm sorry. Let me start over." His smile is creepy, like this whole thing has been rehearsed. "When you told me you were pregnant, I reacted badly. I think we should start over. As a couple, and as a family. I want to do the right thing, Amber. I want us to get married."

I huff a laugh, feeling half indignant, and half tickled. You know when your brain finds something funny that definitely shouldn't be funny? This is one of those times. I slap my hand over my mouth, trying desperately not to laugh. I swallow down the laughter bubbling up my throat, forcing myself to be composed.

Theo takes this as a sign to continue. "I know it's surprising, and you're in shock. But I'm here, Amber. I'm ready to do the right thing."

Theo's mother stands behind him. She nods her head, looking pleased with her son.

I finally find my words. "Theo, I hate to tell you this…but I'm already married." I hold up my hand, wiggling the finger with the giant diamond on it. "But even if I wasn't, I wouldn't marry you."

His face turns an angry red, and I take a step back. "You left me when I needed you the most. You probably didn't even realize this, but childbirth was hard on my heart, and we found out I had a heart condition. Since you left me—over a year ago—I've become a mother, I've had heart surgery, and I've moved on. You can't just show up a year later and decide you're ready to be a husband."

Theo holds a hand up. "Wait, you're telling me you married Ford Remington? The best friend you always told me not to worry about?"

"Don't insinuate I was unfaithful to you, Theo. I didn't see Ford in that way until you were long gone. And guess who was there to pick up the pieces? Guess who was there to be a real father to my child? And who was there to take care of me after my surgery? Ford was."

Theo's mother is slack-jawed, watching the conversation unfold. I honestly don't know the woman well enough to tell if she's shocked, or angry, or something else.

Theo laughs, and it's a sardonic sound, like a true villain. "This is what I get for dating a hairstylist, and not someone more high-class. You ran off with the first man to throw you a bone." He steps forward, and I step back. "I will get custody of *my* daughter, just you wait."

Theo has always had a quick temper, but he would get over things just as quickly. Usually. He never put his hands on me in anger, but his furious expression makes me withdraw. I expect my back to hit the front door any moment, but instead, I feel Ford's hands grasp my shoulders. I close my eyes and exhale. Feeling so much safer with him behind me.

"If I were you, I'd be careful how you speak to *my wife*." Ford's voice is steady, and colder than ice.

Theo grits his teeth, coming closer to us. Ford holds out one of his giant paw-like hands, and Theo slams into it with his forehead. Ford holds him there easily, cupping his face like it's a measly little melon. "That's close enough, I think," he says, his voice low and authoritative.

Theo's mother steps forward, her stilettos clacking against the sidewalk with each step.

"I think we need to leave and cool down. Come, Theo." She orders him like a dog, and he turns and follows with his head down. Her body language is terse and hard, but I'm not sure whether she's upset with me or her son. Probably me.

I notice the silver Mercedes parked in front of Ford's house. How did they even get into this gated community? Theo turns back to glare at us before slamming the passenger-side door.

Once the Mercedes has turned a corner and is out of sight, Ford spins me to face him. "Are you okay?"

I nod, but the tears streaming down my face are traitors to my words. Ford cups my face and uses his thumbs to wipe away my tears. "I don't want to overstep here, Ambs. What can I do to help?"

Wrapping my arms around him, I hide my face in the safety of his chest. He rubs my back and lets me soak his shirt. The same one I was admiring earlier.

"I don't know what to do," I sob. "I never thought he'd put up a fight about Nella."

Ford effortlessly picks me up, one hand behind my knees, and the other cradling my upper body. I hear the front door close behind us, and I realize this is the first time he's carried me over the threshold. It feels like such a newlywed thing, and it makes me cling to him a little tighter.

Ford sits on the couch, still holding me. Letting go of him with one arm, I use the back of my hand to dry my tears.

The man holding me looks pained, tortured, like someone ripped out his heart. He glances behind me, avoiding eye contact. And I bring my hand to his jaw, guiding him back to me.

He swallows, his jaw ticking in that way it does when he's upset. "Ambs, I need you to know that I realize this marriage is fake, that we said two years and done. But my feelings are real, they always have been. Even though it would hurt like crazy...I would step away." He pauses, trying to compose himself. "If you wanted to be with Theo, if you think that's what's best for you and Nella, we could end this now." His words are a broken whisper.

We could end this now. Those words feel like a fist clutching my newly remodeled heart.

I know he's trying to help, the way he always does. But

what I want is for him to fight for us. I want him to hold on tight, like no one ever has before. I need him to fight for me. I've had enough people give up and throw me to the wolves.

So, as caring and patient as I know he's being, it pisses me off. I'm not sure I've ever been angry at Ford. And it feels strange and unsettling, but I want to slam my fists against his chest, knowing he's strong enough to take it.

CHAPTER
FORTY-SEVEN
FORD

AMBER LOOKS madder than a hockey player in the penalty box. And I don't know what I said to put that look on her face. I love when her face gets all pink and flushed, but this isn't a flush. This is something else.

For the first time in our friendship, the fiery temper that rarely comes out—a temper that could only belong to a redhead—is directed at me. And I do *not* like it.

Amber pushes away from me, scrambling off my lap, so she's standing and looking down at me. I've never felt so small.

She closes her eyes; I think she's trying to calm herself. Maybe I should offer her the coin in my pocket?

Finally, she opens her eyes. "Ford, I know you're trying to play peacemaker like you always do, and I love that side of you. That you can deescalate a situation even when your own feelings are running rampant on the inside. But this isn't the time to make peace. I don't want you to smooth over the situation. I want you…no, I *need* you to fight. For me. For Nella." Her chest rises and falls rapidly, and for a second, I fear for her heart.

"I know you, Ford Remington, and I know that for some reason, you probably think we'd be better off without you, or that you're not good enough for us. But that's ridiculous. Do you seriously believe we wouldn't choose you?"

Before I can answer she blows out a deep breath, one hand coming to rest on her hip. She looks furious.

My head falls, looking down at my feet. I imagine I look similar to Moose—my old friend—when Mom would yell at him for chewing up her shoes.

"Look at me," she says, her voice like steel but not unkind. "I want you to pay attention when I say this to you, because I'm not going to repeat myself again."

I look up, meeting her green-eyed gaze. My eyes widen when I see the tears falling onto her freckled complexion. The urge to move closer to her, to wipe those tears away, is so strong. But I stay where I am and let her say what's on her mind.

"There's no way in this world, or even in the next world, that you weren't the one meant to love me and Nella. Ford, no one could love us better than you." Her chin wobbles, but she continues. "The way you take care of us, the way you jump in to help, the way you hold her, and she immediately stops fussing. The way you hold *me*." She blows out a deep breath. "This might have started platonically; I might not have realized at first how I could feel for you…but now there's no way I can ignore it. It's impossible for me to love anyone else the way I love you."

She kneels in front of me, bracing her hands on my thighs. "And no one else's love would ever compare to yours. Do you get that?" Her voice is pleading, begging me to understand. "Do you get that this connection between us isn't normal? Ford, this is a once in a lifetime…once in a universe, type of love." Her voice cracks on the word love. "And if you ever talk about leaving again, thinking you're doing what's best, then you're a fool. Because *this* is what's best." She gestures with her hand between the two of us. "You and me." Another tear trails down her cheek. "No one else will do."

I feel a wet drop land on my shirt, and I realize I'm crying too, at hearing these words I never thought I'd hear from any woman, let alone the one I've dreamt of my entire life. How is it possible for me to get this lucky? To have attained everything I ever wanted in life? It seems too good to be true. But I'm going to roll with it anyway and thank the stars every day for being the luckiest man on earth.

"I'm sorry," I say, reaching for her, cupping my hands around her gorgeous face. "It would be my honor to stay. I'll stay forever. I'll stay for eternity." I kiss her hard, the only way I can with a lifetime of dreams swirling around us. "I love you, Ambs. I loved you when we were eight years old, and I love you still."

She climbs onto my lap, settling her legs on either side of mine and wrapping her arms around my neck. "I love you too, Ford. And I'm never letting you go. Not in two years, not ever."

We sit there, wrapped up in each other for what feels like an hour. I have no clue how many minutes pass, because this moment seems to exist outside of time. It's a pocket in the world that opened just for us, a pocket where time stopped.

Nella's cry from the baby monitor in the kitchen, somewhere on the island along with the subs we never ate, is what finally draws us out of our little bubble.

Amber moves to get up, but I hold her to me, looking into her eyes. "We'll figure this out, okay? We'll get the best lawyer money can buy. There's no way a judge will give him custody —or even partial custody—after he's been out of the picture this whole time."

She nods, resting her forehead against mine. "We'll get through it together."

I lean in, pressing a kiss to her mouth, then loosening my grip on her so she can get Nella.

I spend the rest of the day putting together all of Nella's furniture and arranging it in her room. It seems like a sign of permanence and stability, and I hope it helps Amber not to worry. I hope seeing all this furniture will show her I expect Nella to live here forever, and Theo won't get a thing. Amber needed time with her daughter today, which is understandable. Someone threatened to take her, so of course she needed time alone with Nella, to hold her and remind herself she's not going anywhere. I gave them their mother-daughter time and was happy to distract myself by building furniture.

When I hang the last picture on the wall, one of Amber's paintings of a Pink Piano rose, I hear Amber's gasp from the doorway. I turn and smile at my girls, both seeing the room all put together for the first time.

"Ford, it came together so nicely."

Nella coos, clueless as to what's happening. I step toward them, carefully taking Nella from her mother's arms, then walking her over to the picture I just hung. "See this, Nells?" I glance up and study the artwork. "These flowers are your mommy's favorites."

She stares at the painting, then abruptly stretches her arms above her head and yawns. It's the cutest thing I've ever seen.

Amber sighs. "It's time for her evening nap."

"Can I rock her to sleep?" I ask, eyeing the new linen swivel rocker in the corner of the room. The linen and the white wooden furniture are the only neutrals in a room full of pink. Pink stuffed animals, pink wall hangings, pink sheets, and even a pink and white Turkish rug. It sounds chaotic but it's girly and cute. And if Nella decides she hates pink when she gets older, she can redecorate as many times as she wants.

Amber smiles. "Of course. I'm going to take a shower."

She leaves us, and I turn on Nella's nightlight, then turn down the main light shining from a mini, crystal chandelier. Nella stares at the twinkly stones dangling from it with her mouth open.

I chuckle and sit down in the comfortable rocker. Adjusting her in my arms, I make sure she's comfortable and grab her favorite blanket off the dresser beside me. She grabs the edge of the blanket with one of her chubby hands and uses the other to squeeze my index finger. Before Nella, I never understood the bond someone has with a child but being here in this nursery with this tiny girl holding my hand, I get it. I might not be her father by blood, but I'll be her dad if she'll let me. Thankfully, she seems fond of me, so I don't think she'll mind.

I lean down, brushing a kiss against her soft downy curls. Her eyes flutter closed, those little baby eyelashes resting against her plump cheeks. Cheeks that will one day hold a multitude of freckles, just like her mommy's.

Nella falls asleep quickly, her grip easing its tight hold on my finger. I continue holding her and looking at her, long after she's asleep, soaking up this time with her, and steeling myself for a battle with Theo. A battle he's going to lose.

CHAPTER
FORTY-EIGHT
AMBER

FORD APPEARS somber when he comes into our room after putting Nella to sleep. I can tell this whole Theo thing is bothering him too. I'm dressed in a nursing nightgown and standing by the dresser that has now become mine. There's a mirror attached to it and I'm combing my wet hair and doing my skin care. I moved some items out of the bathroom, knowing Ford would probably want a shower too after assembling furniture all day.

I hope it's quick, because all I want is to fall asleep, safe and sound in his arms after this endlessly long day.

I'm slathering on my facial moisturizer, when the spaghetti strap on my nursing top breaks, pulling right out of the seam. I groan. "No, this was my favorite one!"

Opening a dresser drawer, I rummage through. All my pajamas and nightgowns are dirty. I meant to do laundry today but was distracted by my ex-fiancé.

I yank the nightgown off and toss it into a trash bin Ford has in the corner of the room, then walk into his gigantic closet to find a comfortable oversized tee to wear to bed. He has his t-shirts neatly folded and stacked on a shelf, and I bend at the waist to snag one when I see a glossy, black shopping bag.

My eyebrows shoot up and I'm too curious not to investigate. I move the skates in front of the bag and pull it out. Removing the fancy tissue paper, my jaw drops when I see the most beautiful piece of lingerie I've ever set eyes on. As soon as my fingers glide over the fabric, I know it's a hundred percent silk. The good stuff. My heartbeat quickens, and the blood in my veins warms until I feel like my whole body is on fire. I pull out the receipt and see he purchased this a week after we got married. Meaning he totally got this for me. But before we'd even kissed.

The thrill that runs through me is electrifying and probably a little silly. But after this hellish day, this was just the confidence booster I needed. I grab the white tee on top of the stack and tug it on over my head.

Then, with the black silk negligee in hand, I waltz into the bathroom. I can see my husband clearly through the glass doors of the large shower, and I'd be lying if I said I didn't take a moment to admire him. His physique is really something to behold, and the other day we were under the covers when we explored each other's bodies. This time I have an undisturbed view of the man I get to call *husband*.

And what the hell...

"Ford Douglas Remington, you got a tattoo and never told me?"

He jumps, spinning to look at me. He turns off the water and grabs a towel from the rack, wrapping it around his waist as he steps out of the shower. But I can still see the top of his tattoo peeking out, right above where the defined V muscle meets his hip. Ford swallows, looking nervous, and runs a hand through his wet hair. Drops of water trail down his face and torso, and I am mesmerized.

I could sit here and study his body all day, but I really want to know more about this tattoo. "Why didn't you tell me?"

He looks down, then his gaze locks on mine through his dark, damp lashes. "I was embarrassed to tell anyone. I got it right after I moved from Ohio to D.C." He sighs. "I missed you so much, Ambs. I just wanted a piece of you with me all the time. It sounds so stupid." Ford groans and lowers the towel, just enough for his hip tattoo to be completely visible.

When the simple pink rose, outlined in black, comes into view, my vision blurs. I move forward, gently running a finger over the inked petals. The memory of all those times he brought me Pink Piano roses floods back to me. I can remember the way they smelled, and the summer breeze that tickled my skin when we would sit in Sally's backyard garden with Moose.

"I love it," I tell him, and his face softens...until he sees what's in my hand. His eyes grow so wide, I have to laugh. "You've been keeping a lot of secrets, husband."

"I can explain."

I cross my arms over my chest and tap my foot, waiting for him to do the explaining.

"On our away trip, the guys wanted to shop for their wives, and you and I weren't...you know. But they didn't know that, and they were all, *Come on, Remy, buy something for Amber.* So, I just grabbed something and checked out."

I bite my bottom lip, trying not to laugh. I can totally picture the whole scenario playing out, and Ford blushing the entire time. "So, you just picked the first thing you saw?"

He swallows thickly, his damp skin turning red. "Not exactly." He tightens the towel around his waist. "I might have shopped around...a little. I wanted to be convincing." Ford's eyes drop down to the negligee in question.

"And you never pictured me wearing it?"

Ford scrubs a hand down his face. His tongue pokes the inside of his cheek as if he's deeply pondering how to prove his innocence.

But I don't want him to be innocent. I want him to admit that he pictured me wearing this, and that's why he bought it.

"You know," I start, bringing one finger to his bare chest and pressing lightly. "If you had asked nicely, I probably wouldn't have even complained about wearing it for you."

His eyes snap up to my face. They're impossibly wide, like a cartoon character.

"Really?"

"Yep." I remove my hand, spinning on my heel and walking out of the bathroom.

Ford wastes no time. He's hot on my trail. "What can I do to get you to wear it now?"

I give him a coy smile over my shoulder. "Hmm. Let me think."

He comes up behind me and picks me up, gently laying me on the bed and lying next to me. "I'd do anything for you. I'll get you whatever you want. just tell me what it is, and it's yours."

Bringing my hand up, I cup his jaw, relishing the rough feel of the stubble on his face. "I don't need anything, Ford. Just you."

Ford takes my chin in his thumb and forefinger and tilts my head up. He kisses me slowly. Tenderly. With more tenderness than anyone would think this big, brutal hockey player could muster. "It's always been you, Ambs." He pulls back, smirking. "Now, will you pretty-please wear that black silky thing to bed tonight?"

My head falls back as I laugh, and Ford joins me. Laughing after this emotional day feels so good, and I know that all our days will be like this. That even on the worst days, we'll find things to laugh about, things to take joy in.

Life with Ford will be a full life indeed.

CHAPTER
FORTY-NINE
AMBER

THE FOLLOWING MORNING, Ford is at practice before his game later tonight. This is the first game Nella and I will be attending and I'm nervous but excited. I've followed the team and watched games long enough to know that everyone is fascinated about the players' spouses. There will be photos captured, probably even posted on the Eagles' social media accounts.

I still need to rifle through Ford's closet in hopes to find something to wear tonight. Maybe I can style one of his Eagles jerseys as a dress since his shirts are gigantic on me.

Loading the last of the breakfast dishes into the dishwasher, I throw a detergent pod in and turn it on. Nella is down for her morning nap, and I walk toward the large front window in the living room, taking a moment to soak up the quiet. The sunlight streaming in through the windows is almost too bright, but I bask in its rays, letting the warmth and light soak into my skin, my soul. Taking away all the fear and worry, replacing it with something brighter.

When I open my eyes, that brightness is dashed by a silver Mercedes pulling up in front of the house.

"Not again." I groan. Ford isn't here to protect me this time, and the fear starts creeping in. Thankfully, Theo's mother steps out of the vehicle, no Theo in sight. He doesn't appear to be with her.

She's more casual today, in dark skinny jeans and a pale blue, collared shirt. She looks like a regular woman instead of a lawyer who just got out of court.

I meet her at the door, not wanting to wait around for her to knock.

Mrs. Peregrine seems startled when I open the door. I'm sure I'm quite the vision in my leggings and the baggy t-shirt I borrowed from Ford last night. But this is what she gets when she comes over—uninvited—at eight-thirty in the morning.

"Amber," she says politely, stopping before she reaches the front stoop leading to the impressive front door of this big house. "I came by to apologize about yesterday."

My eyebrows shoot up, betraying how surprised I am by her apology.

She straightens her shoulders and takes a deep, fortifying breath. "My son wasn't quite forthcoming with me about how your relationship ended. I'm afraid he made it sound like you ended things when he wasn't sure if he was ready to become a father. That he asked for time, and you dashed his hopes. But yesterday it was obvious that wasn't the case." She glances down at her black flats, then back up at me. "Not having all the information, I told him he should try again, try to make things right. My brother lives in this neighborhood and said he'd seen you, but none of us realized you'd gotten married. I apologize for the stress my son has brought you."

"Um, thank you."

"As a lawyer, I know my son could get partial custody of your daughter—his daughter."

My breathing stops. Air is no longer moving through my lungs.

"But as a mother—one who has gone through her own custody battle before—I have no desire to put you, or your daughter, through that. Especially after speaking to my son late into the night last night. It's obvious he doesn't desire custody or want to pay child support at this point in his life."

I exhale a deep breath, the urge to hug this woman almost overwhelming.

Theo's mother toys with her wristwatch, appearing self-conscious. "But, if I may be so bold, I do have a favor to ask."

I nod, urging her to continue, but also dreading what she might ask.

"I wondered if you might be willing to send me a photo of her, maybe once a year? Just for me, not for my idiot son. And maybe a small update about her life…how she's doing."

I smile, hoping to ease her nerves. By the look on her face, I think this is the most terrifying request she's ever made. "Of course. I'd be happy to."

Her shoulders slump in relief. "Does she look like Theo at all?"

I hold up one finger, urging her to wait a moment, and run inside to grab my phone before returning to her. "Here's a photo I captured of her smiling."

Holding up my phone, I show her the photo and her eyes brim with tears. She composes herself, and not one tear flows over.

"She has his dimple." Theo's mother grins, and I realize for the first time that he got that dimple from her. "Thank you, Amber." She pulls a business card out of her back pocket and hands it to me.

Reading it quickly, I see it has her work address and email on it.

"Thank you," I say, locking eyes with her, trying to convey that I'm thanking her for much more than just the business card. I'm thanking her for letting me live my life in peace with my daughter when she could've made our lives difficult. She could've fought, could've dragged us to court. But she didn't.

With a soft smile, she turns and walks back to her car. I head inside, feeling like I'm floating…back into the sunlight, and enjoying the feeling of everything being right. My heart is fixed, my baby is safe, and I'm with the man I love.

I haven't felt this safe in…maybe ever.

CHAPTER FIFTY
FORD

AFTER PRACTICE, I rush home. Amber called me earlier and told me about her conversation with Theo's mom, and now I feel a hundred pounds lighter.

I'm so anxious to be with my girls, and I came bearing gifts. Last time I gifted Amber something to wear, it worked out really, *really* well for me. So, I'll buy her all the gifts she wants. Even though she never asked me to or expected it. But that just makes it more fun.

I find Amber and Nella in my walk-in closet—and it's a disaster. Every red piece of clothing I own is on the floor. Nella is on a fluffy blanket on her tummy. She rolls now, and she's been enjoying tummy time.

"Are you looking for more lingerie? Because I only purchased that black one."

Amber gasps. "You scared me!" She rushes over and hugs me. "I'm looking for something to wear tonight."

I grin. "Well, you're in luck. I bought something for you both."

Amber juts out a hip and pops her fist onto it. I know she's trying to look sassy, but it just makes me want to take her to bed.

"Would you stop buying me stuff?"

"No."

"Ford! This constant present thing is unfair, and until I start working at the salon next week, I won't have money to buy presents for you."

"I don't want presents." I shrug.

With a sigh, Amber picks Nella up off the floor and walks into our room, sitting down on the bed. "All right, what did you buy me now?"

I hold up the bag from the Eagles' Fan Shop. "You *and* Nella."

Her face lights up, and she looks at Nella like she understands what's happening. "Did you hear that, baby girl? A present for you too!"

She smiles at her mom, and I hand over the bag.

Amber pulls out the long-sleeved red onesie with a giant number 10 on the front. A sparkly red tutu is attached to the waist, and it says "Remington" on the back.

"Stop! This is the cutest thing I've ever seen." Amber's eyes sparkle with what I hope are happy tears. She pulls the other item out of the bag and gasps. "Oh, my gosh. I had no idea they had such feminine sportswear!" Amber holds up a red satin jacket. It resembles a vintage baseball jacket and has white trim around the edges. There's a white number 10 embroidered on the front pocket, and of course, my last name on the back. Which is also her last name.

She jumps up, handing me Nella, then pushing her arms through the sleeves and running into my closet. I follow her and find her spinning in front of the full-length mirror. "I'm never taking this off."

I quirk a brow, and she laughs, then shoots me a wink.

"Don't be mad, but there's one more thing. Kind of a small accessory."

Amber crosses her arms and glares at me. But it's way more adorable than she probably realizes. "Fine, let's have it."

My heart speeds up, and my palms feel suddenly sweaty. I wipe my free hand on the front of my black joggers, then bend on one knee. Shuffling Nella in my arms, I reach for the box in my pocket, right next to my coin. I cradle Nella in one arm and hold out the box with the other.

Amber studies me, not knowing what to think. "Um, Ford. It's a little late to propose. We're already married."

I chuckle at her words. "You're right. But you have the wrong ring."

Her mouth gapes open. "You didn't."

"I did." I nod my head slowly. "This all started out as temporary…a temporary ring for a temporary marriage. But it's forever now—I'm not letting you two go. Ever. And that requires a forever ring."

I flip the box open with my thumb, and her hands go up to her face, covering her gaping mouth. Inside the box is the ornate, whimsical ring that she wanted so badly. The ring that was perfect for her. And there's no way I'll let her wear anything else on that pretty little finger.

"Tonight, everyone will know we're married. And I couldn't feel more honored that you're my wife. But *this* is your ring, Ambs."

She drops her hands and kneels in front of me. I'm sure we look ridiculous, both of us kneeling inside my closet, which looks like a tornado tore through it.

"You're too good to me."

"You deserve everything good, and I plan to remind you of that frequently."

Amber leans in and kisses me softly before taking the box

from my hand and slipping her old ring off and replacing it with the new one. It looks perfect on her hand, just like I knew it would.

"It's gorgeous." She kisses me again.

Nella fusses, arching her back to push away from me. Amber laughs and takes her daughter, snuggling her close. "Your daddy is so good to us, baby girl."

Daddy. I like the sound of that. No, I love the sound of that.

We walk out of the closet together, and Amber turns to me. She narrows her eyes and asks, "If you've purchased any other over the top items for me, can you tell me now? I'm not sure I can handle any more surprises."

I roll my lips with my teeth. I hadn't planned on outing myself just yet.

"Ford Remington. What did you do?"

I scratch the tip of my nose, thinking of a way out of this conversation, knowing there isn't one.

Amber sighs. "Out with it."

I blow out a breath. "You know the salon?"

Her eyes widen, looking like they might fall right out of her head. "Ford."

"It has a new silent owner."

"Ford!"

That night, when we skate onto the ice for pre-game warmup, all the nerves I feel at facing the Atlanta Cyclones—one of our toughest competitors—fades away.

Because my eyes shoot straight to the area behind our net where the families always sit. Every game I see Mel, Andie and her little brother, Noah, and even Noel. But the way my heart pounds when I see *my* family there...it's unreal.

My girls are dressed in my number—and my name. Amber is wearing my ring—I can see it twinkling in the overhead lights. She beams when she sees me, and she makes Nella's hand come up in a wave. Amber's hair is done in bubble braids, which I know the name of because she tried them on Nella last week, but her hair wasn't long enough.

I blow them each a kiss and notice the cameraman behind the glass snapping photos furiously. Amber acts like she's going to kiss the glass and I laugh. Martie, the social media manager who takes all the photos during our games, is eating this up.

As odd as it might seem to me, fans will go wild when they learn their team captain is married. Fans feel a certain amount of camaraderie with us, even following our wives or girlfriends on social media, wanting an inside look at our lives.

And the knowledge that tonight, everyone in the world will know that Amber is mine makes my chest puff out. Just a little.

I stare into Amber's eyes, and she smiles a secret smile.

A smile that promises a lifetime of love.

And I smile right back.

EPILOGUE

AMBER

I'M BACK in the closet, but now I have one whole side for my things. Yes, in the last week Ford has cleared out his dresser and one side of the closet for me. And he took me shopping for work clothes. He says I have to get used to him spoiling me and that he won't apologize for it.

Since I needed work clothes, I didn't argue.

I now have a plethora of black and white pants and shirts I can mix and match for work. Even though my husband is apparently the silent owner, I'll still happily follow the dress code.

He did get me a pretty great schedule, though. I'll work only three days a week, leaving me plenty of time to spend with him and Nella.

I glance in the mirror checking my outfit one last time. A white bodysuit tucked into black pleated trousers with black wedge boots. My hair is down and curled in loose waves, and my makeup is simple—a little concealer under my eyes, and winged eyeliner.

Ford likes my freckles, so I didn't want to cover them up

with foundation. Plus, I like my freckles too, and I want to show Nella it's okay to embrace them.

I'm about to head downstairs when my phone vibrates from my trouser pocket. I take it out, shocked to see an incoming call from the last person I expect.

My mother.

"Hello? Mom?" I answer, feeling unsure since she hasn't spoken to me in a year.

"Amber!" Mom says. "I saw the good news!"

My eyebrows draw together, unsure what she's talking about. She didn't consider my pregnancy good news, so what *would* she consider good news?

"You did it. I'm so proud. You married a rich man, just like I always taught you. Now we can live the life we deserve."

I scoff. "We?"

"I know you'll take care of your own mother." She laughs, and it grates on my nerves. Her laugh has the opposite effect of Ford's joyfully warm chuckle.

"Goodbye, Mom," I tell her, hanging up the phone and setting her on "Do Not Disturb." She doesn't want me and Nella—she wants money. And I won't have her bringing us down.

Sliding my phone back into my pocket, I silence all thoughts of her. I won't let her bring me down. Not anymore.

Grabbing a lint roller, I carefully head downstairs, not knowing exactly what I'll find. When I'm at the bottom of the steps, to my surprise, and delight, Nella is in her bouncy chair and Rose—the rescue puppy Ford was photographed with during the Eagles' calendar shoot—is licking her face.

Farrah gasps and rushes over, gently scolding the adorable puppy. "No, no, Rose! We do not lick the baby." She arrived two nights ago, ready for her new role as part time nanny.

"Good luck with that." I laugh, and she turns to glare at me.

Nella is grinning at the puppy and making grabby hands.

Farrah blows out a breath, causing her long dark hair to fly around her face. "I think the puppy is going to be more difficult than the baby."

I grimace. "Probably. Sorry about that."

I ducked out first thing this morning to finish up paperwork on Rose's adoption, right after Ford left for an early morning practice. He'll be back any minute, and I cannot wait to surprise *him*, for once.

Did I use the last measly bit of my savings to purchase the fluffy little dog? Yes. But thankfully, I'm married to a professional hockey player, and I don't really need that savings account anymore.

And it'll be worth it to see the look on Ford's face.

The rumble of the garage door makes Farrah and I jump. "He's here!" I half whisper, half yell.

She widens her eyes. "What should we do?"

"I don't know!" I shake my hands around. "Act natural."

Farrah scurries to the kitchen, grabbing the bag of flour and acting like she's about to start a fresh batch of bread.

I nod approvingly.

The door of the mudroom opens, and my husband walks inside. He sees me decked out for my first day on the job and whistles. "Wow, Ambs. You look beautiful."

"Thank you," I say, my voice breathless. I look around, searching for Rose, and I don't see her anywhere.

Looking to Farrah, I widen my eyes, silently asking where the puppy went. She widens her eyes right back, as if saying *I don't know*.

My eyes drift back to Ford, then I hear the tapping of a puppy's claws against the tile floors. Ford looks down just in time for Rose to appear in front of him. She looks up and whimpers, like she knows this is her dad and wants him to give her pets.

Ford drops down to his knees and picks up the tiny dog—who won't be so tiny in a few months. He buries his face in her furry neck and the sight brings back memories of him with Moose.

I swallow, and my eyes prickle with tears.

Ford sniffs, standing up with the puppy still in his arms. A tear streams down his face. "Does this belong to us?" he asks, his voice cracking.

I walk across the kitchen and into the mud room, wrapping my arms around them both. "She's ours. Her name is Rose."

Farrah sniffles from the kitchen, and I know she's crying too.

"She's so cute. Is this the puppy from the photo shoot?" he asks, wiping his face on his shoulder.

I nod.

"She reminded me so much of Moose when I saw her then. I love that Nella will get to grow up with a dog like I did."

"Me too. She already loves her."

Ford leans in and kisses me, then strides right over to Nella's bouncy seat. He sets Rose down, and she immediately licks Nella's face, making her giggle. Ford's laughter erupts, filling the whole house with his deep, thunderous chuckle.

"Don't encourage the licking!" Farrah yells from the kitchen.

Rose turns and licks my dress pants, jumping up and covering the bottom of my black pants with fur. It's okay—that's what the lint roller is for.

Ford picks her up, allowing Rose to lick his nose. "Don't ruin Mommy's fancy outfit before her first day of work."

The puppy licks him again. He sets her down and settles

his hands on my waist. "You look amazing. Are you ready for your first day?"

"Honestly? I'm so excited. It's been too long since I activated my creative brain. And my schedule is full since Andie, Noel, and Mel all made appointments."

"You'll probably be employee of the month in no time." He raises his eyebrows.

I roll my eyes. "I'll probably get employee of the month every month, seeing as I'm sleeping with the boss."

He laughs, and Farrah groans from the kitchen. "Gross, I can hear you guys!"

Glancing at her, I see she actually *is* starting a batch of bread. I shake my head.

Ford glances at Nella and Rose, then back at me. His expression is soft, and maybe a little somber.

I step into him and wrap my arms around his neck. He wastes no time circling his arms around my waist and hugging me tightly. His mouth brushes against my neck, and he hums contentedly.

"You okay?" I ask, leaning back to look at him. Taking advantage of his nearness, I stare into his warm brown eyes—the same eyes that brought me comfort when I was a girl. I'm a woman now, and they still bring me comfort, as well as love and protection.

"Never been better," he responds, closing the distance between us and kissing me softly, tenderly, endlessly.

ALSO BY LEAH BRUNNER

Under Kansas Skies Series

Running Mate

House Mate

Check Mate

Cabin Mate

D.C. Eagles Hockey Series

Passion or Penalty (prequel novella)

Desire or Defense

Flirtation or Faceoff

Betrothal or Breakaway

Secret or Shutout

ACKNOWLEDGMENTS

Thank you so much to my amazing, lovely, talented BETA readers! Madi, Katie, Amanda, Meredith, and Gila. You guys rock! Your input helped me make Ford and Amber's story so beautiful!

To Leah's Leading Launch Ladies… have I told you lately that I love you? You gals make the world a brighter place.

To my ARC readers, thank you for being so pumped about this book! I love how EXCITED you guys were for this book! You guys are the best. Every post, every share, every TikTok, every comment… it all makes a huge difference and I appreciate you so much! Without you, this job would be WAY less fun.

To my sensitivity reader, thank you, thank you. Your help with Ford's character made him what he is now.

To my lovely publicist, Jen. Thank you for being my sounding board and for running things behind the scenes! You're awesome!

To my husband and children, thank you for being my biggest fans and supporters. Thank you for watching all those hockey games with me. I love you.

ABOUT THE AUTHOR

Leah is a Kansas native, but currently resides in Ohio with her family. She's a proud military spouse and has moved all over the country, (and hopes to move a few more times)!

When she was a child, she dreamt of writing children's books about cats. Even though she ended up writing romance, she's pretty sure her childhood self would still be proud.

Learn more at leahbrunner.com

instagram.com/leah.brunner.writes
bookbub.com/profile/leah-brunner
tiktok.com/romcomsaremyjam

Made in the USA
Monee, IL
22 March 2025